ALSO BY
KATHLEEN IRENE PATERKA

Saturday Night Sisters
The Other Wife
Royal Secrets
Deep Fried Reservations
For I Have Sinned
Lotto Lucy
Home Fires
Fatty Patty

NONFICTION
For the Love of a Castle
For the Love of a Castle II … The Romance Continues

DON'T OPEN THE DOOR

KATHLEEN IRENE PATERKA

DEDICATION

Grandchildren fill a space in your heart
that you never knew was empty

~ Unknown

Desmond and Ryan Carter, this one is for you.

AUTHOR NOTE

This book has been long in the making. Nearly three years, but who's counting, right? Except that I was, and perhaps you were, too. *When's your next book coming out?* readers would ask, forcing me to admit that I just didn't know. Talk about embarrassing. I was constantly dreaming up imaginary conversations my readers were having. *You'd think, after eight books, she'd know what she's doing. She should be a whiz at drafting plots, writing rough drafts, dealing with all those pesky edits...yada, yada, yada.* But here's the thing: when I started writing Reet's story of **Don't Open The Door** in 2020, I was also committed to another writing project. A non-fiction work with a firm deadline. *It shouldn't take long,* I reasoned. *I can write two books at the same time.* But guess what? I couldn't.

Poor Reet. **Don't Open The Door** started strong but floundered as I grew more focused on the other writing project. And with a deadline looming, it became obvious I needed to put Reet's story aside and focus solely on my non-fiction work. When **For The Love of a Castle ~ The Romance Continues** was published in the summer of 2022, I was ecstatic. No more divided loyalties. No more scrambling to find time for both books. I could concentrate all my time and efforts on Reet.

And finally, one day, ***Don't Open The Door*** was finished. I hope you love Reet's story as much as I do.

But before we start the story, please indulge me as I offer a few words of thanks.

First and always, to my readers. Thank you for being there with me on the journey. Thank you for helping me remember why I do this in the first place, and that my words and what I do are making a difference. That's all any of us can ask.

I owe a great debt to certain individuals who provided backstory and feedback on the plot and character development, including Barb Godwin, Chris Krajewski, and Catherine Chant. I know absolutely nothing about guns, but happily for me, my friend Katie Bee does. Katie deserves a huge shout out for instructing me on how to safely handle a weapon, followed up by an afternoon on the firing range. Beta reader commentary proved crucial to Reet's story. Special thanks to Peggy Kusina, Haley Georgi, and Deb Aeling, especially in those final chapters as I struggled to find my way to The End.

I've been working with the same editor for years. A talented author in her own right, Catherine Chant is a brilliant editor. She knows me, she understands my writing process, and she catches all those irksome boo boos. Best of all, she's not afraid to tell me when things aren't working. I've done my best to make things right. Any mistakes you find in this book are mine alone.

A note about the language found in this book. My apologies if you find it offensive, but I'm afraid it couldn't be helped. The world is full of people spouting profanity, and Lloyd Walsh is one of those people. If I'd tried to tame the words coming out of his mouth, he wouldn't have been Lloyd, and it wouldn't have been the same story.

Finally, a word about my guy Steve. The fact that he loved books and reading just as much as I did was what immediately attracted me to him when we met in March 1979. We married in September 1980, and we've been writing our own version of Happily-Ever-After ever since. Steve's my biggest critic, my biggest fan, and none of this would be possible without his patience, encouragement and support. I love you, Steve.

Kathleen Irene Paterka
September 25, 2023

There's no place like home, except Grandma's house.

—Unknown

*There is a bit of good in the worst of us
and a bit of bad in the best of us.*

*—Big Book of Alcoholics Anonymous,
pg. 417*

PROLOGUE

F ONLY.

If only our UPS driver hadn't been running late. If only I'd taken time to peer through the peep hole. If only I hadn't opened the door.

I was in the kitchen when I heard the doorbell ring. *And about time, too!* I thought to myself as I headed into the hallway toward the front door. I'd been expecting the UPS driver since that text *Out for Delivery* popped up on my phone yesterday morning. Twenty-four hours later, I was still waiting for him to show up on my front porch with his customary smile, friendly nod, and my package in hand.

Signature required, I'd noted when placing the order for this special delivery. A very special gift, from all the way across the ocean. I neared the door, thinking about the delivery guy on the other side. Out in the cold, shifting back and forth on his feet, waiting for me to sign for my package. Poor guy. I didn't envy him, driving around in that big drafty truck, delivering packages in all kinds of weather. It must be a tough job, especially in winter. Here in the Midwest, only an hour or so from Chicago, we've already seen a few snow flurries, despite the fact we're barely into November. Thanksgiving is still a few weeks away, but tomorrow is Tiffany's birthday.

Birthdays are special, especially for sweet little girls like my granddaughter. I've been planning for weeks, determined to make her birthday dreams come true. A fancy cake with frosted pink roses and *Happy 6th Birthday Tiffany!* in elaborate swirls. Balloons, streamers, and party hats all around for the three of us. And Tiffany's birthday present, ordered weeks ago, now finally arrived all the way from England: a vintage-style ballerina doll, just like the one I had as a child. A sparkly ruffled tutu, jointed legs and arms, a jeweled headpiece as a crown. I couldn't wait to see Tiffany's face when she unwrapped her present. Tiffany loves ballerinas and that little girl deserved to have an extra special birthday. Especially given the past few months, with all the things she and her brother LJ have been through. Life is tough enough for adults; kids shouldn't have to suffer.

"Am I glad to see you!" I yank open the wide wooden door. "I'd started thinking—"

My words disappear as I come face to face with the man. Not the UPS driver, not a substitute. Not a stranger, either. He's broader, bulkier, since the last time I saw him, and sporting a buzz cut. But I know who he is. Four years has done nothing to erase the sullen frown on his face or vanish the mean glint in his eyes.

A warning not to cross him.

And I won't…so long as he doesn't step foot in my house.

"Hello, Marguerite. Been a long time."

Not long enough, I think, and grip the doorknob tighter. Lloyd Walsh is the last person I'd expect to see at my front door. The faster he's off my porch, and out of our lives, the better off we'll all be.

"Aren't you going to ask me in?"

"No." I step forward, plant myself firmly in the doorway, cursing my foolishness for not taking the extra minute to peer through the peep hole. One look at his scowling face, and I would have thrown the lock. The front door is made of good solid wood. The deadbolt would have held. He has no business being here. No business in my life. Not in any of our lives.

Lloyd Walsh can go to hell.

He scuffs a hand against his head, as if trying to stir up something inside an empty brain. He shifts on his feet, peers over my shoulder into the house.

"Where's Dee? She here?"

"No, she is not." I have no intention of volunteering information. Hopefully, once Lloyd figures out that he's reached a dead end, he'll go away.

"That's not what I been hearing," he says in a deep threatening baritone. "They tell me Dee and the kids have been staying with you."

"She isn't here. She isn't…and she hasn't been," I reply, slightly fudging the facts. My daughter DeAnna hasn't been here for more than two weeks.

He squints at me suspiciously, then plants a massive foot halfway over the threshold. His grimy leather jacket reeks of dirt and stale cigarettes. I step backward as he leans in closer.

"Wanna know what I think, Marguerite?"

The nasty half-smile on his face sends a shiver down my spine. "Not particularly. But you're going to tell me anyway, right?"

Lloyd's smile broadens. "I think you're lying."

I bristle. He's got some gall, calling me out like that.

"I don't appreciate being called a liar."

He hangs there another moment, silently quizzing me, then draws back.

"What about the kids?" he asks.

"They're not here, either. Not right now."

That much is true. They missed the bus this morning, and I had to run the school bus route. I'd dropped Tiffany and her big brother LJ off at school more than an hour ago. But once the school day is over, they'll take the bus home, to me. Lloyd needs to go.

He folds his arms across his chest, leans against the door frame.

"I got time. Guess I'll wait."

"Don't bother," I say, summoning up all the bravado I can muster. "I already told you DeAnna isn't here. But even if she were, it wouldn't matter. This is my house, and I'm the one who gets to say who can come in, and who can't. And I don't want you here, Lloyd. I suggest you turn around, walk down the driveway, get in your car and drive away."

He chuckles. "That's what you suggest?"

"I do," I say, taking note of the grimy four-door parked curbside. Typical Lloyd, to show up in a rust bucket replete with dings and dents. So much for DeAnna's knight in shining armor.

"You're not welcome here, Lloyd. You need to leave."

His eyebrows arch high over the smirk on his face.

"What I *need*, Marguerite, is for you to quit telling me what to do."

If Lloyd Walsh thinks that making a few intimidating threats will scare me into doing what he wants, he should think again. He might have no intention of leaving, but I have no intention of allowing him to get under my skin…or into my house. I've had enough of him swaggering his way through our lives. For years he's been bullying my daughter, scaring my grandchildren, doing his best to destroy our family. The best way to deal with bullies is to stand up to them, hold your ground. Whatever it takes.

Lloyd towers over me, but I draw myself up straight and tall, fix him with a cold gritty stare.

"We're done talking, Lloyd."

"I don't think so, Marguerite," he says cooly. All the studied amusement drops from his face, leaving him with a flat deadpan look. "In fact, I think our little conversation is just getting started."

"Go away." I move to shove the door closed, but he proves too fast. His one-foot-in-the-door gives him extra leverage and his other foot quickly follows. Reaching inside his jacket, he pulls out a gleaming piece of cold, hard steel and aims it at my chest.

Gun in hand, he forces his way inside.

CHAPTER ONE

WHEN I WAS LITTLE, I'D drift off to sleep at night dreaming of the happy life promised to good little girls. *Sugar and spice and everything nice,* Aunt Sis would say, *that's what little girls are made of. Little girls just like you, Reet!,* she'd add, and wrap me in one of her big hugs. Aunt Sis was my mother's sister. She lived alone in an apartment near downtown Chicago, and she gave the best hugs. I loved Aunt Sis as much as if she were my very own mother. Even more, though that was something I never dared say out loud. It was painfully obvious, even to me as a child, that there was no love lost between my mother and Aunt Sis. And while I thought Aunt Sis was one of the most wonderful people in the world, it was my mother who made up the rules that governed my everyday life. Rules I was constantly breaking, according to her. No wonder I loved Aunt Sis. She seemed to think I could do no wrong, and I worked hard to live up to her image of me. I tried my best to be kind and good, each and every day. And every night, after climbing into bed, I'd close my eyes, rest my head on the pillow, and dream of all the bright and beautiful things Aunt Sis promised were surely in my future.

Some of them came true.

The first day of first grade, and a beautiful blue dress plus a brand-new pair of glossy black patent leather shoes, all courtesy of Aunt Sis. *Way too fancy for school*, my mother fumed, quickly banishing the shoes to the dark prison of my closet floor. And though she allowed me to wear the new dress to school, she insisted that on my feet would be the same ugly oxfords I'd been wearing for months. *Much more sensible*, she proclaimed as I silently laced up my scuffed shoes and headed off to school. I wasn't about to sass back. My mother had a quick temper, and her frequent tirades were often accompanied by a sudden smack of her hand against my bottom. And while my mother the warden had decreed that my new shoes must remain doomed in their closet prison, I often snuck out of bed at night, creeping to the closet and drawing out the shoes. Putting them on, I would parade around the bedroom, admiring how the patent leather gleamed in the moonlight. I would have slept in those shoes if I thought I could get away with it. But I didn't dare. I wasn't brave enough. But I loved those shoes. Wearing them gave me a thrill and made me feel as if I was someone different than my mother's daughter. That I counted for something. That, despite what my mother said, I could do anything. Anything, that is, except wear those shoes to school. The night I discovered them finally too small to fit my feet, I cried myself to sleep.

My very first kiss. Too bad it wasn't Alan who was doing the kissing. Ralphie Bennett and I had been practicing kissing out behind his father's garage since Kindergarten. But Ralphie's kisses didn't count. First, because he lived next door. Second, because I'd known him all my life. I had no intention of growing up and marrying Ralphie. How could I?

Everyone knows the man is supposed to be older and smarter than the woman he marries. But I was two weeks older than Ralphie and knew tons more stuff than he did. Plus, Ralphie picked his nose.

My future husband would be handsome, heroic, and the perfect man for me. And after our wedding—me in a shimmering white gown and flowing veil, him in a snappy tux— and a glamorous honeymoon, the two of us would settle down in a cute little house and live a life of happy bliss. I'd learn to cook, and our house would be filled with fragrant smells of delicious dinners and fresh baked goods. I would also learn to sew, and I would fix up our little house exactly as I pleased. Arriving home from work, my Handsome Heroic Husband (HHH) would pronounce my efforts *brilliant*!

Except that's not the way things turned out. I'm not sure how and where and when my life veered off kilter. Yes, the designated HHH did appear, but Alan's flaming red-orange hair and some deep facial scars due to a severe bout of teen-age acne completely shut him out of the Handsome category. Not that I cared. Alan was my husband and hero (HH) for over thirty years. Alan's been dead nearly three years now, but I still wear his wedding ring and I always will. There'll never be another man for me. Alan was kind and decent, a generous man who everyone loved, and most of all, me. Together we made a happy home where I could putter to my heart's content. Children would make our lives complete, but Barry, our firstborn, caught us off guard. The surprise news that we were expecting so soon had family and friends busy ticking off the months on their fingertips. Barry arrived ten months after our wedding, and despite all the gossip, every-one was delighted. He was a perfect baby, the kind of son any parent wishes for. Eventually, after years of trying, DeAnna arrived to join our family. A precious baby girl to cherish and adore. A little sister for Barry, people gushed. How sweet! But not all little girls are sugar, spice, and everything nice. DeAnna grew up pushing the limits, constantly testing our patience right from the get-go.

And now, because of DeAnna, there's a man in my living room.

A man with a gun in his hand.

A gun pointed directly at me.

"Sit." Lloyd uses his gun to point at the couch.

It's a command, not a choice, given the gun in his hand. I quickly obey, drop onto the floral cushions before my legs give out. They're feeling wobbly and I'm feeling frantic, trying to remember where I put my phone. I cast a wild glance around the room. *Where is it? Where is it?* I'm not the type of person who has their phone permanently attached to their hand, but usually it's nearby. Where did I put it? I glance down at the sweater I'm wearing; it's an old one, my favorite, and it has no pockets. My corduroys have pockets, but they're way too snug for a phone. I sink back against the cushions, usually so comfy and embracing, but not today. My heart is pounding hard and heavy in a way that scares me, hammering against the wall of my chest. I force a deep breath, then another, try to slow my breathing. How much stress can a heart take before calling *time out* and going into heart-attack mode? I try not to panic. I know little about cardio health and hearts.

And I know even less about guns, only the little bits here and there that I've picked up from TV crime shows. The police, detectives, and crime scene experts are constantly flouting their knowledge. And while I'm no expert, Lloyd pointing his weapon directly at me has upped the danger level. I'm not scared of Lloyd, but I can't say the same about his gun. I have no clue if it's loaded or not, but I'm not about to take any chances.

If he pulls the trigger, I doubt his gun will be firing blanks.

Lloyd takes a long sweeping glance around the living room, as if he's never seen it before.

"You alone in the house?"

What does he expect me to say? *Yes, I'm alone… for now. But wait a few hours and the kids will be back. Wait two more weeks and DeAnna might be back.*

"There's nobody here but me."

I watch as he stalks the room, halts at the curved archway, glances into the formal dining room. An antique sideboard, six wooden chairs gathered round an oval table, a small glass chandelier hanging above. I'd planned to turn the dining room into party central later tonight, once LJ and Tiffany were asleep in their beds. I'd decorate by hanging streamers from the chandelier and drape the table with glitzy beads and ribbons. Balloons, party hats. I'd stashed all the decorations and party supplies in the tiny pantry off the kitchen. If Lloyd were to venture into the kitchen and open the pantry door, he'd see the party favors and know what's up. Lloyd isn't stupid. He might not remember tomorrow is Tiffany's birthday, but seeing the decorations will jog his memory.

He'll know the kids have been around.

He'll know they're coming back.

"What do you want, Lloyd?"

He doesn't bother answering, but steps away from the dining room arch and heads to the living room staircase. He pauses at the bottom, glances upward, past the landing, listening intently.

I hold my breath, wait for his next move. All he has to do is take a good look around and it will be obvious the kids are staying with me. The house is loaded with clues. Once he climbs those stairs, searches the bedrooms, he'll spot the evidence. Tiffany's clothes neatly arranged on hangers, her few pairs of shoes lined up underneath. My granddaughter likes things neat and tidy, but her big brother LJ is a different story. When it comes to messy, he's definitely DeAnna's son.

Lloyd shrugs out of his leather jacket. He's dressed casually in worn jeans and a black t-shirt under a faded flannel shirt. One side of his neck is covered in ink; an elaborate tattoo of a fierce black snake slithers from underneath his shirt collar, up the side of his neck, behind his ear. He tosses his jacket over the banister, but it slides to the floor. He turns back to face me without bothering to pick it up.

Poor LJ. There's little hope for him, stuck with a messy mother, and a messy father, too.

"Like I said, I'm looking for Dee. I been trying to call her, but something's up with her phone. She ain't answering."

They'd taken her phone away, I silently reflect, and she wouldn't get it back until the day she left. But he doesn't need to know that. He doesn't need to know anything about DeAnna.

But *my* phone! Where is it? What did I do with it? My eyes sweep the living room, but I come up empty. Did I leave it in the kitchen? Maybe on its charger?

"I hear Dee and the kids have been living with you."

"That's true," I reply. "DeAnna stayed here for a few months. But not anymore," I add. "She's gone."

He turns, gazes up the stairs again.

"I already told you, there's no one here but me. But go ahead, look around all you want."

It's a gamble, giving him permission to search my house. Then again, what choice do I have? Lloyd doesn't need my permission. The gun gives him that. But if he goes upstairs, then surely he'll insist on me going with him. And if I somehow manage to slip away, I might be able to get into the bedroom, lock the door, call 911.

There's still an old-fashioned rotary phone, hooked up to a landline, on the nightstand next to my bed.

Lloyd turns away from the stairs to face me.

"So, if Dee's not here, where is she? When did she leave?"

"Almost two weeks ago." I answer his second question while ignoring the first, watching carefully as he prowls throughout the living room. It's almost as if he finds it impossible to remain still. He puts me in mind of one of those tigers LJ loves to watch on our frequent visits to the zoo. Confined to its cage, stalking the perimeter, eyes wary and alert as it paces back and forth. Lloyd obviously has been sprung from a similar captivity. How long has he been out of prison?

I ransack my brain for details of his sentence. He was nothing but a small-time drug dealer, looking to make some fast money by getting involved with big-time dealers. But Lloyd hadn't counted on the undercover narcotics squad also in play, which is what eventually took him down. Hard drugs equaled hard time. He'd been sentenced to ten years in a maximum-security prison.

"I didn't realize they'd let you out already," I venture.

He lifts one shoulder, blows me off. "I got out yesterday. I had to get some things straight before seeing DeAnna and the kids."

"It hasn't been ten years," I say, ignoring his reference to his family. "Not even five."

He shoots me a hard look. "You ever hear of parole?"

I'll bet it wasn't for good behavior. I'd love to fling the taunt right in his face, but I bite back my words, swallow my anger. The last thing I need to do is make him madder than he already is. Especially given the gun in his hand.

I nod at it. "I thought once you're convicted of a felony, you're no longer permitted to own a firearm. Is that true?"

"Maybe. Guess I forgot to ask," he says with a sly smile. "I left in a hurry."

I gasp. "You escaped?"

"Same old Marguerite, never cutting me a break." His eyes narrow. "Assuming I'm the bad guy, up to no good. But someone has to be the bad guy in your world, right? That someone will always be me."

Lloyd is right. As far as I'm concerned, he's always been the bad guy. I've never liked him, not since the day we met. It was a rainy Sunday evening when DeAnna brought him home after work, nervously joking *meet the parents* as she introduced him to Alan and me. We'd already heard plenty about her new boyfriend. He flipped burgers at the fast-food restaurant where DeAnna worked. It was my fault the two of them had met. I was the one who insisted she get a part-time summer job. It would be a good thing, I'd told Alan; it would give her some pocket money and hopefully teach her some responsibility, too. She's still in high school, he'd cautioned, but I'd persisted, and eventually got my way.

Hamburgers and French fries brought DeAnna and Lloyd together, but their romance was fueled by alcohol and drugs. He'd wreaked havoc from the get-go, and nearly destroyed our daughter's life. But I'll be damned if I'll simply stand aside and allow him to destroy my grandchildren's lives, too. Tiffany and LJ are barely more than babies. They deserve better.

I take a deep breath, try to gather my wits together before speaking.

"I'm sorry if you took what I said the wrong way," I say. "That's not what I meant. And please don't think that I'm judging you, either. Because I'm not. The truth is, Lloyd, what I meant to—"

"The truth?" he chortles, slapping his thigh in glee. "Marguerite, you wouldn't know the truth if it bit you in the ass. Don't go getting pissy with me…and don't sit there preaching about what I'm supposed to think. I don't need you yapping at me. And I'm not answering any of your stupid questions, either."

"But—"

"Maybe I got paroled. Or maybe they let me out early for good behavior. Bet you never thought about that, did you?"

"No," I admit.

He's right about one thing. The minute I saw him, I automatically jumped to the worst conclusion. Then again, who would blame me? This entire situation is his fault. Lloyd used force to barge his way into my house this morning. He's been here numerous times throughout the years, but today is different.

Today he is armed and dangerous.

"Do me a favor? Please put the gun down."

"You don't like it?" he challenges with a sneer.

"No, I don't. Would you please put it down? It's making me nervous."

His smile widens. "Here's the thing, Marguerite: making people nervous is what guns are designed to do."

"If you won't put it down, would you at least not point it at me? Please," I add softly, lifting my gaze to meet his.

We stare at each other for a long moment before he finally lowers his weapon.

"Thank you."

Thank you, thank you, dear God! Now please help me find my phone!

"Man, it's hot in here. How about turning down the heat." He runs a finger under the collar of his flannel shirt.

"It's that time of year. We had snow on Halloween." Neither Tiffany nor LJ had been happy when I'd insisted they wouldn't be stepping one foot outside the house for trick-or-treating without their winter coats. It was a blustery night, with high winds and a wintery rain/snow mix. The last thing I wanted was one of them getting sick. *Either you wear your coats over your costumes, or you don't go out at all*, I warned, despite their loud protests and teary faces. I hated playing the bad guy. One of the best things about being a grandparent is having the time to play and have fun with your grandchildren, indulging their whims and desires, while letting someone else handle the disciplining. Except in this case, I was the one responsible, and would be for the foreseeable future. God forbid something should happen to one or both of those two little kids on my watch. I'd never forgive myself, and guaranteed DeAnna wouldn't forgive me, either.

"The thermostat control is over there, on that wall by the stairs," I say, directing him with a nod.

Lloyd moves to the wall, resets the control, then throws me a quick sideway glance.

"Well?" he prompts.

He's waiting for something. But as to what that might be, I have no idea.

"Come on, Marguerite. I just did you a big favor. You got nothing to say?"

His words fill me with an uneasy dread. What favor?

"I'm sorry, Lloyd." I shake my head slowly, completely baffled. "I'm not sure what you mean."

"*Dial down that thermostat*, isn't that what they say? I figure, I just probably saved you a couple dollars, right? And I'm thinking a little gratitude is in order," he continues in a happy drawl. "I'm thinking, right about now, what I oughta be hearing out of your mouth is *Thank you, Lloyd.*"

"Thank you, Lloyd," I say, gritting my teeth. What a small, petty man he is. The heating bill is the last thing on my mind right now.

"You're welcome," he says with a smug smile. "See how easy that was? That's the way it works, Marguerite. You be nice to me, and I'll be nice to you. We can get along, right? Just don't go doing something stupid to make me mad. If you do that, whatever happens next will be all your fault. Remember: I'm not the bad guy here. Do what I say, and nobody gets hurt." He shoots me a meaningful look filled with menace. "*Capisce?*"

"*Capisce*," I reply in a faint voice.

His grin widens, and he nods. "Good. We understand each other."

"Yes, we do," I say, exhaling slowly in small, shallow puffs as I watch him draw the gun's aim off me. Until that moment, I hadn't realized I'd been holding my breath. I squirm where I sit, shifting side to side for a better seat. Though Mother Nature has provided plenty of padding to my bottom half, I can still feel the couch's springs poking through the cushions.

"Where's your phone?" he asks abruptly.

I draw in a deep breath.

"Come on, no stalling," he warns. "Let's have the phone."

"I'm not sure where it is," I say carefully. "Somewhere here in the house. Maybe on the charger?"

He checks the window once more. "So, you're all alone."

"I am."

"Alan at work?"

Lloyd's words stopped me cold. He doesn't know that Alan is dead? Oh, but if only he wasn't! Alan would know exactly what to do, how to handle this situation. He'd always been good at managing people. Managing me, managing Lloyd. The two of them had gotten along as much as anyone could get along with Lloyd. Plus, Alan would know what to do about that gun. He'd been a peace-loving man, but he'd also enjoyed hunting trips with his buddies.

"Alan's been gone nearly three years."

"Ha! He finally got up the nerve to leave?" He slaps his thigh with a loud chortle. "Good for him!"

I flinch. Lloyd might think he's being funny, but I'm not amused.

"Obviously, no one told you. Alan is dead."

"Dead?" He halts mid-step, glares at me in seeming disbelief. "You gotta be shitting me."

"No, I am not *shitting you*." What is the matter with him? Doesn't he know any decent language? Right now, I'd like nothing better than to—

"What the hell?!" Lloyd sputters as a shrill whistle begins shrieking from the kitchen. He flinches at the unexpected noise, and I cringe as he whips around and once again points his gun directly at me.

"It's a clock," I quickly tell him. "It's a little train clock hanging in the kitchen. DeAnna gave it to Alan one year as a Father's Day present. It has a little engine on the hour hand; it chugs around the face of the clock, and it whistles when it reaches twelve. That's what you just heard."

"Pretty stupid, if you ask me," he mutters.

I nearly laugh out loud. For once, Lloyd and I can agree about something. That stupid little train clock drives me crazy, too. Such a silly thing, but Alan had always loved it, especially since it came from DeAnna. He'd hung the clock on a wall near the kitchen door, and I didn't have the heart to take it down after he died. Seeing it was a daily reminder of what a good man he'd been. Plus, Tiffany and LJ had always been fascinated by Grandpa's clock. It had a little switch on the back that I normally kept set to silent, but when they were around, they'd beg *Grammie, turn on the whistle*! I'd turned it on the day they moved in with me, and it was on now. Anything to keep those kids happy.

Thank God for that stupid clock. It's a good reminder not to waste time.

Clocks run on schedule. Trains run on schedule.

So does the school bus.

Five hours until school is finished, and the bus drops the kids off here at home.

Five hours is all I have to get Lloyd out of this house.

"There's an on/off switch for sound. I can turn it off if you like," I offer.

"Doesn't matter." He rubs his neck with his free hand, wipes the sweat beads from his forehead with his shirt sleeve.

He's nervous, I suddenly realize. Maybe as nervous as I am. But why should he be nervous? Lloyd's the one calling the shots. He's the one who pushed his way inside my house. He's the one with the gun.

But what if my gut reaction when I first saw him was correct? What if Lloyd did escape from prison, and now he's on the run?

Which makes total sense, especially given how he looks. He's sweating profusely, with big wet stains spreading under his shirt sleeves and across the back. His eyes dart continuously back and forth around the room, and I suddenly wonder if he's scared that he might be caught.

If I were in his shoes, I'd be scared, too.

"How about some coffee?"

"Coffee?" I stutter, surprised by the ask.

"Yeah, I could use some." He gives me a pointed stare. "You got coffee, right?"

"Sure I do." I nod. "Why don't you sit down? I'll run into the kitchen—"

"…and straight out the back door?" Lloyd taunts with a grim smile. "I don't think so. You get me that coffee, and pour yourself a cup, too. We'll sit together at the kitchen table, and we'll talk about old times. And you can tell me where Dee went." He waves his gun toward the back of the house. "The kitchen's that way, right?"

What would it hurt, him being in my kitchen? He won't find any sign of the kids. I'd wiped down the counters, loaded their cereal bowls in the dishwasher before driving them to school. *Cleanliness is next to godliness*, my mother always preached, and today I'm glad I heeded her lecturing. Being a clean freak might help keep his suspicions from growing.

"Don't go trying anything funny," he warns as I inch my way off the couch. "No fast moves."

As if! What does he think I might do? Throw him a body chop? Kick the gun out of his hand? It's not as if I have a black belt in karate or spend my evenings attending Self Defense classes. The only class I attend with any regularity is a knitting class at our town's community center every other Thursday morning. My neighbor Millie loves to knit, and the two of us usually end up driving together. We trade gossip and knitting patterns with other members of the class, knitting needles flying as we work up our latest creations. I think about the chunky cable sweater I'm making as a Christmas gift for DeAnna. I'm using size fifteen needles; they're nice and thick. Perfect for stabbing someone in the neck.

"How do you like your coffee? Black?" I ask, conscious of Lloyd close behind me. I wrack my brain, trying to remember where I've stashed my knitting bag as I shuffle baby-steps into the hallway. Dragging my feet is the only way I know to stop myself from acting on my instincts, which are currently shrieking *Run! Run! Run!*

"I don't buy cream, but I think there's some flavored vanilla half-n-half," I add as we reach the kitchen. "The caramel was better, but it's all gone." LJ likes to dump it on his cereal, something I personally consider quite gross. Then again, I'm not ten years old. "And I have milk."

"Just sugar." Lloyd halts at the kitchen table. Grabbing one of the chairs, he turns it around, straddling it so he can watch me.

I move to the counter, turn my back to him, purposely blocking his view. I don't want him to see how bad my hands are trembling, how I'm shaken to the core. Lloyd is like any other bully, relishing the power he thinks he has over me. But I refuse to give him the satisfaction of seeing me scared. And I am scared. More scared than I've been in my life.

The coffee is still hot and fresh from when I made it earlier this morning. I pull a clean cup from a cupboard, reach for the coffee pot, and stop dead as I see my phone. It's sitting exactly where I left it, next to the coffee pot. I feel a hot flush race up at my face at the glorious sight of freedom directly in front of me. Reaching out, I slowly, softly, finger the phone. Do I dare take the chance? I've never been particularly brave. Grabbing it will require every single ounce of courage inside me. And if by some miracle I do manage to dial 911, the police would never get here in time to prevent Lloyd from taking his revenge.

I'm suddenly aware of how small my kitchen is. There'd be plenty of time for Lloyd to grab me, hurt me, before the police show up. Not to mention the damage his gun could do. Maybe it's best not to tempt fate.

Meanwhile, I have to keep my options open.

I use a finger to nudge the phone partially out of sight behind the coffee pot. I don't dare chance making a further move, or he might notice. I pour us both generous cups, spoon a few tablespoons of sugar into his. On second thought, I dump the same amount into my own. Normally I drink my coffee black, but I could use an energy boost. What with the late start this morning, getting the kids off to school, playing chauffeur, I had no time for breakfast.

"Here you are. Coffee, sugar." I stand in front of him, his coffee cup in hand. Briefly I consider throwing it in his face. The steaming coffee would stun him momentarily. Long enough for me to bolt out the back door, make my escape.

But what if my aim is off? I've never been good at baseball or contact sports. What if, instead of scalding him, the coffee only splashes his shirt? Lloyd would be furious. He'd point his gun at me. Maybe this time he would pull the trigger.

"Careful, it's hot." I place the cup directly before him, then slowly back away. Back to the counter, back to the sink. Back to my phone and the promise of freedom.

"You think I'm gonna sit here all by myself? I don't think so." Lloyd uses the weapon like a traffic wand, signaling me back to the table. "Grab your coffee and take a seat, Marguerite. The two of us aren't done talking."

The last thing I want to do is rile him up. For now, at least, I need to do what he says. I collect my cup, pull out the chair directly across from him. It's my chair, the one I always sit in. It's a comfy chair and I like this spot. From here, I can easily see the stove, keep an eye on whatever I'm cooking. Sitting here also offers me a good view of the backyard and its elaborate playset. Alan built it one weekend for LJ and Tiffany, and they love playing on the swings and slide. I glance through the kitchen window, gazing at the slide which stands in empty silence; the swings, which hang abandoned, clinking together as they catch a faint breeze. The morning sun frames the backyard lilac bushes. Lush and fragrant in the springtime, their twisted wooden branches are bare. How could everything outside look the same as it did yesterday, while inside the house, things are so very different?

Lloyd changed everything.

I steal a glance at him over the rim of my coffee cup. Being confronted with a gun (especially when it's pointed directly at you) makes one painfully aware of how short and sweet and fragile life can be. If provoked, who knows what Lloyd might do? In the blink of an eye, anything could happen. I never realized how good I had it. Tucked away in my cozy little house, surrounded by the familiar comforts of an ordinary life, I took it all for granted. And then, in one brief moment, I ruined everything. Poof! The doorbell rang and stupid me rushed to open the door without looking.

What if this turns out to be the last day of my life?

Things like this aren't supposed to happen to people like me. If I'm being totally honest, I'll admit that, until today, on some subconscious level I'd assumed that I deserved the normal peaceful life I was leading. I didn't go looking for trouble. I didn't put myself in harm's way. So how could it happen that I'm the one who ends up sitting in my kitchen staring down a gun? How is this fair?

No one ever promised life would be fair, my mother liked to lecture. Thanks a lot, Mom.

I do my best to be a good person. I try to be kind and loving, generous to everyone I meet. Even to people who constantly try my patience. People like Lloyd. I'm as civic minded as anyone else. Rummaging through closets, bundling up old clothes for donations to local shelters. Volunteering is easier than writing a check, especially now I'm retired from my job with the school lunch program. Money is a concern, but I do what I can to support various charities and causes. Donating empty soda bottles to the Veterans of Foreign Wars. Buying a poppy from The American Legion. And I never pass by the Salvation Army Christmas kettles without searching my purse for spare change. So many people need help. They struggle to find jobs, to try and keep themselves and their children warm and fed. How can I not help?

But there are other people out there, too. People beyond the fringe. People who've dropped out of society and will never show up on a do-gooder's radar. Shadow people. Vicious people. People who wouldn't think twice before lunging out in anger, burying a knife deep in someone's chest. People who are coldblooded and ruthless, who could aim a gun, pull the trigger, go for the kill.

Is Lloyd one of them?

I stare at him over my coffee cup, watching as he slouches in his chair. One hand holds the gun, and the other his coffee mug. He takes a fast sip, winces, re-parks the mug on the table.

"Do you need more sugar?" It's critical that I try and keep him happy, at least until I can come up with some kind of action plan that will save me and the kids. "I used three spoonsful, but—"

"Too hot."

"Sorry. Let me get you some ice. That will cool it down." I start from my chair. "I'll—"

"Stay where you are," he barks, training the revolver back on me. "I'll drink it when I'm good and ready. You sit there and keep your hands on the table where I can see them. The two of us need to finish up our little chat, remember? You got the answers, Marguerite, and you better start talking."

"What do you want to know?" I ask, blinking in innocence even as my heartbeat accelerates into guilty overdrive.

"I got lots of questions." A smoldering anger slides across his face. "Let's start with Dee. Is she still in town? Or did someone tell her I might be getting out, and she went into hiding? And don't go pretending like you don't know what I'm talking about," he adds. "You can't fool me. You know where she is, and you better tell me."

"But I—"

"Has she got the kids with her? LJ and Tiffany? I'm warning you, Marguerite: if you don't start talking, things are gonna get ugly. Real ugly." Lloyd's eyes narrow in a dangerous squint. "Where's Dee? Where are my kids?"

CHAPTER TWO

DeAnna's unexpected news ten years ago exploded through our lives like a firecracker, shooting dangerous sparks in every direction.

"I'm pregnant," she said, glancing back and forth between Alan and me.

We greeted her words in stunned silence. To say we were shocked was putting it mildly.

"I know it's not what you wanted to hear," she rushed to fill the bleak stillness blanketing our living room. "And it's not what I wanted to tell you. But I'm running out of time, and soon it will be too late. I don't know what to do! I need your help." The words rushed out of her mouth as the dam of tears broke, flooding down her cheeks. "I'm so scared."

No doubt, I thought. Any girl would be scared. Especially a girl like DeAnna. Unmarried, uneducated, under the age of twenty, who suddenly finds herself *enceinte*. I trained my eyes on my daughter's face, resisting the impulse to glance at her tummy. For weeks now, I'd suspected she might be pregnant. Finally hearing it confirmed came as somewhat of a relief. At least the truth was finally out in the open. There was no longer any need to pretend I didn't know or to hold my tongue. Some discussions can be put off to another day, a better place and time.

But not babies.

Babies don't wait.

"Well." Alan dipped his head and stared at the floor. He drew a handkerchief from a pocket, wiped his lips, cleared his throat with a thick harumph.

"I'm sorry, Daddy. I know you're disappointed," DeAnna's words tumbled out. "Please don't hate me."

"Of course, we don't hate you," I quickly replied, shooting a look toward Alan. Settled in his recliner, he'd been reading the newspaper until our daughter announced her desire to talk. He'd set aside the paper, donned an amiable smile, and turned a listening ear to what she had to say. Now, newspaper still in his lap, he looked anything but comfortable. His face was stoic, but after thirty years of marriage, I was an expert at figuring out what was going on in that mind of his. He might not say much, but Alan had always been a pushover when it came to his little girl.

My little girl, too, I reflected. My baby, DeAnna. Our little girl, barely a woman.

Woman enough to be carrying our first grandchild.

"And the father?" I hated myself for asking. The truth was easy enough to guess. Lloyd and DeAnna had been sneaking around for months. "It's Lloyd, right?"

DeAnna nodded.

"Do you plan on getting married?"

"I don't know," she offered, stealing quick glances at her dad. "He hasn't asked me. Not yet. But even if he does, I'm not sure if I'll say yes. I'm not sure I love him."

"Seriously, DeAnna?! You slept with him, but you don't know if you love him?" I blurted without thinking. We hadn't raised our daughter to act like that. DeAnna knew better. I'd shared the facts of life with her when she first started asking questions. Alan explained things to Barry, and I'd been responsible for instructing DeAnna. And now DeAnna was pregnant. Either I'd failed her as a teacher, or she hadn't been listening.

But had she ever listened to anything I said?

"What were you thinking?" I pressed.

"Obviously, I wasn't," DeAnna replied defiantly, even as her tears increased.

Alan was out of his chair in a heartbeat. He dropped onto the couch next to DeAnna and slipped his arm around her shoulder.

"Shh, it doesn't matter, that's all behind us now." He consoled her with soft little pats. "Right now, the only thing that matters is getting you the help you need. You were right to come to us. Your mother and I—"

"Love you very much," I interrupted in a shaky voice.

Alan nodded.

"We sure do," he echoed. "We love you very much."

"How can you love me?" DeAnna mumbled, her face buried against her father's chest. "I know how much I've disappointed you."

"Well, naturally we're surprised," he conceded. "But we're not the ones you need to be worrying about, honey. You need to concentrate on taking care of yourself, and that little baby. Your life is going to change in a big way. It's already changed."

"You're so young," I added. "You have your whole life ahead of you. Think about it, DeAnna. You just started college—"

"Community college," she pointed out. "But it's not a big deal. And it's not like I'm losing out on a big important scholarship. Besides, I hate school. I thought college would be better than high school, but turns out it's just as boring, too. In fact, I'm not even sure I want to keep going. I'm—"

"You're dropping out?" I sucked in a quick breath at hearing her sad retreat into what would probably end up being total surrender of a better life. I'd had such high hopes for my daughter, especially since I myself had never been to college. I'd thought maybe if she managed to stick it out, get herself through that first year, things might even out. She'd make some new friends, people other than Lloyd, and be exposed to new ways of thinking. College would expand her horizons. Now the only thing expanding would be DeAnna's waistline.

"I knew it! I knew the minute I said anything, that you'd start in on me." DeAnna's eyes flashed with malice as she shot me a reproachful glance. "You never change, do you?"

"Let's not make your mother out to be the bad guy here, okay?" Alan urged softly. "You do what you have to do, DeAnna. And if that means you leave school for a while, then so be it."

"Oh, Daddy, I knew you'd understand." She gave him a quick hug. "Besides, it's not like it's the end of the world. Once the baby is born, I can still go back to school."

But not back to the way things had been, I thought to myself. DeAnna was so young. She had no clue what she'd be giving up, how her life was about to change. How it had already changed. She could never go back. Babies change everything.

"You've got some big decisions ahead," Alan said. "Adult decisions. But remember one thing, honey: no matter what happens, your mother and I will never stop loving you. You're our daughter, and we'll always love you. So, whether you marry Lloyd or not, whether you go back to college, whatever you decide to do…we'll stand by you."

DeAnna lifted her head, glanced back and forth between us through tear-stained eyes.

"Do you think I should keep the baby?"

I drew in a sharp breath. Was she seriously considering other options? For years, Alan and I had co-existed with anxiety and heartbreak thanks to DeAnna's reckless behavior and irresponsibility. But no matter how disappointed we might be, confronted with this latest proof of our daughter's insistence to live life on the edge, this time things were different. And different for us, too. Whatever decision she made would impact us, too. This baby was our grandchild.

Our first grandchild.

"How about Lloyd? What does he say about all this?" Alan asked softly. "This is his baby, too."

"I don't know," she replied, and wiped away fresh tears.

My heart ached for her, and all she was going through. It was painfully obvious she was miserable. I thought about reaching out, wrapping my arms around her…but I stayed where I was. Probably the last thing DeAnna wanted right now was me trying to comfort her. She never wanted that.

"I always thought Lloyd was so smart, that he had all the answers. Until now." DeAnna's voice was hesitant. "He's not being helpful. I've tried to talk to him about it, but he shuts me down. And I know this is going to sound stupid, but it's almost as if he thinks that by not talking about it, then it's not really true. Except that it is! We're having a baby.

"And then…yesterday, he told me he isn't sure he wants to be a father," she added. "He said it's too soon, and that maybe he's not ready."

Maybe Lloyd should have thought of that while he was busy sweet talking our daughter into sleeping with him. Ditto for DeAnna. Neither of them had been thinking. At least, not about the important things like finishing school, getting a good job, setting goals, establishing priorities. Life wasn't just all about having fun, getting high, doing whatever you wanted simply because it felt good. Having choices means accepting the responsibilities and consequences. That includes having sex.

"Lloyd says that having a baby will be expensive. He thinks we should look at our options, that we shouldn't get married just because someone says we should. He says we need to figure out what works for us. Lloyd says…he said…"

DeAnna halted, as if struggling to find the right words for what came next.

"Lloyd said that if we could get some money together, that I could do something…and then we wouldn't have to worry about it anymore. He said maybe that would be best. But I don't know." DeAnna shook her head and glanced away, avoiding the subject, avoiding our gaze. "I don't know."

I didn't dare look at Alan. Was he as horrified as I was? Wrapping our brains around the idea of an unplanned pregnancy is one thing, but the mere thought that this tiny little being growing inside our daughter might never make it into the world is more than I can bear.

More than any of us could bear, as it turned out, when the three of us silently agreed to shelve any further talk, at least for the moment. DeAnna sought shelter in the safety of her bedroom, shutting the door, shutting out the world. Alan disappeared between the pages of his latest read, and I disappeared into the kitchen and made a dinner which none of us wanted or ate. Afterwards, ignoring the dishwasher, I handwashed the dirty dishes. Anything to keep my hands busy and my mind preoccupied from thinking about DeAnna and her dilemma. Except it didn't work. I spent the evening in front of the television; if someone had asked, I wouldn't have been able to recall any of the shows we watched. My nerves were raw, my thoughts twisting and turning, over and again returning to what our daughter had shared. Only when the very last late-night show signed off the air did I finally climb the stairs, pull on my nightgown, brush my teeth, and climb into bed.

Alan was already in bed, the blankets pulled up high around his ears the way he liked. I stretched out on my back, feeling the mattress sag beneath me. Sooner or later, we'd have to break down and buy a new one, but obviously now wasn't the time to be spending money. If DeAnna kept the baby, she was going to need lots of support, including financial. She didn't have any money, and Lloyd wasn't exactly rolling in the dough. And babies were expensive; Lloyd was right about that when he'd warned DeAnna. They'd need a crib, changing table, stroller, car seat. Alan could help them pick one out. He was good at researching the latest in consumer advisories for the best product with the highest safety ratings. And they'd need baby clothes, too. Diapers. Disposable or cloth? Given global warming and environmental concerns, how did parents today decide which was the better choice? Washing machines versus landfill.

And DeAnna would need a good doctor, too. My own OB/GYN retired last year, and I had no clue who to recommend. Maybe one of my friends would know. I'd call around tomorrow.

My brain refused to give over to sleep. I sat up in bed, my eyes adjusting to the darkness as I listened to Alan's slow, steady breathing. Obviously, our daughter's predicament wasn't keeping him from getting a good night's sleep. I leaned over, placed a hand on his shoulder.

"Alan?" I whispered softly. "Alan, are you awake?"

A few seconds passed with no response, and I shook him a little harder.

"Alan?" I hissed as I poked him in the ribs. "Are you asleep?"

"Not anymore, I'm not," he said with a deep sigh and rolled over to face me. He propped himself up on one elbow and squinted at the luminous alarm clock on the nightstand. "Good Lord, Reet, it's two o'clock in the morning," he groaned. "Why are you still awake?"

"I've been thinking about your sister. I might give her a call tomorrow."

"Mary?" He scrubbed his face with one hand, as if trying to rub the sleep away. "What about her?"

"Remember that bassinette we bought before Barry was born? And once DeAnna came along, she used it, too. But then, Mary borrowed it. Do you think she still has it? Or did she give it back and we put it in the attic? I can't remember."

"I don't know, Reet. Does it matter?"

"Of course it does! Don't you even care?" I fumed.

"We can't do anything about it tonight."

"You could go up in the attic and look," I suggested.

"Not right now, I can't."

"Why not?"

"Because I'm going back to sleep. You should, too." Alan sank back into the pillows.

"But—"

"I'll look tomorrow," he promised.

"This is important!" I insisted. "We should do this! DeAnna needs our help."

"This isn't about us," he said through a big yawn. "DeAnna's a grown woman. She'll make up her own mind. And if she wants our help, she'll let us know."

"But—"

"I love you, Reet. Now go to sleep."

I felt him yank the covers back up around his ears and settle down in the darkness. I gave my pillow a fast punch or two, then flopped back down next to him. How he could sleep at a time like this, I'd never understand. I stared up at the ceiling. There was so much to do. So many plans needed to be made. And we didn't have much time. The baby clock was already ticking.

What name would they give the baby? He wouldn't be a *Lloyd*, for that was much too old-fashioned a name for modern day parents. Maybe they'd name him *Alan*, to honor his grandfather. That would be a lovely choice. Names were so important, and you had to choose wisely. Poor Barry, who'd been legally stuck with *Aloysius*, due to Alan wishing to honor his father. *Aloysius Carey*? With our son's middle name left up to me, and with Barry Manilow my favorite singer, it was a no-brainer. I called him Barry, and eventually everyone else did, too.

Or maybe DeAnna's baby would be a little girl. Annabelle, Amanda, Cecilia, Penelope. Beautiful names, all of them. I'd been named after my maternal grandmother, Marguerite, who'd died long before I was born. When our daughter was born, we settled on DeAnna, a combination of Alan's mother's name Deidre, and my mother Anna. Alan's mother had been touched while mine hadn't said a word, one way or another. Still, at the time, it had seemed like a beautiful tribute, and the right thing to do.

Adult children nowadays didn't seem much inclined to honor anyone or do the right thing. They did whatever they wanted. Maybe DeAnna and Lloyd would dream up some crazy name like Cosmo or Crash, Moonbeam or Dandelion. Who in the world would want to name their baby after a weed? I wouldn't put it past them, especially DeAnna. Maybe the next time I was near a bookstore, I'd stop in and buy her a book of baby names. Or maybe I'd hop online tomorrow morning, order a book for her. It could be here within a day or two and I would give it to her before she and that imbecile she was dating fell in love with a name everyone hated.

Merely thinking about Lloyd and everything else was giving me a headache. No wonder I couldn't fall asleep. I thought of a recent article I'd read about the health benefits of a good night's sleep for seniors, a category in which Alan and I definitely qualified. I lay there in the darkness, wracking my brain and trying to recall any of the meditation exercises they'd touted as aids to assist in falling asleep. I forced myself to concentrate, willing my body and each of my limbs to relax.

Breathe in, breathe out.

Breathe in, breathe out.

I thought about DeAnna. Did she have problems sleeping?

Breathe in, breathe out.

Breathe in, breathe out.

How old was that bassinet? Maybe it should be replaced. I made a mental note to talk it over with Alan tomorrow morning before he went up and searched the attic.

Bassinet, crib, stroller. I definitely needed to start a list.

Breathe in, breathe out.

Breathe in, breathe out.

Why couldn't I focus? At this rate, I'd never get to sleep. Alan, meanwhile, seemed to have had no problem. I lay there listening to the soft steady sound of his breathing, his occasional snore. It was monotonous.

Alan was still snoring when I woke up in the morning.

CHAPTER THREE

"QUIT WASTING TIME," LLOYD SAYS. "Where's Dee? Where are my kids?"

How much do I divulge without giving away her whereabouts? Lloyd is obnoxious and irritating as hell, but he isn't dumb. If I tell him where DeAnna is, he'll immediately know the kids aren't with her, and he'll assume LJ and Tiffany are living with me.

And he would be right.

"It's hard to think with that thing pointed at me." I eye his pistol, steel myself for what comes next.

Lloyd stares me down, his eyes cold and black. I force myself to remain still, painfully aware that at any second, he might choose to pull the trigger. I could die right here at my very own kitchen table, spill my blood in the same spot where I've mopped up only-God-knows how many cups of spilled milk and juice throughout the years. But if sacrificing myself is what it takes to keep those kids safe, then I'll do it. There's no telling what Lloyd might do if he manages to get hold of LJ and Tiffany.

I promised DeAnna I would protect her kids, no matter what.

Promises are important. Promises matter.

I always keep my promises.

"Where are they?" he demands.

I stare back and forth between Lloyd and his gun.

"Son of a bitch," he suddenly mutters, and lowers his weapon. "You really know how to piss a guy off, Marguerite."

"I'm sorry." I breathe a sigh of relief and sink back in my chair. "I can't help it if guns make me nervous."

"Your problem, not mine," he shoots back. "You grow up around guns, you learn how to handle them."

"Your father taught you?"

"He taught me how to shoot when I was a kid."

"Alan used to go to deer camp with his buddies," I say, remembering. "When Barry got older, Alan took him along. But they stopped after a few years. He never was much one for hunting."

"Barry's always been a wimp," Lloyd says with a snort.

I don't bother correcting him, despite the fact I'd been referring to my husband, and not my son. But in the grand scheme of things, what does it matter? Neither Alan nor Barry had much to do with guns.

"Speaking of your father," I say, "I was very sorry to hear about his passing."

Six months ago, if memory serves correct. None of us attended the funeral. And, according to DeAnna, neither did Lloyd. I find myself suddenly curious as to whether staying away had been his choice, or a decision forced on him by the prison authorities.

"We sent flowers," I add. A subtle reminder that our two families are connected can't hurt. It might even help bring him to his senses…enough so that he decides to ditch the gun and end this ridiculous scenario of holding me hostage.

"It's difficult when a woman loses her husband. How is your mother doing? I haven't seen her in some time."

No surprise. The only thing Margo and I have in common is our grandchildren. We move in different circles, in different worlds. She's a businesswoman, a sharp dresser, with an even sharper tongue. I've learned to keep my distance. But that doesn't mean I don't feel compassion for what she's been through. The last time I saw her was four years ago, in a crowded courtroom. Margo never flinched as she stood by her son, listening as he was accused, duly tried, convicted on drug-related crimes. She never wavered, not even as the judge sentenced him to ten years in prison. I watched as the guards led Lloyd away in handcuffs. I watched as Margo finally began to weep. I felt like crying, too. *There but for the grace of God*, I reminded myself. DeAnna hadn't been with Lloyd at the time of his arrest, and the police never did come looking for her. But that didn't mean she wasn't complicit, that she hadn't been a willing participant in his drug dealing. I hadn't dared ask her if she'd been involved, for I feared her reaction. Knowing DeAnna, she would have berated me for accusing her, then stormed off in a huff. But ultimately, I suspected I already knew the truth. It was buried deep in my mother's heart. The truth that my daughter, too, could also have been led away in handcuffs. Margo's tears could have been my own.

What a sad, sorry situation. There was no love lost between Lloyd and me, but the fact remained that he was the father of my grandchildren, and he was heading to prison. None of their lives—Lloyd, DeAnna, LJ, Tiffany—would ever be the same. I leaned into Alan, close beside me, felt his arm around my shoulder, pulling me close, grateful that at least the two of us had each other for support. Margo and Donald had been in the courtroom in support of their son, but Donald had seemed indifferent to anything surrounding him, including his wife. They'd sat side by side on the same wooden bench, no words between them spoken, never showing the slightest interest in each other. Donald's attention was focused on the judge, glaring at him as if Lloyd's incarceration was solely His Honor's fault. Alan and I hadn't spent much time socializing with their family. The few interactions we'd had, it was painfully obvious Lloyd and his brothers and sisters had grown up in a much different environment than our own children.

Then again, I think to myself, sparing another glance for Lloyd: who am I to be passing judgment on him and his parents? Our own family life isn't covered with roses. We've suffered our share of thorny issues and painful troubles.

Not to mention that the only reason Lloyd was in my house today was because DeAnna had gotten involved with the wrong crowd and the wrong man.

What a mess.

"Do you mind if I warm up my coffee?" I ask, while still in my chair. Until he puts down that pistol of his, I'm not making one move without his permission.

Lloyd shrugs, and I take it as a yes. At least he hasn't specifically flat-out told me *no*. I stand up, cross the room, stretching my legs as I go. Every muscle aches from holding myself so still. Nearing the counter, I spot my phone peeking out from behind the coffee pot. I will myself to ignore it, acutely aware that his eyes are probably tracking my every movement. I'd never have time to dial 911 before he was out of his chair and on me. Lifting the coffee pot, I refill my cup.

My hand trembles, which comes as no surprise for I'm way past my daily caffeine limit of two cups. How much longer before my bladder insists on calling timeout? I'd been thinking about the bathroom earlier when the doorbell rang.

Reaching the table, I'm relieved to see Lloyd has put down his revolver. It rests on the table, close at hand, his fingers mere inches from the trigger.

I stand next to my chair, offer him a hesitant smile. "Thank you."

He jerks his head in the direction of my chair.

"Sit down."

I'm quick to obey.

"Let's cut the happy talk bullshit, Marguerite." Lloyd stares me down. "No more stalling. I wanna know where Dee is. And my kids." His eyes narrow. "If you don't start talking, you're gonna be sorry."

I pull in a deep breath, trying to center myself. The situation is terrifying in and of itself; if any other man were making these threats, I'd be scared silly.

But this is Lloyd. I'm afraid of his gun, but I'm not afraid of him. The good news is, I don't have a sense that I might be in mortal danger…not yet. Hopefully, that won't change.

"I'll tell you whatever it is you want to know. Whatever you want, Lloyd."

"Damn right," he says smugly.

"But before I do," I say, with some hesitation, "I hope at least that maybe you'll be willing to share what you're planning to—"

"You think I'm gonna tell you?"

"Because if I were you—"

"Good thing you're not, right?" he says with a smirk.

"Because if I were you," I bluster on, "I'd be thinking about how all of this ends. If what you said is true, that you've been released and you're out on parole—"

His scowl deepens. "You don't believe me. I shoulda known you wouldn't."

"Did I say you lied? No, I didn't. All right, for the sake of argument, let's assume you're telling the truth. They sentenced you to ten years, then paroled you after four. Now you're a free man."

"Damn straight."

"So why on earth would you jeopardize that?"

"What?" His head jerks up.

"You barge your way into my house. You're holding me hostage with a gun." I nod at the pistol, still on the table. "You threatened me with a loaded weapon. Think about it, Lloyd. You're not doing yourself any favors. But it's not too late. You can end this right now. Before something bad happens. Before one of us gets hurt."

"If anybody gets hurt, it ain't gonna be me," he predicts.

His grim words of warning send a chill down my spine.

"If you hurt me," I force myself to go on, "things won't end well for you. You'll never get away with it."

"You think you're so smart?" he snarls.

Not smart enough, I silently admonish myself. A smart woman would have used the peephole first. A smart woman never would have opened the door. A smart woman wouldn't be in this mess. And while maybe I'm not so smart, hopefully I'm smarter than Lloyd. If he hurts me, they'll find plenty of forensic evidence to indict him. He's left his fingerprints all through the house, including the front door and the stairway banister. Not to mention the DNA he's unwittingly provided, all around the rim of his coffee cup.

"If you do anything to hurt me, they'll know it was you. They'll come looking for you. And eventually, they'll find you."

But they'd find me first…my cold, dead body sprawled out on my kitchen floor.

"Let's think about this, Lloyd. Let's take a minute to calm down, and to think about what we're doing. What *you're* doing. Because honestly? Threatening me won't solve anything. You and I, we've always had our differences. But showing up here, barging into my house, threatening me with a weapon? That won't go over well, Lloyd. The last thing you want to do is something—"

"Go ahead, Marguerite," he croons in a soft dare. "Go ahead and say it. You know you want to."

I do! I do!

And if I dared, I'd fling the word directly in his face!

Stupid! Stupid! Stupid! It perches on the tip of my tongue, but I pull it back inside my mouth unspoken. Calling him names will only escalate the situation.

Lloyd's dark eyes glow with menace.

"It seems we've reached a standoff." I finally break the silence.

"Not for long," he predicts. "You still haven't told me where Dee is, and my kids. You're trying to keep them from me."

"I'm trying to protect my family."

"*My* family!" he roars, slapping his palm so hard against the table that the gun jumps.

I shrink back in my chair at the naked rage on his face. How much Lloyd must hate me. And me not telling him what he wants to know is only making matters worse.

Curling his fingers, he raises his thumb above his fist, pointing his trigger finger directly at me.

"They're *my* family, Marguerite…and you better not fucking forget it."

As if I could.

CHAPTER FOUR

"**G**ET THIS BABY OUT OF me!"

"It won't be much longer now, I promise." I leaned over my daughter's hospital bed, gripping her hand tighter. "You can do this, sweetheart. I know you can."

"I can't!" DeAnna screamed, banging her head from side to side against the pillows. Her long blonde curls were drenched with sweat, her face red with rage, her eyes swollen from crying. "Can't you see I'm dying here?"

"You're not going to die." I brushed back strands of hair from her forehead with a damp washcloth. "Just a little longer, and then you can push."

"No! Something's wrong! I'm going to die!"

"Reet?" Alan, hovering at the foot of her bed, shot me a nervous glance.

One look at my husband and I knew he needed to leave the room, which was stifling hot despite continuous clanking and humming from a ceiling vent. Alan was sweating profusely, nearly as much as DeAnna, and his face was tinged in an ugly shade of green. The last thing we needed was him passing out.

"Would you go find the nurse?" I suggested. "Ask her to come check on DeAnna. And tell her someone needs to check the air conditioning, too."

I watched him make a hurried escape through the door into the hospital hallway. Poor Alan. He'd been such a trooper through this all. Driving us to the hospital hours earlier, then joining us in the maternity ward at DeAnna's request. She'd insisted he be there, and eventually he'd agreed to her demands. But once we were settled in the birthing room, his excitement had quickly paled, replaced by nervous dread. For the past ten hours he'd hung back in a corner, witnessing his little girl's distress. I didn't blame Alan and his nervous panic. He hadn't been allowed anywhere near the delivery room when Barry or DeAnna were born. Things were different now. Men were encouraged to participate.

But childbirth was still an intense, messy, bloody experience. Alan wasn't prepared.

Neither was DeAnna.

"It's taking too long!" she'd first complained, then climbed from her bed at the nurse's suggestion that walking might help speed up the labor process. Soon the floor beneath her feet was littered with big blue rectangular paper pads; some were damp, but others were soaked and stained with streaks of blood.

"Why is there so much blood?" she shrieked. "No one warned me there would be blood!"

"It's probably some of the fluids leftover from your water breaking. The nurse said it might happen, remember? She said it's completely normal and nothing to worry about."

It was DeAnna's first time giving birth. No wonder she was anxious. Despite my words of comfort and reassurance, there was real fear in her eyes. Real fear in Alan's eyes, too, especially as the hours wore on and DeAnna's cries intensified. More than once I suggested he might be more comfortable in the waiting room. Alan's role was minor. He was an innocent bystander, a soon-to-be grandfather.

And as for the soon-to-be father? I'd gladly wring his neck if I ever got my hands on him. Real men didn't abandon their extremely pregnant girlfriend to go out drinking and drugging with friends while that same girlfriend was due to give birth to their first child. Real men didn't ditch their responsibilities for cold beers on a hot humid day. Then again, all I had to do was consider the source. It came as no surprise that Lloyd had gone AWOL.

Dammit, where was he?

Then Alan was back, this time with the nurse. She approached DeAnna's bedside, quickly examined her, then drew back with a confident smile.

"Guess what? I think it's almost time for you to have this baby."

"*Almost*?" DeAnna howled. "I've been ready for hours! Get this baby out of me!" Then she halted, grimaced, and banged her head from side to side. "Oh, God, make it stop! It hurts!"

"Don't fight the contraction," the nurse warned. "Grab my hand and focus. And don't push, not yet!"

"I'm going to push!" she screamed.

"No! Just pant, pant, like they taught you in prenatal class. Come on, DeAnna, you know what to do. Breathe your way through it. You can do this."

"I can't," she whined.

"Yes, you can," I piped up from the opposite side of the bed. I grabbed her hand and squeezed hard. "Hang on to me, DeAnna. Hang on tight as you can. Now, breathe! Breathe!"

The two of us stood watch as DeAnna struggled, panted, and whimpered her way through the intense contraction. When it finally passed, the nurse reclaimed her position close to the foot of the bed.

"You made some good progress with that last contraction," she advised. "In fact, you might be ready to start pushing."

The nurse was right, and with the next contraction, all of us encouraged DeAnna to push. For once in her life, she offered no resistance but gladly followed directions. Within thirty minutes, the number of people crowded into the birthing room had swelled to six: DeAnna, the doctor and nurse, Alan and me, and our newborn grandson.

"What a fine looking little fellow," the doctor said with a hearty smile as he placed the baby on DeAnna's tummy. "Good job, Mama."

"Hello, little man." DeAnna cooed, a rapturous look on her face as she traced a finger against his cheek. "It's your birthday today. Happy Birthday."

Alan, at my side, reached for my hand. He clasped it in his own and squeezed tight as we stood together at our daughter's bedside. His face was wet with tears, and I was crying, too. DeAnna and I had always had our differences, but miracles happen when babies are born.

The baby—our grandson!—mewed softly, making sweet little sounds like the same ones I'd heard so long ago from my own children.

The nurse moved in and gently gathered up the baby. "Just need a few measurements from this little one. I'll give him right back, promise."

I leaned down and placed a soft kiss on DeAnna's forehead.

"You did a magnificent job," I said. "He's such a beautiful baby."

"He sure is," Alan murmured. "We're so proud of you, honey."

"I'm proud of me, too!" She glanced up at us, her face flush with sweat, pride, and the glow of new motherhood. "He *is* beautiful, isn't he?"

"He certainly is," I agreed.

"There's not a finer baby anywhere in the world," Alan replied.

"Alan, sweetheart, don't you think he looks like you?" I said as the nurse returned with the newest member of our family.

"Lord, I hope not!" he replied with a grin. "For starters, he's got way more hair. Did you ever see a baby with so much hair?" he asked the nurse as she carefully placed the baby into DeAnna's waiting arms.

"He gets the blue ribbon," the nurse laughed.

"Does this little guy have a name yet?" the nurse asked.

"He sure does," DeAnna replied. "Hello, little man," she cooed, cradling her son close. "Hello, LJ."

"El-jay?" The name made no sense to me.

"LJ," she confirmed, reverently touching his nose, the tips of his ears, gently stroking the soft downy hair covering his head. She glanced back up at us. "We already talked about it. His name is LJ."

We? I had a sinking feeling as to exactly who made up the other half of the equation.

"We're naming him after his daddy," she proudly announced. "Lloyd James Walsh. And we're calling him L.J. That's short for Lloyd Junior. LJ Walsh."

Hearing my grandson's name was the first major upset of this glorious day. And I didn't dare look at Alan. What a disappointment this had to be for him. Though we'd never discussed it, I'd suspected that he had similar hopes as mine that DeAnna would name our grandson after him. And if not Alan's first name, then definitely his middle. Names were important, and if anyone had bothered to ask (not that they had), I would have confirmed that *Alan* got my vote. Not only was he DeAnna's father, but he'd already proved to be more of a father to her baby than Lloyd could ever hope to be. Our pregnant daughter deserved better than some lowlife who breezed in and out of her life, including the apartment they shared. Eventually she'd moved back in with us, at least until the baby was born. The final weeks had been touch-and-go, especially with DeAnna's constant Braxton-Hicks contractions. All those false starts had rubbed our nerves raw, and we'd been looking forward to the day the baby finally arrived.

And now here he was, and such a beautiful little boy, too. I wouldn't have missed out on this moment for all the money in the world. I assumed Alan felt the same.

As for Lloyd? It was anyone's guess. Despite our calls, the numerous messages we left, both voice and text, he'd never bothered showing up.

Typical.

"Mom, have you seen my purse? I need it. I want my phone. I need to text Lloyd."

"I'm sure he'll be here soon," I said. Though quite honestly, if I never laid eyes on him again, that would be fine with me. I placed her purse on the foot of the bed. She'd need to relinquish the baby before she could reach it.

"Daddy, can you find him? Lloyd probably doesn't even know that I'm in the hospital. He doesn't know about LJ."

"Sure thing, honey," Alan said. "Let me go make some phone calls and see if I can track him down."

"Thank you, Daddy," DeAnna said with a loving smile for Alan as he left the room. She placed a tender kiss on her baby's forehead. "Just think, LJ: you're going to meet your daddy soon."

I bustled around the room, plumping her pillows, smoothing down the bedsheets. The room had grown quiet since the medical staff cleared out, but sooner or later it would fill up again. Lloyd would make an appearance. Maybe his parents, and his friends and family, too.

"Isn't he the most gorgeous baby you've ever seen?" DeAnna breathed, her eyes still focused on her newborn in her arms.

"He certainly is," I said, pausing to admire my grandson. Such a precious baby boy. And he *did* look like Alan, despite what anyone else thought. "Years ago, I thought you and your brother were the most beautiful babies in the world," I told DeAnna, "but seeing this little man of yours—"

"His name is LJ, Mom," she prompted. "Call him LJ."

"LJ," I repeated, swallowing the moniker quickly to avoid a nasty aftertaste. I can't blame the baby. It wasn't this little guy's fault that he's named after a deadbeat.

"Why don't you get some rest," I suggested. "Your body's been through so much. You must be exhausted."

"I guess I am kinda tired," she admitted. "I didn't sleep much last night."

"Try closing your eyes," I said. "I'll watch the baby…I'll watch LJ." Hearing no protest, I leaned in and gathered the baby in my arms.

"Don't leave, okay?" DeAnna rested her head against the pillow. Within a few seconds, her eyes were closed.

"We're not going anywhere, are we, LJ?" I smiled down at the baby drowsing in my arms. "We're going to sit right over here in this comfy rocking chair and get to know each other."

I took a seat, cradling him close, stroking the dark fuzzy hair covering his head. Then suddenly he flinched, his body going rigid, and I held my breath until he slowly relaxed once again to lay peacefully in my arms. The air conditioner's clanking and humming was the only thing breaking the silence, and I was fine with that. I didn't want to talk, or even hum a little tune. I didn't want to do anything that might disturb the peace I felt inside. I'd forgotten the softness of a newborn's skin, and how perfectly delicious babies smell. I sat and rocked, marveling at the perfect little creature in my arms, and all was pure bliss.

Until the door abruptly opened, and Lloyd blew into the room.

"Hey!" he cried with jubilation. "I hear we got ourselves a baby!"

By nightfall, the room was crowded with balloons and flowers, and family and friends offering DeAnna and Lloyd good-natured ribbing of what to expect now *baby makes three*. Alan and I quietly made our way home and collapsed.

Four years later, the scenario was repeated. The same cast of characters, the very same hospital, and a very pregnant DeAnna supported by Alan and me. And once again, an irresponsible Lloyd was nowhere to be found until hours after his daughter was born. When he finally deemed to make an appearance, my frustration and resentment had moved well past simmer and was nearing the boiling point.

"My little girl," he cooed, snatching up his daughter from her hospital crib to cradle her close. "Hello there, little girl. I'm your daddy. Whatdya think about that?" He fingered the fine wisps of baby hair. "You've got blonde hair, so soft and silky. Like pure gold." Lloyd's eyes brightened. "Hey, that's it! We should call her Tiffany!" He strutted toward the hospital bed, bouncing the baby in his arms. "Whatdya think, Dee? Tiffany Walsh!"

DeAnna frowned. "I thought we were going to call her Sarah. Or Mary. I like both those names."

"Nope, she don't look nothing like a Sarah," he firmly replied. "This one's a Tiffany."

"Tiffany?" DeAnna repeated the name, as if testing it on her tongue, then wrinkled her nose. "I don't like it. It sounds cheap."

"Ha! You think that stuff they sell at Tiffany's comes cheap?" Lloyd smirked and cuddled his daughter closer. "Sorry, baby girl," he crooned, "but your mom don't know nothing. Stick with me. I'll teach you what you need to know."

But time wasn't on his side. Before Lloyd had a chance to teach her much of anything, the authorities had caught up with him, convicted him of dealing drugs, and sent him off to prison. Tiffany had just turned two, and from then on her contact with him had been limited at best. DeAnna had full custody and she controlled Lloyd's access to the children and they rarely saw their father.

And unless I managed to find a way out of this, LJ and Tiffany would find a big surprise waiting when they got home from school.

CHAPTER FIVE

"**B**ARRY. DeAnna. Stop it. Please." We'd buried their father less than five hours ago, yet here they sat, bickering at each other the same way they've been doing since they were kids. I closed my eyes and rested my head against the back of Alan's worn leather recliner. I'd hoped that by claiming my seat in his favorite chair, I'd feel embraced by him. But that wasn't happening. Mostly I felt tired and numb. *Probably from the shock*, Alan's sister Mary had advised earlier at the funeral home. *It's your body's way of protecting you.* But I knew the feelings would set in, sooner or later, and I was not looking forward to it.

"As usual, everything needs Barry's stamp of approval." DeAnna, slouched deep in the couch cushions, folded her arms across her chest and scowled at her brother. "I don't understand why you think this is such a big deal."

"*A big deal?* Maybe because it's a big ask," Barry lobbed his reply. "You've got a lot of nerve, coming over here to-night and demanding money like you're entitled to it. Mom doesn't owe you anything. Not one dime."

"Kids, stop it," I said. "And keep your voices down. Do you want to wake LJ and Tiffany?" My grandkids were upstairs, finally asleep, and now it was just the three of us, gathered in my living room on the night of Alan's funeral. I'd assumed this would be a simple conversation about us moving forward, with some much-needed healing for our family. Instead, thanks to both my children, it had quickly dissolved into a caterwaul of grievances.

"If *you* were the one who needed money, *you* wouldn't hesitate to ask." DeAnna said, ignoring me, accusing him. "Raising kids isn't cheap."

"Is that why Lloyd started dealing drugs?" Barry countered.

"What a shitty thing to say," she retorted.

"Sorry if the truth hurts. If Lloyd hadn't been dealing drugs, he wouldn't have ended up being sent away to prison. He'd be home and working a job like everybody else. He'd be making money so he could feed his kids. That's the way the world works, DeAnna. Normal people don't sit around waiting for other people to pay their way. We work for our money."

DeAnna's face contorted with rage as she glowered at him.

"Why don't you do us all a favor and shut the fuck up?" she shouted.

"Now who's talking trash? Take a look in the mirror, sis," he coolly advised.

"Stop. Just stop it," I pleaded. "I'm not up to hearing this. Not now. Not tonight."

"Great, DeAnna. Are you happy now? See what you've done," Barry warned.

"So it's my fault? I'm the one to blame?" she demanded. "Screw you, Barry. That's not fair. And it's not true, either.

Things aren't always my fault, and especially not this time. Daddy died, but I'm not the one who killed him."

I opened one eye and peered at my daughter. Alan's unexpected death had ripped away the covers and left us shivering in our grief. DeAnna, perhaps, more so than any of us. He'd doted on her, and she'd blithely taken his love and support for granted. I hadn't been sure how she would handle herself, with Alan no longer around to bail her out. But tonight, I had my answer. She expected me to take his place; she expected me to meet her demands.

But I didn't have what she needed. Not money, and not much else, either.

Nothing changes if nothing changes.

I dragged in a deep breath. All of us would need to make changes. And it wouldn't be easy.

"Today has been hard," I said. "And we're all hurting. But we can't let it destroy us. Your dad wouldn't want that."

"Mom's right." Barry held up his hands, palms outward, to DeAnna in a gesture of conciliation. "She doesn't need to hear this."

"Barry, please." I held up my own hand in an effort to silence him. "I can speak for myself."

"Sure, Mom, sorry," he quickly replied. "And you're right. Today has been hard. But you look exhausted. I don't want to see you overdoing it."

"I appreciate that, honey, but you need to let me do things my own way. I need to learn how to do that, and you need to learn how to let me."

I couldn't fault Barry. This past week had been a nightmare, but he'd never complained. He'd been with me from the start, arriving at the house less than an hour after my frantic call with the news his father had been in an accident. Barry was there with me, holding my hand, crying with me as the authorities confirmed Alan's death. He was the one who made the necessary arrangements, contacting the funeral home, overseeing the retrieval of Alan's body from the hospital morgue following his autopsy.

And after that first day, when all I wanted to do was hunker down in bed, pull the covers over my head and give in to my grief, Barry refused to let me get away with it. He pushed me to get up, to take care of myself, to do the things that would help me get through it. DeAnna promised, then bailed, pleading child-care issues. It was Barry who helped me select a casket and flowers, notify our family and friends. And in the middle of all the insanity, it was Barry who urged me to contact a lawyer, to ensure my case would have legal standing in the eyes of the court should it come to that. The attorney had been kind and calm, and blunt. Alan and four others—including the semi truck's driver—had died that night, and the issues surrounding the matter of fault would most likely be argued ad nauseum by numerous insurance companies before any final resolution was reached. Ultimately there would most likely be some type of financial settlement, he advised us, but we shouldn't count on seeing any money soon. It could take months, years even, before things were resolved to everyone's satisfaction.

But it would never be resolved, as far as I was concerned. Black ice. An Act of God. They'd eventually assign a monetary value to Alan's death, but what did it matter? Alan was gone.

"I hate to ask, Mom. But look, I don't need much. Only a little bit to tide me over." DeAnna's face flushed. "If it weren't for the kids, I wouldn't ask. But my government check won't show up till next week, and I'm nearly out of groceries."

There's no doubt in my mind that she's telling the truth. After Alan's funeral service and burial, we'd come back to the house for a funeral feast courtesy of our friends and neighbors. LJ and Tiffany had descended on the homemade casseroles, breads, pies, and desserts like baby vultures, devouring it as if they weren't sure they'd be eating tomorrow.

Were there days when my grandchildren went hungry?

"There's plenty of food in the kitchen," I told her. "The neighbors have been so generous. Take some home with you. In fact, take it all. I don't want it. I won't eat it."

"You've got to eat," Barry warned me. "You need to keep your strength up."

"Don't worry about me," I replied. "I'm packing plenty of extra pounds. Those should keep me going for a while and then some."

"Thanks, Mom," she said. "That's great. The kids will love it. I'll grab some stuff before I go. But…"

"There's always a *but*, isn't that right, sis?" Barry said.

She shot him a cool glance, before turning back to me.

"I appreciate the food, Mom, I do. But the thing is, there are still a couple of bills that need to be paid. That is, if you could see your way to loaning me some money."

"Yep, and now we're right back to the money," he said dryly.

I was too tired to argue with either of them. "How much money do you need?"

DeAnna's eyes and face lit up.

"What's your problem?" Barry pressed. "I can't believe you, coming around here, trying to sponge off Mom. Especially today, after we just buried Dad. You make me sick. For once in your life, DeAnna, why can't you do the decent thing? Don't you have any pride?"

"Pride goes out the window when your kids can't eat," she spit out the words.

"You need money?" He stormed to his feet, yanked his wallet from his hip pocket. Drawing out some bills, he thumbed through them, quickly counting. "Ten, twenty, forty, sixty, eighty…and here's another fifty. How much do you want? How much will keep you happy? How much will make you shut up?" Grabbing the wad of bills, he threw them in her face. They fluttered to the carpet around her feet. "One hundred and thirty bucks. It's all I've got, but it's all yours, sis."

"You are such a fucking prick," she screamed, even as she crouched down and snatched up the dollar bills. "I hate you!"

"Hate me all you want," he said, "but I'll bet it won't stop you from taking my money, right?"

DeAnna glared at him as she lifted herself off the floor, shoved his money in her pocket.

"And not even a *thank you*," he taunted.

"Thank you," she said, spitting out her gratitude in no uncertain terms.

I had nothing left inside me. This day has left all of us crushed. My children are adults, but they lost their father and they're both hurting. But I was hurting, too. I'd buried my husband today. Why didn't they go home and leave me in peace?

"Is it enough, DeAnna?" I asked. "Do you have enough with the money Barry gave you?"

"Well…" she hedged, leaving me to realize that there was still an ask with my name on it.

"I wouldn't ask if I didn't need help. But the thing is," she admitted, "I got a little behind on the electric bill. Plus, the gas bill is due on Friday. They've already threatened to cut me off if it's not paid in full. I mean, what am I supposed to do? Lloyd's not here to help with the rent, and that stupid apartment where we live is so cold. It costs a fortune to keep it heated. But I don't want the kids getting sick."

Neither did I.

"How much, DeAnna?" I asked.

"Five hundred dollars should cover it," she said without meeting my eyes.

"Five hundred bucks!" Barry shouted. "I just gave you money, and now you're begging her for even more? You think she's made of money?"

"You want to know what I think? I think it's none of your business," she snapped back at him. "Butt out!"

"DeAnna, go get my purse," I said. "I'll write you a check."

"Where is it?"

"In the kitchen, I think. On the counter."

"You shouldn't give her money," Barry said as we watched his sister disappear toward the kitchen. "When it comes to money, DeAnna knows what's up. And she also knows you'll probably get a nice settlement from the insurance company because of Dad's accident. Give her money now, and she'll only be back for more."

"Barry, she has children. LJ and Tiffany, remember? What am I supposed to do?"

"Don't give her money," he firmly repeated.

"If you needed money, if you were the one asking for help, I would gladly give it to you."

"I know you would. But that's the thing, Mom: DeAnna knows it, too. You and Dad, you've always treated her with kid gloves, like you were trying to protect her or something. Dad, especially. When it came to DeAnna, he was always an easy touch. Maybe if she'd been allowed to make some mistakes, see what the real world was like, then she—"

There was truth in what he said, but this wasn't a conversation that was meant to be. Barry was my son, not my husband, and it wasn't up to him to dictate the things I should be doing. Not that Alan had dared tell me what to do. That's not the way things had worked between us. We'd been partners, Alan and I, and we'd figured things out together, the way it's meant to be between husband and wife. And while I knew Barry loved his sister, I was also aware that things hadn't been easy between them since Lloyd entered the picture.

"Barry, I love you dearly, but I really want you to drop this. Your sister knows all too well what the real world is like...maybe even more than you do. She's struggling to raise two kids, and she's doing it all by herself. Her life can't be easy."

"Probably not," he agreed. "But maybe she should have thought about that before she let herself get involved with that creep."

Did he actually believe I hadn't had the same thoughts? It was a struggle not to play into Barry's cynicism. It would be so easy to do. But I had two adult children, not just him.

"I know how you feel about Lloyd. I don't like him, either. But what's done is done. And for the time being, or at least while he's still in prison, he's not around to mess up her life. She's trying to do this alone. I think we should cut her a break."

"All I'm saying is, don't give her cash. You have no idea what she'll do with it."

"She has bills to pay."

He stared at me without answering, which in itself was answer enough.

"You think she'll use the money to buy booze," I accused.

He shrugged. "Maybe booze. Maybe drugs."

"She's done using drugs."

"Once an addict, always an addict."

"Barry, this is your sister we're talking about."

"You think I don't know that?" he replied. "Do you have any idea what enabling someone means?"

"I know what it means. But I also know what it means to show someone a little kindness and compassion. One day, when you and Holly have children of your own, maybe you'll understand. At least, I hope you will."

"Here's what I understand," he hissed quietly as DeAnna sauntered back into the room with my purse. "She'll play you every chance she gets. Mark my words: she's here for the money. Once she gets it, she's gone…until the next time she runs out of cash."

It wasn't that I had much to give. It was crucial that I watch my money, especially now Alan was gone. The life insurance policy we'd carried on him hadn't been large, and there wouldn't be much left once I covered the funeral costs. Hopefully if or when an insurance settlement was reached, there'd be enough funds to see me through. Not that I was expecting a windfall; just enough to live on. And one day, after I was dead and buried, any money that was left would go to my children.

Eventually they would get the money anyway. But DeAnna needed help now. Why not give her what I could?

If Barry had children, he would do the same.

I wrote out the check for five hundred dollars, scrawled my signature, and handed it to her.

"Thanks, Mom. You're the best." DeAnna leaned in for a quick hug.

I wrapped my arms around her. The two of us might have our differences, but she would always be my daughter and I loved her very much. There were times when I did not like what she was up to, or the choices she was making, but I would always love her. No matter what.

And I loved my grandchildren, too. Why should they suffer because of mistakes their mother made?

"It's getting late," DeAnna said, ignoring her brother as she shoved the check in her pocket. "I'm gonna take off. I've gotta get home, get the kids to bed."

"Why not spend the night?" I offered as she started for the stairs. "After all, the kids are already asleep. Why disturb them? We have enough room."

"They'll sleep better in their own beds. And LJ has school tomorrow. It's easier if I take them home tonight."

"If you think that's best."

"She wouldn't know what's best even if it bit her in the ass," Barry remarked as we watched her rush up the stairs. "She wants to get out of here before you start thinking twice about giving her that check."

"Don't forget to grab that food in the kitchen," I reminded her a few minutes later when she reappeared with the kids in tow. Three-year-old Tiffany, flushed and drowsy from sleep, was in her arms, with LJ dragging behind. Getting up, I started towards the three of them. "Or maybe I'll pack it up for you. You have your hands full with the kids. Let me do it, it will only take a minute."

"No, I'll get it," she said.

"Why do we havta go home?" LJ cried, rubbing his eyes as he dropped to sit on the second-next-to-bottom step. "I wanna stay."

"I don't care what you want, you're coming with me." DeAnna reached out and yanked him to his feet, pulling him down the rest of the stairs. "Put on your coat. Now!"

She flung the jacket at him which only made LJ cry even harder and caused Tiffany's sobs to start.

"Dammit, what is wrong with you kids!?!" DeAnna cried.

"Let me help." I plucked LJ's jacket from the floor where it had fallen.

"I got him." Barry, right behind me, took the jacket and helped LJ pull it on.

I bent and put my face close to Tiffany's as DeAnna struggled to zip her snowsuit.

"Sweet little girl," I said, thumbing away her tears. "You're so tired and sleepy, aren't you? You need to go to bed and sleep. But come back soon and visit Grammie, okay?"

"Me, too!" LJ cried from behind me. "Grammie, me, too!"

"Yes, you, too." Still crouching, I twisted to kiss his cheek. "You're a brave little boy, LJ. You go home with your mama and sister tonight. And come back whenever you want."

"I love you, Grammie." He wrapped his arms around me and buried his face against my chest.

"I love you, too, LJ."

Poor little guy. He was only a little boy. All of this was so unfair for him, for Tiffany. I hated to see either of my grandchildren in distress.

"Let's go," DeAnna said, breaking things up and rushing them both toward the door. "Bye, Mom." She bussed my cheek with a quick kiss. "Take care. Talk soon."

"Bye, kids," Barry said. "See ya, sis."

Her brother, she purposely ignored as they shuffled out the door.

"I hate to think what kind of a life those kids are in for," Barry predicted as we watched them head down the driveway to her car.

"Don't worry. The kids will be fine. Things will look much better in the morning," I said, trying to reassure myself as well as my son, for I had my own qualms about the situation. We watched from the doorway as DeAnna shepherded her children through the snowy night, loaded them into the car, fastened their seatbelts. "All she needs is a good night's sleep. She's had a rough day."

"We all have," Barry reminded me. "Especially you, Mom."

He put his arm around me, and the two of us watched in silence as DeAnna backed down the driveway onto the street.

And as her car rounded the curb and disappeared, I suddenly realized Barry's prediction from earlier had come true.

DeAnna took my money, but she left the food behind.

CHAPTER SIX

"**D**eAnna is my daughter." How can Lloyd not understand my position? "I'd do anything to keep her safe. *Anything*. And I'm sure most mothers agree. When it comes to protecting our children, we'll do anything. Your mother, too, Lloyd. I'm sure if you asked, she'd say she feels the same…about you."

"Keep my mother out of this," he cautions.

"Have you talked to her since you were paroled?" I press on despite his warning. "Have you seen her?"

He lifts a shoulder, dismissing my ask. "She lives with my brother now."

I frown. "What happened to her house?"

"She sold it after my dad died."

"I didn't know," I say. "I'm sure she must miss it. It was a very nice house."

His parents' home had been much nicer than the one where Alan and I lived. More spacious, more *everything*. Including a basement game room with champion sized pool table, and a sprawling backyard with hot tub and pool. Then again, Lloyd's parents had five children. Kids needed space.

"The first time Alan and I met your parents was at that house," I add. "Do you remember? They invited us to a barbeque. It was summertime, a holiday. Memorial Day, I think…or maybe it was the Fourth of July."

My memories from that night are fuzzy. His father Donald stationed at the grill, loud and rambunctious, downing beer after beer as he flipped burgers and brats. His mother Margo, wine glass in hand, doing her best to match her husband drink for drink. She stumbled around the pool, fussing and cajoling people to *enjoy, enjoy, enjoy*, even as she and Donald kept up their continuous bickering about whether or not he was burning the meat.

"The food was delicious," I add. "And after dinner, your dad shot off fireworks in the backyard."

A gloomy look slides across his face.

"I think maybe you, and one or two of your brothers were out there helping him. Oh! And someone burned his fingers."

"Jimmy," he replies with a fast nod. "He was always playing with matches. One time, he was up in his bedroom, and he almost set the house on fire. My dad got it out in time before one of the neighbors called the fire department. Jimmy was always doing stupid stuff like that."

I think about my own neighbor Millie, and one of her favorite phrases. *There but for the grace of God…* Alan and I had been lucky. Damned lucky. Barry and DeAnna had pulled some ridiculous stunts, but at least neither of them had tried to burn the house down. And while our family had its share of ups and downs, and while DeAnna and I certainly had had our struggles, we'd done the best we could. Our kids knew they were loved, and that they could count on us. What kind of family had Lloyd grown up in? What had Donald and Margo been doing while their son played with matches? They both had careers that demanded their attention: Margo in real estate, and Donald in some type of insurance, often shifting from job to job. Finances seemed to be a constant struggle, according to DeAnna, and she'd mentioned something once about a possible bankruptcy. Not that it was any of my business.

I have no business sitting in judgment of anyone. Including Lloyd's parents.

Not with my own daughter locked away in rehab.

CHAPTER SEVEN

"**T**HEIR TIMING SUCKS! AND IT'S totally not fair!" DeAnna's blue eyes brimmed with tears. "Why are they insisting that if I'm serious about rehab, I need to go today? Don't they realize I have plans? How can they expect me to drop everything and leave? I mean, I have a life!"

"I know, honey. And I agree, the timing is unfortunate." I did my best to console her while keeping my words and tone of voice as preachy-free as possible. "But let's think about it. We're lucky that a room opened up for you. Plus, remember what the Residential Director told us: they can't hold the room for more than twenty-four hours."

"But what about Halloween? I was going to take the kids trick-or-treating. Now I'm supposed to tell them that I can't go? They'll hate me," she wailed. "I don't see what the big deal is, about me waiting another week or so. The room will probably still be there. I just need a little more time."

Time for DeAnna to maybe talk herself out of going to rehab? We'd been waiting for this chance at recovery for more than a month, ever since she voluntarily committed herself to the In-Patient Residential Treatment Program at a facility fifty miles away. A facility with a waiting list. Today a bed had finally opened up. An open bed with DeAnna's name on it.

"You know how much Tiffany's been looking forward to Halloween, especially since she missed it last year, on account of being sick with that stupid corona virus. And remember how I promised her then that I'd take her trick-or-treating this year? I did! I promised!"

I pressed my lips together and held my tongue. DeAnna's life was littered with promises she'd failed to keep. The ones that cut deepest, the ones that hurt the most, were all the broken promises she'd made to her kids.

No more drinking. No more drugs. Mama's all better now. Never again.

"And what about Tiffany's birthday? How can I miss that? I always help blow out the candles on her birthday cake!" She stuck out her lower lip. Big fat tears threatened to spill down her cheeks. "It's not fair," she said with a dramatic sniff. "I want to go to rehab. I want to get better…but I want to help my kids, too."

"Taking care of yourself is a good way to help them."

"But maybe now isn't the right time. Maybe I should stay home. I mean, I can always go to rehab later. Sooner or later, an open bed will come up again. Maybe next week. I could go then."

Maybe. Or maybe not. But I kept my mouth shut, despite the misgivings I felt deep inside and the growing urgency that it had to be today. That if she didn't go today, then she would never go.

But it wasn't my decision to make.

DeAnna sighed, stared at me across the kitchen table.

"I don't know, Mom. What should I do?"

"I can't tell you what to do. It's your life, DeAnna, and it's your decision. But I will promise you this: if you do go, then I'll do my best to take good care of Tiffany and LJ while you're gone. I'll make sure they get to school, and I'll help them with their homework. They'll never go hungry, and I'll make sure they get enough sleep at night. And as for Halloween, I promise I'll take them trick-or-treating. We'll go around the neighborhood and visit every house until there's no more candy left and people shut off their porch lights."

DeAnna still didn't look convinced.

"Tiffany was going to be a fairy princess, and so was I," she said, pouting in pure DeAnna fashion. "We were going to be fairy princess sisters. I bought us sparkly crowns at the dollar store, and I was going to do our nails with some fancy glittery pink polish."

"There's always next year," I said softly, hoping that it's true.

"Okay, fine," DeAnna finally said with some reluctance. "I guess I'll go."

My heart filled with gratitude, soaring with happy relief at hearing her decision.

"I think you made the right choice," I said. "And I think, once you get there, you won't be sorry."

"I still think it's not fair." She turned away and stared out the window.

I followed her gaze. This time of year, our backyard didn't offer much of a view; only a bleak glimpse of the small vegetable garden I planted each spring in hopes of harvesting a few green beans, peppers, and tomatoes. The garden was empty now and would soon be buried under snow. But come next spring, the sun would shine, the snow would melt, and once again I'd be down on my knees, hands in the dirt, planting seeds deep in the ground. It was a ton of work, keeping things watered, culling weeds, shooing away pesky rabbits. Every year I swore I was done with gardening. But each year saw me back on my knees doing the same darn thing, hoping and praying that my hard work would pay off, that those greedy little rabbits would keep their distance, and that things would sprout and eventually blossom into wonderful and tasty produce. *Have faith*, I reminded myself daily as I yanked up fresh weeds. If a person didn't have faith, then what was the point?

I had faith in my daughter. I had faith that she would follow through, make the phone call to rehab, tell them that her bags were packed, she was ready, willing, and waiting. Later that day, my hopes were even higher as I kissed her goodbye. There were tears all around, especially from Tiffany and LJ. The three of us watched as the van with their mother inside pulled away from the curb. I bent down and gave them plenty of reassuring hugs and kisses.

"I know it's hard, but your mama will be back before you know it," I told them as we started back inside the house. DeAnna was on her way, on her journey. A promise fulfilled, a new beginning for my daughter.

And as the days passed, my hopes grew stronger and brighter.

Until DeAnna's phone call from rehab yesterday.

"This place is unbelievable," she sputtered. "I made a mistake. I never should have come here."

"You're giving up already?" All the hopes which had been lifting me higher and higher these past few days suddenly deflated, flying circles in my mind like popped balloons. "Oh, DeAnna, please don't say that. Please don't give up on yourself."

"Don't go getting all preachy with me," she warned. "You do that all the time, and you have no frigging clue what this place is like."

It wasn't easy, ignoring her accusations. DeAnna has always known how/when/where to flip the switches that set me off. But this time, she happened to be right. I would never be a candidate for rehab. I have no taste for alcohol or drugs. One glass of wine induces a dreadful migraine headache, and the sour smell of beer convinced me long ago it wasn't worth it. Two hits of weed in high school and the nauseous roller coaster ride that followed persuaded me to never touch it again. Nowadays, the only regular drug I took was my thyroid medication. That, and the occasional ibuprofen for when my knees get to aching.

"This place is filled with losers." DeAnna's grumbles continued. "Why I thought coming here would be good for me, I'll never know. I'm not as bad as any of them. I don't belong here."

"Remember the first time you were allowed to phone home? You sounded thrilled. You were so happy that day."

They'd taken her phone when she arrived in rehab and she hadn't been allowed any phone privileges during the first crucial week. The second week proved a different story. While her personal phone had been confiscated and wouldn't be returned until the day she left, there was a community phone which she could use. And use it DeAnna did. And with each daily phone call, her complaints grew.

"Lots of people are here under court order. None of them had a choice. It was either go to rehab or go to jail."

No one had coerced DeAnna into signing up for rehab, I silently reminded myself.

"I've had it with this place. I want to come home."

"Why not give it a little more time? It's only been two weeks."

"Two weeks too long," she groused.

Typical DeAnna, bailing when the going gets tough. Now that her days in rehab were beginning to form a pattern, whatever assumptions and expectations she'd originally had were probably beginning to fall far from the mark. But rehab never promised her an easy stroll through a bountiful garden. She was on a journey down a path lined with crooked boundaries that probably included some dead ends. But DeAnna was the one who'd put them there, and she was the only one who could remove them.

"I want to come home."

Not a good idea.

"Maybe you could drive over and pick me up? Today?"

"DeAnna, I'm sorry, but I can't. Not today."

Not today, not tomorrow, not next week.

"I can't stay," she whined. "I have nothing in common with these people. How am I supposed to relate to them? You should hear the things they say during group sessions. I've never been arrested. I've never been in jail."

There but for the grace of God, the thought filtered through my mind yet again.

"And there are all these stupid rules that they make you follow. *Make your bed, hang up your clothes, yadda, yadda, yadda.* The list goes on and on. It's almost like being five years old again." DeAnna spit a laugh. "Okay, I know this sounds weird, but being here almost feels like when I was a teenager and living at home. Except this is worse. *Way* worse. At least you and Daddy weren't constantly ordering me to pee in a cup."

I closed my eyes, whispered a prayer. DeAnna had finally landed in a place meant to help her. Hopefully, she'd give it the time and space needed for the cure to take, for the miracle to happen.

"Did I tell you they searched me? The day I got here, right after I walked through the front door. First thing they did was grab my suitcase. Then a woman took me into a little office and patted me down. And then, when I finally got to my room, I found my suitcase on my bed. Wide open on the bed! It was obvious someone had pawed through my stuff. I mean, they have no business doing that, right? They went through my personal belongings without my permission. They never even asked! Is that legal? I don't care if it's rehab or not. This is still America, right? What's mine is mine, and nobody should be allowed to touch my things unless I say so."

"I'm sure it was frustrating," I said. Then again, what did she expect? She'd signed up for rehab, not a five-star hotel. "Did you notice anything missing?"

DeAnna hesitated. "Some candy," she finally admitted. "They said it wasn't allowed, and that I should have known better than to bring candy and stuff along."

I remembered paging through The Residential Guidebook they'd provided to DeAnna before she left home. The book had been quite specific with its list of *Do Not Bring* items.

Candy, sugar, and foods of any type had been included. Hadn't DeAnna noticed?

"I guess they had a problem with ants last year, and that's why they made the rule," she continued. "Okay, so I guess that rule about no food makes sense. I don't want ants crawling around in my bed! Ick! And it's not like I'm missing the candy. We get plenty to eat. But it's the principle of the thing, you know? My roomie had it worse. She brought along her iPad, but they found it and took it away. Supposedly they've got it locked up in an office somewhere around here, that it's safe. At least, that's what they told her. We're not sure if she should believe them. Anyway, she's still mad about it, and I don't blame her. She's thinking about leaving. And if she goes, then so will I. She's the only friend I have in here. If she leaves, then who am I supposed to talk to? I'll be all alone. That won't be any fun."

Was rehab supposed to be fun? I couldn't remember if that specific topic had been addressed in the Guidebook.

"Hopefully, if she does leave, you'll get a new roommate. Someone that you like."

"Maybe. Oh, I forgot to tell you! Guess what…you'll never believe it!"

DeAnna sounded thrilled, and I was left wondering at her abrupt switch. One minute she was demanding that I drive over and pick her up, and in the next breath she was laughing and sharing some giddy girlfriend gossip. The emotional whiplash was overwhelming and left me convinced that she needed to stay exactly where she was.

"Come on, Mom! Guess!" DeAnna demanded.

"All right," I said, deciding to play along. Anything to keep her happy. "You mentioned you're getting plenty to eat. Are you gaining weight? Is that it?" DeAnna had always been thin, and her drinking and drugging had aggravated the condition. Rather than encouraging the munchies, her addictions had robbed her of an appetite.

"Wrong!" she crowed. "Guess again."

"Honey, I'm sorry. I don't know. You'll have to tell me." All these years of living topsy turvy through DeAnna's daily dramatics, I simply had no more guesses left in me.

"Spoilsport!" she groused happily. "Okay, fine. Believe it or not, I now do my own laundry!"

"Imagine that!" I was delighted at her news. DeAnna had always been a slob. I'd spent countless hours throughout the years begging her to do things for herself, only to ultimately give in and do her laundry, hang up her clothes, and clean up her messes in the kitchen and elsewhere, too.

"They set me up with a Big Sister. That's what they're called; she's like a mentor, you know? Her name is Susie. She knows all about this place and how things work. It's nice, having someone to talk to."

And nice that our conversation had shifted, too. Minutes ago, she'd been complaining about the various rules and restrictions of residential life, how she had no friends, how she wanted to come home. But sometime while we'd been talking, her voice had shifted upward into a lighter and happier gear, and suddenly we're zooming along discussing things on a brand-new level. And while I was more than willing to go along for the ride, I'd made sure to buckle up and keep my eyes wide open. When it came to DeAnna, it was better to be safe than sorry. She'd crashed our lives one too many times.

But maybe this time, things would be different. Being in rehab could make all the difference, if only DeAnna decided to stick with it, embracing the opportunity she'd been given. To treat recovery seriously and see it as a gift. But she was the only one who could do it. Everything hinged on that. And if she did decide to stick with rehab, if she gave it a chance, gave herself a chance, then surely life would be better. DeAnna's life. LJ's and Tiffany's lives. My life. All our lives.

Including Lloyd's.

I stare at the revolver on the table between us, grateful that it's no longer in his hand. The cold hard steel gleams in the sunlight. Sunshine always makes a person feel better. So does coffee.

Maybe the sunshine and coffee are working their magic on Lloyd.

Maybe there's a chance I can talk my way out of this.

After all, I've already convinced him to put down the gun. That's a start.

High on the wall, a whistle suddenly shrieks, causing us both to flinch.

"What the fuck?!?" Lloyd cries out.

"It's the clock." I point to the wall.

Together we watch as the little train chugs its way into time.

CHAPTER EIGHT

"THAT STUPID CLOCK," I MUTTER as my heart rate settles into I-can't-believe-this-is-happening-to-me range. It won't register anywhere near normal again until Lloyd and his gun are out of my house. But eleven o'clock! He's already been here an hour. Time isn't on my side. Four hours from now, the school bus will show up with LJ and Tiffany. And just as they do every day, they'll burst through the door and into the house, drop their backpacks, and run through the rooms to find me.

They'll find Lloyd instead.

But I can't think about that right now. There's a much more urgent problem demanding my attention. I screw up my courage. Let Lloyd say what he wants, but I can no longer wait.

Mother Nature has a rotten sense of timing.

"Lloyd, I need to use the bathroom."

"Yeah, right, like that's gonna happen." He snickers. "Too bad, Marguerite. You'll have to hold it."

Does he think I'm kidding?

"Lloyd, I'm serious." The urge to empty my bladder is increasing by the minute. "It's not as if I have much choice."

He shrugs, gulps his coffee.

"If I sit here much longer, then I'll pee my pants…and that's the truth, so help me God." I raise my right hand with a solemn nod. "I was headed for the bathroom when you showed up today."

He stares at me for a long moment, and I squirm under his scrutiny. Finally, he cedes with an eyeroll.

"Go ahead. But make it quick," he warns.

Standing, I push back my chair.

Lloyd stands, too.

"There's no need for you to tag along," I assure him. "I'll be right back."

"You gonna try and stop me?" he challenges.

When he picks up the gun, I realize I have no choice but to capitulate. I turn and head for the hallway without another word. For now, I'll let him go right on thinking that he's the one in charge. But no way is he coming in the bathroom with me. I don't care if he does have a gun. I deserve some privacy.

I head down the short narrow hallway, aware of Lloyd close behind me. Close enough that I can feel his breath, hot and heavy, on my neck. How in the world DeAnna put up with him all these years is beyond me. The bathroom door is ajar. I push it open and start inside.

He grabs my forearm, pulls me backward.

"Not so fast."

My heart speeds up into overdrive as I catch sight of the dark glower spreading across his face.

"Gimme your phone," he demands, and holds out one hand.

"My phone?" My voice squeaks as I hear myself playing dumb. "I'm…I'm not sure where it is."

I watch his eyes travel the length of my body, searching for a telltale lump of cellular technology. Thank God I followed my instincts and resisted the urge to grab the phone from the charger while I had a chance. I wouldn't put it past him to do a strip search.

"Lloyd, honestly, I don't know where it is. Maybe it's upstairs? You can check my pockets if you don't believe me. But please, make it quick," I plead. "I need to pee."

He stares at me a long minute, then suddenly relents, letting go of my arm.

"I'll be right outside," he warns. "Don't go trying anything funny. And don't lock that door."

The urge to pee is all I can think about. I dash inside and close the bathroom door, shutting him out. I scurry past the sink, but not before reaching across the vanity to turn on the faucet full blast. I've always had a hard time tinkling when there's a remote chance someone might be listening. Older restaurants and shopping malls are the worst, with the stalls close together. I yank down my pants, sink onto the seat and close my eyes in blessed relief. Finally, I let go.

When the pressure on my bladder begins to diminish, I reopen my eyes and focus on my surroundings. The guest bathroom, as I prefer to call it, is barely larger than the hallway closet, with only a sink and toilet for doing one's business. DeAnna once accused me of being pretentious, but I refuse to call it a washroom, even in my head. A washroom or toilet sounds like something you'd find in a grungy factory or a crowded gym. My little guest bathroom features scented soaps and fluffy hand towels.

And directly to my right, a little window overlooking the side yard.

I eyeball the window as I reach for some tissue to wipe myself. This window could be my salvation. I could make an escape *if*—and this is a big *if*—I somehow manage to wiggle through it. Once on the lawn, I could hightail it through the side yard, across the driveway, and into my neighbor Millie's yard next door.

Do I dare try it?

Yes!

Will I fit?

I contemplate the logistics for another few seconds. That's all it takes for reality to set in. Who am I kidding? The window is much too small. I'd never be able to squeeze through the narrow opening. LJ or Tiffany, maybe…but not someone my size. And even if I was small enough, the window is at least five feet off the floor. No way I'd be able to boost myself up and through it. I have zilcho upper body strength, and even a simple task like opening a pickle jar can prove quite the challenge. Plus, there's a not-so-small matter of those thirty extra pounds I've battled for years. I should have taken better care of myself. I should have stuck to a diet, lost weight. Karma sucks. My flabby thighs might be the very thing that ends up killing me.

The door shudders under heavy pounding on the other side.

"Time's up," Lloyd insists.

"I'll be right out," I call, cursing him under my breath as I hastily wipe and pull up my pants. Never in my wildest dreams did I ever think I'd be reduced to *peeing on demand.*

I flush the toilet, stand at the sink, wash my hands. Precious moments pass as I take one last wild look around, searching for something—anything!—I might use to defend

myself. Soap sachets or hand towels won't do much good…
but what about an aerosol can of scented air freshener?
Tucked hiding in my hand, a can would make the perfect
weapon. I could charge out of the bathroom in a surprise
frontal attack, whack Lloyd on the head before he realized
what was happening. Better yet, I could spray the can's con-
tents directly in his face and temporarily blind him, hopefully
providing enough time for me to dart for the front door and
freedom.

I yank open the cabinet door underneath the sink, peer
inside.

Empty, except for one measly roll of toilet paper.

"Open this door, or I'll kick it open," Lloyd growls from
the other side.

"Don't do that!" I open the door, and once again come
face to face with him. I offer a tentative smile, though smiling is the last thing I feel like doing. "Thanks. I feel much
better now."

"Good. Maybe now you're ready to give me what I
want."

"What do you mean?" I ask warily.

"All this yap-yap-yap coming out of your mouth, and
you still haven't told me where DeAnna and my kids are. I
want some answers, and you're gonna give 'em to me."

"I will," I promise. "Let's go back to the kitchen. I'll pour
us more coffee and I'll tell you where they are."

"Screw the coffee. Start talking, right now." Lloyd raises
the gun, centers it mere inches from my belly. "Where are
they?"

And at that precise moment, my phone in the kitchen
begins to ring.

CHAPTER NINE

T HE HOUSE WHERE I GREW up wasn't big, and the walls were thin. My parents' bedroom was next to mine, and I often woke to the muffled shriek of my father's alarm clock. But not this morning. I was awake, happily daydreaming about the day ahead when I heard his alarm. The bedsprings squeaked and I waited for the familiar creak of the loose floorboard as his feet hit the floor. That was my cue. I threw off the blankets and leapt out of bed in a tizzy of energy and excitement. If I hurried and dressed, I could get downstairs and have breakfast with him before he left for work. Having breakfast with my father was always special and made the day start right. But today was already special in a way other days weren't.

Today Aunt Sis was coming to visit!

I heard my father murmur something and my mother briefly answer as I skipped across the bedroom floor. While he showered, shaved, and dressed, my mother usually chose to roll over and go back to sleep. It made no sense to me. Early spring, the sun shining, the birds singing, and the glorious promise of a fresh new day ahead. How could anyone choose to close their eyes to a day such as this? Maybe that's what happened when people got older. And if that were true, then I didn't want to grow up. I loved being ten years old. It was the best age in the world. I was old enough to pack my own lunch (no more of those yucky carrot sticks my mother insisted I eat); old enough to walk to school by myself; old enough to know when to keep quiet during adult conversations. If you're quiet enough, and sit very still, they often forget you're in the room.

I've overheard some interesting things, especially when it was my grandmother doing the talking. She loved to gossip, but some of the things she said were downright weird. Like the time she mentioned my mother and Aunt Sis being Irish twins, which made no sense to me. They had different birthdays, plus no one in our family had come from Ireland. Later on, my grandmother explained to me that *Irish twins* simply meant that my mother and Aunt Sis were sisters who'd been born less than a year apart. And while that was true, the idea of them linked together in any way stuck in my head, causing further confusion. For one thing, the two of them looked nothing alike. Not to mention, Aunt Sis was smarter, despite being younger than my mother. They also had completely different personalities. You never saw Aunt Sis's face covered in scary scowls, and you never heard her lash out in screaming fits. Which she surely would have done, according to my mother, if Aunt Sis had had children of her own, and especially a child like me, to give her constant grief.

She's nothing but a lonely, bitter woman with nothing better to do, my mother would say with a haughty sniff when Aunt Sis extended one of her frequent invitations for me to spend the night. I did my best to ignore my mother's pronouncements. Whatever the reasons behind the invitations, I could not have cared less. My aunt loved me and I loved her. Knowing that Aunt Sis wanted to spend time with me, and seemed to truly enjoy having me around made me feel wanted and special in a way that I instinctively realized my mother could never begin to appreciate or comprehend.

I've no clue why you want to spend time with her. Oh, but I knew why. Even my ten-year-old brain could figure that out. Aunt Sis was kind, and patient, and listened carefully to whatever I had to say about whatever I wanted to talk about. She was everything my mother wasn't.

Plus, she was great fun!

Aunt Sis hated cooking and loved going out to dinner. She'd take me out to one of her favorite Chicago restaurants whenever I stayed with her, and she always let me choose where we should eat. Usually I picked the fancy Italian restaurant, with its cushiony black booths and smoky red candles flickering on the tables. Its big menus, printed in Italian, had totally confused me until Aunt Sis pointed out the word *spaghetti*. After that, I felt much better. The last time we were there, we both ordered the spaghetti carbonara, which I thought was delicious and Aunt Sis agreed.

Often after dinner, we'd go to the movies. Big, spacious movie theaters with plush velvet seats and massive screens. And what glorious movies they were. No shoot-em-up westerns like my father enjoyed; no dark mysterious murder mysteries such as my mother craved. Aunt Sis preferred comedies, especially the musical variety type. Those were my favorites, too. I loved music, and anything that made me laugh. She also enjoyed the occasional romance. *A little romance is good for the soul,* she liked to say, *and lots of romance is even better.* Personally, I found the kissing scenes on the big screen disgusting. I'd scrunch up my face and wrinkle my nose, which never failed to make Aunt Sis laugh. All that hugging and kissing was ridiculous, I told her, but she assured me that someday when I grew up and fell in love, I'd surely change my mind. I wasn't too sure about that.

Once we saw a movie about a big ship that hit an iceberg and sank to the bottom of the ocean with lots of people still on board. The movie was good until the ship began flooding, and everyone started screaming and fighting over life jackets and lifeboats. And when people started jumping off the ship, I scrunched down in my seat and closed my eyes tight. I didn't want to see anyone die. People thought they were taking a nice trip, but they ended up at the bottom of the ocean. Everyone knows you aren't supposed to die on vacation. That's not the way vacations work. Aunt Sis grabbed my hand, squeezed it tight, asked me if I wanted to go home. But I shook my head, opened my eyes and kept on watching. It helped that Aunt Sis held my hand for the rest of the movie.

Later that night, safe in her apartment, we sat around the kitchen table eating store bought cherry pie topped with vanilla ice cream and talking about the ship and all the people on it. It was a real-life adventure story, she said, which left me totally fascinated and absolutely convinced I would never ever step foot on a big boat, let alone sail the ocean! And just as she always did whenever I asked questions, Aunt Sis had answers. She had a way of explaining grown-up things in an easy way that made sense to a kid like me. Plus, she never made fun of me for being scared. When she took me home the next day, Aunt Sis hugged me close, thanked me for visiting, and told me that I was her favorite niece. Which was crazy ridiculous, seeing as how I was her *only* niece, but

I laughed anyway. I knew what she meant. She was saying that she loved me.

And that was the thing I loved most about Aunt Sis. Her words could be trusted. If she said something, I knew that she meant it. It wasn't like when my mother said something borderline nice, which always put a little hope in my heart and made me think that maybe this time, I could actually believe her. But then I'd catch sight of that squirmy little scowl running across her forehead and I'd remember the reality of what living with my mother was like. That little scowl was a harbinger of things to come, and I'd be much better off if I didn't believe anything coming out of my mother's mouth.

But not Aunt Sis. When *she* said something, you knew what she meant.

I did one of my special little happy dances in front of the chest of drawers. Today was a most important day, and I'd already planned what to wear. I yanked open a drawer, found clean underpants and undershirt, quickly pulled them on. Being the only girl in fourth grade whose mother still made her wear an undershirt was downright embarrassing. My best friend, Sally McMaster, started developing last summer, and the perky little nubs poking through Sally's shirt were a topic of endless discussion and fits of giggles between us. Sally, three months older than me, was the first to develop. The thought that both of us would someday grow breasts was something we found hilarious. Sally's mother, however, had no sense of humor and said there was nothing hilarious about the way nature worked. The very next day, Mrs. McMaster whisked Sally downtown to the lingerie section of her favorite department store. Sally was fitted with a training bra, which she proudly modeled for me the next day. It was the sweetest thing, frothy white lace with a tiny pink rosebud embroidered in the middle, and it sparked a fit of strange new feelings inside me. Feelings I wasn't sure what to do with. I longed for a bra just like Sally's. But first, I needed breasts, and that meant going through puberty. Thinking about all the changes my body would soon be going through—developing breasts, growing hair in places where there had been none, starting my period (*gross!*)—was scary in a way I couldn't put into words. So many things about growing up were scary, including my friendship with Sally. I'd never been jealous of her, not once…until I saw her parading around in her new bra. Our friendship might have been ruined if not for Sally's assurance that wearing a bra was no big deal and actually quite inconvenient. Still, I longed for the day when I could ditch my undershirts and begin wearing a bra (or *brassiere*, as my mother insisted on calling it), just like Sally. And nylons, too, I groused, pulling on my white anklets. Sally had been shaving her legs since the beginning of third grade. Why couldn't my mother be more like Mrs. McMaster, who seemed confident and knowledgeable about how these things worked. Didn't my mother understand that I was growing up? I'd be in fifth grade next year, and after that came middle school. I wasn't a baby anymore!

I pulled my favorite blue dress from its hanger and slipped it over my head. *That dress matches your eyes,* my father always said when he saw me in this dress. I smiled every time. He liked saying it, and I liked hearing him say it…and I had a funny feeling that one of the reasons he said it was to put a smile on my face. My father was like that: the kind of man who always had something nice to say about people. To their face, and even if they weren't around to hear him. My grandmother liked to say that my mother should get down on her knees and thank her lucky stars that such a kind, decent man had showed up to marry her. And while my father never failed to smile at hearing my grandmother's words, my mother usually scowled, leaving me to wonder exactly how and why the stars had anything to do with my parents' marriage. What made two people fall in love? Why had my father and mother ended up together? The only thing they had in common was me.

I'd been thinking about bringing it up with Aunt Sis the next time I stayed overnight. I knew she wouldn't mind me asking. We could talk things over, and she'd help me see the bigger picture (as she liked to put it). Then again, the last thing I wanted was to start a family feud, especially between my mother and her Irish sister. After giving it some thought, I finally decided maybe it was better to keep my mouth shut… at least around adults. Kids could get into trouble with adults for saying the wrong thing. That's what best friends were for. I knew I could count on Sally. And when I brought it up, told her that my parents had absolutely nothing in common, Sally said that maybe what was really happening for them was *between the sheets*. Then Sally arched her eyebrows and shot me a sly little smile. *You'll understand when you're older*, she assured me, but my friend's answer only made me madder and more confused than I already was. Sally was only three months older than me. Why was she making it sound as if she knew it all? When would I finally start getting answers to my questions? How much longer before I grew up?

And yet, despite the lure of ditching my ugly undershirts for pretty bras, and finally being allowed to shave my legs, I still wasn't totally convinced that growing up was such a great idea. There didn't seem to be much point. Each morning my father left the house and drove to the bank where he sat behind a desk and gave people money to build their own houses. Meanwhile, my mother stayed home. She spent hours on the phone chatting with her friends, trading gossip. When she wasn't on the phone, she was fussing about the house, fussing at me. A haze of cigarette smoke followed her wherever she went. The cigarettes were tempting until one day last summer when my neighbor Ralphie coaxed me into sharing one. My first and last, I vowed after I finally stopped coughing. How could anyone enjoy smoking? Chalk up another thing my mother and I would never have in common. Though I did like playing cards. She and her friends traded off houses for their weekly card games, and I always looked forward to afternoons when my mother played hostess. There were lovely snacks involved, and the candy box was fair game. Sometimes I tried sneaking a piece without being noticed, but I rarely got away with it. She'd smile, allow me the chocolate, but the indulgent look on her face was deceiving. Once her friends left, she'd slap my hands and face. The candy box was off limits.

What had turned my mother so mean?

Did she even love me? Sometimes I found myself wishing that I had been someone else's little girl. It was a comforting thought, but troubling, too. Would I be doomed to hell for wishing my mother had been someone else?

Someone who wore nice perfume and didn't smoke.

Someone who always had a box of chocolates and didn't mind sharing.

Someone like Aunt Sis, who always had nice things to say about people, even the ones you *knew* she didn't like.

But while my daydreams of a life with Aunt Sis proved a delicious pastime, I also knew they were nothing more. No matter how much I twisted and turned the truth in my head, I belonged where I was. I would always be my mother's child. Besides, life with Aunt Sis would require a sacrifice: life without my father. And that was something I could not fathom. But maybe that was the way things were in life. You didn't always get what you wanted. Maybe the secret to getting along in life was to pick and choose carefully.

Which was what I intended to do, as soon as I grew up. I would take my mother's example and model myself after her by doing exactly the opposite. I would do my very best. I would love my husband and my children, and I would always be there for them. I would cherish and protect them, and my family would know how much they meant to me. We would always be happy. There would be no need for anyone to shout or cry. Why would we? It would be the perfect life.

You think being a grown-up is all fun and games? Just you wait, Marguerite. You'll find out soon enough when you grow up! But no matter how much my mother might grouse, issue stern warnings, I knew things would turn out wonderful. I was determined that when I grew up, my life would be so much better than hers. I would make the right choices and never have reason to be sorry.

I would be the best mother ever, I vowed.

I could hardly wait.

CHAPTER TEN

LOYD SNATCHES MY PHONE FROM its spot behind the coffee pot and punches the speaker button. He glares at me as we listen to the voicemail in real time.

"It's my neighbor Millie," I tell him as I hear the older woman's voice. "She lives next door. I probably should answer," I add. "She's very nosy, always watching out the window, keeping tabs on me. She knows if and when I leave the house."

"A nosy neighbor? Fuck her."

"I'm sure she knows I'm home. If I don't pick up, she'll start wondering why, and probably keep calling until she gets an answer."

He grunts, and I realize my hopes of making any sort of impact on him are quickly fading.

"Who knows? She might even decide to come over and see if I'm okay," I add. "She's done it before."

Lloyd huffs a hard sigh.

"Make it quick." He slaps the phone into my hand.

"Hi, Millie," I say, cutting off my neighbor's message. This is no time for small talk.

"Reet! So, you *are* home! I was starting to wonder. I thought I saw you leave the house earlier, but then you came back. What happened? Did you sleep in late and you needed to get the—"

"Yes, I'm here," I interrupt. My phone is still on speaker, and Lloyd's sure to get an earful if the old woman starts blathering about my mad dash for the car with LJ and Tiffany in tow. "Sorry about not picking up right away," I add. "I was in the bathroom."

"Oh, no problem. Honestly, Reet, can you believe how many people insist on taking their phones with them into the bathroom? All those germs, millions of germs, lurking inside a bathroom. If nothing else, that horrible Covid virus taught us about germs, and how easily they can spread. Germs in the bathroom! Germs on our phones! Talk about unsanitary." Millie happily yaps on without pause. "And speaking of bathrooms, have you ever noticed how some women don't even bother to wash their hands? First they do their business, and then they stand in front of the mirror, putting on their lipstick and fluffing their hair…but they ignore the bathroom sink. You'd think they'd want to take advantage of some hot water and soap. I mean, wouldn't you?"

"Yes, I certainly would," I reply, for once in my life entirely grateful for Millie's constant scatteredness. At least she's moved on from questioning me further about my early morning school bus run.

Lloyd peers at me with a deepening scowl, and motions for me to hurry up. Which I promptly do, seeing as how he's waving the revolver around in impatient little circles.

"Millie, I'm a little busy right now. I'll call you back later, okay?"

"No need. Just give me a yes or no answer. Are you going to our knitting class on Thursday? If you are, I'd like to catch a ride with you. I was driving home from the grocery store the other day when my car suddenly started making these funny little sounds. *Ping-ping-ping*, that's what they sounded like. Well, I'm sure that I don't have to tell you how upsetting it was, hearing those little pings. I mean, what do I know about cars? Nothing, that's what. So I drove home very carefully, very slowly, and once I got in the house, I called the service center and made an appointment to get it fixed. Naturally, they wanted to know what was wrong with the car. I said, if I was smart enough to know that, I would have fixed it myself. Ha! They didn't seem to think that was very funny."

Apparently, neither does Lloyd. He's quit waving the gun around and now has it pointed directly at me.

"Anyway, to make a long story short, I can't get the car in for servicing until Friday. Which leaves me with no transportation to our knitting group. And I was so looking forward to going. Did I tell you that my granddaughter is pregnant again? She's having a little girl this time, and she's so excited! I'm knitting up a baby blanket. I found a new pattern, all frilly and pink. I started it last night, and it's knitting up so pretty. I can't wait to show it to everyone! That is, *if* I can get to the knitting group on Thursday…*if* I can get a ride with you, Reet."

"Yes, of course I'll give you a ride."

"Oh, good. And speaking of cars, do you know anything about that run-down car in front of your house? It's parked at the curb, and it's been there—"

"Sorry, Millie, but I need to hang up now. Bye."

I punch the button disconnecting the call and slump against the kitchen counter. Talking with Millie is an exercise in exhaustion, even on a normal day…which this day isn't. I'm suddenly afraid to look at Lloyd. Obviously, Millie was talking about his car. Nothing escapes her eagle eye.

Millie saw his car. Did she see him?

"Sorry about that." I offer him an apologetic smile. "Millie tends to go on and on."

"A real motor mouth," he says with a grunt. "I thought she'd never shut up."

"Me, too!" I burst out without thinking.

He looks at me and I look at him, and suddenly both of us are laughing, caught up in a surreal moment that defies logic. Lloyd and I are not friends, and we never will be. But we're laughing together, laughing about my neighbor, laughing at the insanity of this bizarre situation in which we now co-exist.

What else is there left to do but laugh?

Cry, or shoot someone.

"Millie's always rambling on about something," I confide.

"Reminds me of my grandma," he says. "She was always yapping about something."

"She's gotten much worse since her husband Frank died," I reply. Maybe if I keep him talking, Lloyd won't notice that I'm still holding my phone. I curl my fingers around it, shifting my arm slightly, allowing it to casually drop down by my side. "It was horrible, the way he died. The two of them were asleep in bed one night, when he had a heart attack. Millie slept through the whole thing. The next morning, when she woke up, Frank was dead."

"Dead?" Lloyd's mouth hangs open. "You mean, dead in bed? With her?"

I nod solemnly.

He winces. "Gross."

"I know, right?" My thoughts tumble back to that awful day, how dreadful it must have been for Millie, waking up to find her husband's body cold and unresponsive. "Anyway, maybe that explains why Millie is like she is. She's lonely. Getting old isn't easy. You start losing things. Your eyes are the first to go. Then it's your hearing, your balance. But once you start losing the people you love? Your family, your friends? That's when things get hard. Some days, it can feel like you're all alone in the world."

I bite my lip, glance down at the kitchen floor, study the patterned tile. Anything to keep my mind off Alan and how much I miss him. I can't risk falling into the doldrums again. Each time I do, the climb back out is that much harder. I take a deep breath, force my eyes back on Lloyd. "Anyway, that's probably why Millie calls so much. She's usually on the phone with me once or twice a day. She's just looking for someone to talk to."

"Next time she calls, she can talk to me." Lloyd holds out his hand, wiggles his fingers in an easy come-on. "Gimme your phone, Marguerite."

So much for hoping he wouldn't notice. Reluctantly I bring it forward and hand it over. I watch forlornly as he drops it inside his shirt pocket.

"Don't be surprised if she calls again soon," I say. "I usually end up letting her talk. It doesn't cost much; only a little bit of my time." I throw him a rueful smile. "I've got plenty of time, now that I'm retired."

"How did he die?" he suddenly asks. "You never said."

Wasn't he listening? I already explained what happened to Millie's husband.

"Frank had a heart attack. He—"

"No," Lloyd interrupts. "Alan."

"Alan? You mean, *my* Alan?"

"Who else?" he replies, vague annoyance sliding across his face. "You know some other Alan?"

Hearing him casually throw out Alan's name makes my legs go wobbly and my stomach suddenly plunge. I'd been about to pour myself more coffee, but now all I want to do is sit down…before I fall down. Leaving my cup on the counter, I head back toward the table, Lloyd right behind me, and we take our seats. He stares at me expectantly. I roll my tongue around inside my mouth, trying to find some spit so I can tell him what he wants to hear. Even three years later, I don't like imagining what would have been Alan's last moments, and I certainly don't like talking about them.

"There was a winter storm," I finally say. "He'd been at work and was driving home. He was on the interstate, in rush hour traffic. A big semi spun out on black ice. Alan and three other people died at the scene."

An immense tragedy for so many families, a television reporter had called it. But actually it was more like an ironic twist of fate. My poor sweet Alan, who despised the drudgery of our bleak Midwest winters and dreamed of the day when he could finally retire to somewhere warm and sunny, had ended up losing his life in a freak winter snowstorm. Over fifty cars had been involved in the pile-up, with the interstate shut down for nearly twenty-four hours. The local news coverage had been extensive, and the national networks had featured footage from the accident during their nightly broadcasts. I'd assumed that everyone, including Lloyd, would have heard about it. Then again, he'd been in prison when it happened. Maybe inmates weren't allowed to watch the news. Maybe their TV time was limited. Maybe they didn't have TVs.

"Hunh." His face sags slightly.

"That was three years ago," I say, "but not a day goes by that I don't think about him. I miss him very much." My heart aches as I speak my truth. Three years has done nothing to diminish the way I feel about my husband. If anything, my love and respect for him has only grown. "He was such a good man."

"Yeah," he replies. "Dee was always saying what a good guy her dad was, how much she loved him."

"She was? She did?" I throw him a sideways glance as something shifts inside me. The notion that Lloyd and DeAnna would have been discussing personal things like that was vaguely upsetting. Some things are meant to be private. Things like family members, family matters.

Then again, DeAnna is family. Family to me and Alan.

She is also family to Lloyd.

My thoughts slide to his own family. From what I'd seen and heard of him, Lloyd's father hadn't been particularly pleasant or kind. What kind of father had he been to Lloyd? What sort of childhood had Lloyd gone through? What must it have been like for him and his siblings, growing up with a man such as Donald Walsh for their father?

"Alan loved DeAnna," I reply. "He loved her very much."

"Right? Just look at that stupid clock she gave him." Lloyd points to the nearby wall. The train clock continues chugging its way toward twelve noon. "Like you said: he hated the thing, but what does he do? Puts the damn thing up where he can see it every day, simply to make her happy." He snorts a short laugh, shakes his head. "My dad would have thrown it in the trash."

Lloyd has the story mixed up. It's me, not Alan, who despises the clock. But in the grand scheme of things, what does it matter? Especially given the slight catch I hear in Lloyd's voice, and that faraway look in his eyes. Despite myself, my misgivings about him and everything he professes to be, I find myself wondering about the little boy he was once upon a time. A little boy, caught up in a swarm of siblings, trying to find his way through the thick of things. He'd started out like all little boys, searching for love and attention and approval from the grown-ups in his life. Time passed, and a young man with a chef hat perched atop his head grilled burgers over a hot stove, cracking jokes and doing his best to impress a new waitress named DeAnna.

I throw him a thoughtful stare. How much of what he says and does is false bravado? Maybe Lloyd isn't as secure in his skin or as confident about his life as much as he'd like me and the rest of the world to believe. What if, in trying to convince all of us that he has his act together, he's also looking to reassure himself?

"Why you looking at me funny?" His eyebrows knit together as his gaze narrows with suspicion. "Something wrong?"

"Nothing. Nothing at all," I reply.

And my phone rings again.

"Look at you, Miss Popularity." Lloyd puts down the gun and fishes my phone from his pocket. "What's Millie want now?"

But it's not Millie. I already know who's calling. He calls every day, Monday through Friday, always at the same time. I steal a quick glance at the clock. Sure enough, the little engine has rounded the halfway mark and is headed up the left side of the track toward twelve o'clock. High noon.

"I guess I should answer," I offer.

"Screw Millie. She can leave a message." Lloyd turns the phone face down on the table next to the revolver.

"But it's not Millie." I shake my head softly. "Barry calls me every day, right around now."

"Barry, hunh?" Lloyd seemed to consider, then swings his head side to side. "Naw, I don't think so."

The two of us listen in a silent void as the call is dropped.

Lloyd breaks out in a wide grin. "Looks like Dee's bro isn't into leaving voicemails."

"He never does," I reply. "But he'll call back. He'll keep on calling until I pick up."

"Too bad. Guess Barry's gonna have to figure out a way to get through the day without talking to his mama."

The phone rings again. Lloyd folds his hands across his chest and settles back in his chair, answering me with a smug smile. But then a third, and a fourth call, come through, continuing to drop, and all traces of his smile abruptly disappear.

"What the hell is his problem?" he mutters.

"Please let me pick up," I reiterate. "I promise I won't say a word about you being here. Barry will never know."

"You expect me to believe that?" he growls. "You think I'm stupid?"

"Of course not," I reply, as the phone begins to ring again. "But I'm telling you, he's going to keep calling. Please let me answer. Please, Lloyd? I won't say a word."

"Why should I believe you?"

"Why shouldn't you?" The words fly out of my mouth before I think to stop them. "I made you a promise, and I'm not someone who goes around breaking promises. If you let me answer, I'll say that I'm busy in the kitchen, and that I can't talk. Barry will believe that. Why wouldn't he? But at least let me answer the phone and talk to him for a minute. If not," I add in an aside, "he might start thinking something's happened to me. That maybe I've fallen. Who knows? Maybe he'll decide to come over and check on me."

No *maybe* about it. I know my son. If I don't answer soon, Barry definitely will be showing up at my house…but not right away. He'll wait until the final bell rang, his school day ended, and his students were dismissed. It will be hours before Barry shows up. But Lloyd doesn't know that.

And I have no intention of telling him, either.

Lloyd eyes me with darkening suspicion as the phone begins to ring again.

I shrug my shoulders softly, even as I cringe. "What can I say?"

He plucks the phone from the table.

"Keep it short," he warns, handing it to me. "And don't try anything funny, either. You don't want to make me mad, Marguerite."

Lloyd's right. Making him mad is the last thing I want to do. He's already halfcocked crazy, and that goes double for me. I'm terrified that the slightest thing might set him off, push him over the edge into who-knows-what-he'll-do-next.

And if I were harboring any thoughts of making the slightest attempt to somehow save myself, the presence of a loaded weapon on the table between us is all I need to keep from breaking my promise to him. He'd fly into a rage, maybe grab the gun, pull the trigger. I would never survive. Not at such short range. And Barry, at the other end of an open line, would hear everything. The sharp crack of gunfire. My screams. Those horrible final moments of my life.

"Put him on speaker," Lloyd commands.

My heart thrums wildly in my chest and I will myself to get a grip. There's no time left to panic. Whatever happens next isn't up to me. I assured Lloyd I could be trusted to keep my promises, and I'm not about to screw things up, and give him reason to doubt anything I might say in future.

If I still have a future.

Then I hit the speaker button, connecting me with my son.

CHAPTER ELEVEN

HOLLY MADE SUCH A BEAUTIFUL bride, and Barry looked so tall and handsome in his tux. My boy was getting married. I blinked back tears. It was hard not to cry.

Thank God for Alan, seated beside me, my hand tucked firmly in his. He gave my fingers a tight squeeze as we watched our son and his bride at the altar reciting their wedding vows in front of family and friends.

"Remember when we did that?" Alan whispered, his head close to mine.

"Yes," I whispered. "It was the perfect day."

Perfect, the same way everything about today had been perfect, I caught myself thinking as the service concluded and the wedding guests streamed out of church. Perfect, though the forecast had predicted rain. Yet the weather held. Golden sunshine embraced them as the newlyweds exited the church to cries of good luck and best wishes. Gossamer soap bubbles floated through the air, settling on their heads as if to crown them with assurances that their hopes and dreams would all come true.

Such a magnificent start to their life together. Everything I could have hoped for my son and new daughter-in-law. Their future looked bright.

Unfortunately, I no longer harbored such hopes for my daughter.

The past few months had been telling. All the wedding plans, choices about the church, ceremony and reception, the food, cake, and music (not to mention who'd made the final invitation list and who'd been scratched) had been time consuming and emotionally exhausting. Yet any fears of Holly turning into a bridezilla never materialized. She remained her usual charming self as the wedding day approached. Not so DeAnna, who'd morphed into a bridesmaid-zilla. Inviting her to be part of the wedding party was a generous gesture on Holly's part, I'd thought, especially since DeAnna would be heavily pregnant with her second baby when the wedding day arrived.

"Why Holly insisted on fresh flowers for the bridal bouquets is beyond me," she scoffed. "Talk about wasting your money. The flowers will be dead in less than twenty-four hours."

"It's her wedding," I replied.

"Well, I think she's making some stupid choices…if you ask me."

I didn't recall the bride or groom, or anyone else, asking for DeAnna's opinion.

"I still haven't made up my mind if I'm going to be in the wedding," she added darkly. "I might not even go."

"DeAnna, you don't mean that!" I cried.

"Oh, don't I?" she replied, eyes gleaming.

My stomach gave an uneasy pitch hearing DeAnna's last-minute threat. "Don't you dare back out now," I warned. "Barry and Holly are counting on you."

"The only thing those two are counting on is the money that you and Daddy are giving them as a wedding present," DeAnna countered. "Anyway, I might be in the wedding, but then again, maybe not. It depends on my dress. I still don't understand why Holly got to pick the dress I'm wearing."

"Maybe because she's the bride?"

"All I can say is, that dress better fit, and it better not itch. And it better look nice. I'm not showing up in something that makes me look like a big ugly cow."

"You'll look beautiful," I assured her. "The dress Holly chose for you is perfect. Remember how much you loved it when you first saw it?"

"No, I don't. And besides, who cares? I'm allowed to change my mind. Barry might, too, when he sees the tux she's picked out for him. He'll look like an idiot in that monkey suit."

But as it turned out, Barry had *not* looked like an idiot, and DeAnna's dress was the perfect color and didn't itch… though her endless complaints and constant grumbling caused plenty of sleepless nights and some serious fretting right up until the wedding day. I'd held my breath as I watched her struggle to stuff herself into the dress. It had been a tight fit, but DeAnna *was* eight months pregnant.

"As soon as they cut the cake, I'm going home and getting out of this dress." DeAnna, slouched uneasily in her chair, rested her crossed arms atop her baby-tummy-shelf.

"Ladies and gentlemen, put your hands together for our bride and groom!" the DJ in a booming voice announced to the crowd. "Let's watch as they take their first dance together as man and wife!"

"Ugh." DeAnna tossed a withering glance at her brother and new sister-in-law as they headed for the dance floor. "Their first dance? Like any of us care."

"I think it's sweet," I murmured as Alan returned to the table with two flutes of champagne and placed one in front of me. I smiled up at him. Did he remember the two of us dancing at our own wedding so many years ago? Tonight, here at our son's wedding, we would dance together again. The romance continued.

"Mama, did you dance with Daddy when you got married?" LJ, decked out in a little tux befitting the ring bearer, gazed up at his mother.

"Quit asking stupid questions. You know your daddy and I aren't married."

"How come, Mama?" LJ pressed. "How come you ain't married?"

"How come you *aren't* married," I gently corrected.

"That's what I'd like to know," DeAnna said, with a furious look for me as she watched me sip my champagne. "Where's my glass?" she asked her father. But Alan merely smiled, shrugged, and shook his head.

"Can I be the ring bearer when you do?" LJ asked.

"If we get married? Yes."

"When you gonna get married, Mama?" he persisted.

"First, your daddy has to ask me."

"When's he gonna do that?"

"Good question, LJ," DeAnna says. "Why don't you go ask him?"

"Okay." He scooted off his chair and headed across the room toward the bar where his father stood.

"LJ looked so cute on the altar today," I said as we watched him scamper away. I hadn't been thrilled about seeing Lloyd's name on the invitation list, but he was DeAnna's plus-one, and plus he was LJ's father. Including him had been the right thing to do.

And he'd cleaned up much nicer than I'd expected. Almost as if he were trying to make a good impression. Decked out in a nice suit, clean shaven, sporting a fresh haircut, Lloyd looked so handsome that I found myself forgiving him for his lack of a tie.

But any goodwill I felt toward him dissolved as the evening progressed. Lloyd kept his distance, hadn't sat with us during dinner, nor with DeAnna, either, since she'd been seated at the bridal table with the rest of the wedding party. Then again, Lloyd wasn't my problem, I reminded myself for the umpteenth time as I watched him head for the beer keg. There was no way of knowing how much he'd been drinking. Hopefully, he wouldn't end up picking a fight with someone, or make a scene with DeAnna. Those two were constantly arguing, picking at each other about this and that. It was hard to stomach. Lloyd needed to take care. This was a family wedding, and he wasn't family. Not yet. Hopefully, he never would be.

Whatever DeAnna saw in him was lost in translation.

Then again, a nagging little voice piped up in my head, *your daughter isn't such a prize herself.*

"Did you see how LJ turned when he got to the altar and lifted the pillow to show us he hadn't lost the rings?" Alan beamed. "What a good boy."

I nodded. I'd been worried about our grandson, too. But LJ had taken his ring-bearing-duties seriously. Plus, never once during the ceremony had he reached down to scratch himself.

"He's very sweet," I add.

"I'm so sick of all this wedding stuff," DeAnna said. "Barry and Holly should have done us all a big favor and eloped. But *no*, the two of them are all about having their *Big Day*. The only reason they wanted this big fancy wedding was to show off. Barry never should have married her. Holly loves to show off. Look how she paraded down the aisle in that gaudy dress she bought in New York!"

"You don't like Holly's dress?" Alan asked, tapping his foot to the downbeat as we watched the bridal couple waltz their way around the dance floor. "I think she looks perfect."

"She does make a beautiful bride," I agreed.

"She's such a hypocrite!" DeAnna cried. "Look at her, how she's prancing around in that white dress, trying to make us believe she's something she's not. Everyone knows that she and Barry have been living together."

"Yes, we know…and no one cares," I reply.

"Well, I'll just bet you would have had plenty to say about it if this was my wedding and I was the one wanting to wear the white dress," she replied darkly. "You never miss a chance to spout off and let us all know your opinion."

"Stop it, DeAnna. Just…stop it." I flashed my daughter a warning glance. For someone who relished rebelling against authority and resisted attempts at being told what to do, she was doing a great job of sitting in judgment of others. "It's your brother's wedding."

"Right. Good ole' Barry. Sucking up to everyone, like he usually does, preaching his agenda."

"I suggest you sit back and enjoy yourself," I said as the music shifted into a jazzy tune. I watched as Holly set her sights on Alan and crooked her finger at him with a fetching smile.

I gave him a nudge. "That's your cue, remember? The father-daughter dance."

"Duty calls." He clambered to his feet and headed for the dance floor.

"Daddy is such a sap. Look at him out there, at her beck and call." DeAnna reached for his half-filled glass and brought it to her lips.

"DeAnna! Don't drink that! It's champagne! You're pregnant!"

"Really, Mom?" Her eyes widened. "Wow, thanks for the reminder. I had no clue."

"You know what I mean. You shouldn't be drinking."

"And *you* shouldn't be telling me what to do." She tipped the glass, drained the champagne, and set the glass aside. "Yum. I think I'll have another."

I shook my head in dismay. "Sometimes I wonder why I bother."

"But you don't, Mother," she retorted. "You never do."

And right then and there, I decided it was better to keep my mouth shut than say something I'd regret for the rest of my life. The two of us turned to the dance floor, watching as Alan swayed to the music with his new daughter-in-law.

"I don't see why she insisted that Daddy do the honors."

"He was glad to do it. Holly's father died when she was five years old. She grew up without a man in her life. Your dad was honored when she asked him to fill in."

"But he's not her dad." A pout filled her face. "Why insist on dragging him out on the dance floor? Just because she's married to Barry now doesn't mean she gets to be all grabby and try making Daddy into something he's not. Because he's *not* her father."

"She knows that."

"You sure about that? Somebody ought to clue her in."

I caught Barry beckon to me from the dance floor. Thank goodness it was my turn to be in the spotlight. DeAnna had been griping all night and I'd heard enough.

"If I ever get married," she added, "guaranteed I won't be making a big splashy spectacle of myself."

"If and when that day comes, I'm sure you'll do as you please," I replied as I walked away. Hopefully DeAnna's wedding day was somewhere in the far distant future *and* would include a different groom. If she married Lloyd, she'd be throwing away her life, and her children's lives, too. When would my daughter finally open her eyes and see him for the man he was? Lloyd didn't seem the least bit inclined to work towards a goal of providing for a family and giving them the things they needed. Bad enough that DeAnna herself didn't seem to have a clue. She didn't need Lloyd hanging around, dragging her down, maybe fathering more babies with her. Another child between them would just strengthen the ties that bound them to each other. DeAnna needed to get her priorities straight and figure out what she wanted out of life. That would come with time. And if we were lucky, time would also provide the needed space for her to meet someone new. Someone who would treat her right. Someone she could fall in love with.

Someone other than Lloyd.

Anyone but Lloyd, I thought to myself as Barry took me in his arms. I smiled at my son, but my thoughts were still on Lloyd as I watched him approach our table and claim the chair I'd vacated. He sank down beside DeAnna, caressed her bulging belly in long even strokes. She leaned in close, purring a smile as he whispered something in her ear. Whatever he said caused her to break out in peals of laughter, and I tore my eyes away, sickened by the sight. All the men in the universe to pick from, and she'd settled for him. Never in a million years would I understand what our beautiful girl saw in Lloyd.

"Everything okay?" Barry said as he whirled me around the dance floor in a fast two-step. "You look a little green around the gills."

"Too much champagne," I quipped.

"Come on, Mom, you barely drink. What's up?"

I steeled my nerves and guarded my tongue. This was Barry and Holly's wedding reception. No room for doom and gloom in this space. Especially while I was in Barry's arms.

"Everything's fine," I assured him. "Such a perfect day, a perfect evening."

"For a minute there, it looked like you and DeAnna were about to duke it out."

"Well, it's over now," I hedged. I'd go to my grave before repeating any of the horrible things his sister had said about his new bride. "You know how your sister gets sometimes."

"Yeah, and no thanks to that creep she got herself tangled up with," he commented drily. "I wish she'd do herself and all of us a big favor and dump him."

I wholeheartedly agreed with him, but the last thing I wanted was to sink further into the muck surrounding DeAnna and Lloyd.

"Let's not talk about them," I said, tapping him lightly on the chest. "This is your wedding day, remember? You and Holly have such a wonderful life ahead. I hope you'll be as happy as your father and me."

"Thanks, Mom." He bussed my cheek with a soft kiss. "Speaking of which, looks like Dad and Holly think their dance moves are something special." He threw a nod to his wife and father as the two waltzed past us with happy little waves. "How about we give them a run for their money? Hang on, here we go!"

Away we went, before I had a chance to exclaim one way or the other. We swayed to the music, my hand clasped tight in Barry's, his other hand around my waist. We never missed a beat as we circled the floor in a series of complicated whirls, twirls, and dips. The room swirled past us, a dizzying montage of lights and laughter, bright smiling faces, hearty applause. Around we went, circling the room again and again. I threw back my head and laughed. I couldn't remember when I'd had so much fun. Guaranteed I would remember this night for the rest of my life.

And then, as we whirled past the table where DeAnna and Lloyd sat, the fun abruptly ceased. I caught a glimpse of Lloyd's face. He glared at Barry, openly staring in a way that was blatant and rude. What was up with that? The two of them had never had much of a relationship. But if Lloyd's rudeness was any indication of how he felt towards Barry, no wonder my son wanted nothing to do with him. Then suddenly Lloyd's gaze shifted and he turned to focus on me as we danced by, headed for the other side of the room. The music grew faster, with Barry keeping time to the beat. We twirled, round and round, faster and faster, in a complicated spin. I snatched another glance at Lloyd as we flew by again. My face burned under the heat of his naked scowl, the anger and resentment spilling across his face.

He hates me, I thought. *Nothing would make him happier than to see me dead.*

I caught my toe and stumbled.

"Whoa!" Barry grasped me close in his arms.

I struggled to find my balance. If not for my son, I'd be flat on the floor.

"You okay, Mom?"

"I'm sorry, sweetheart, but I think I've had enough. I need to sit down."

"Sure," he agreed. "Let's take a breather."

He led me from the dance floor. Past the wedding guests, back toward the table and my empty chair. Lloyd had vacated it, moved on to once again claim his space at the crowded bar. We traded glances as we passed before him, and I caught the gleeful taunt lingering in his eyes, the satisfied half-smile hovering around his lips.

If nothing else, just by his presence here tonight, Lloyd had sent us a message. He didn't think much of Alan, he didn't like Barry, and he most assuredly particularly didn't like me.

Message delivered, loud and clear.

I was DeAnna's mother, but Lloyd was DeAnna's universe. Their lives would always revolve around each other, especially now there were children involved.

The facts were undeniable.

Lloyd wasn't going anywhere, and neither was DeAnna.

And he would never let her go.

CHAPTER TWELVE

"Hey, Mom." Barry's voice flooding over the phone is heavy with concern. "Everything okay? When you didn't pick up, I got worried."

"Don't be silly. Of course, I'm okay." I keep my eyes focused on Lloyd, who's listening intently to the conversation I'm having with my son. "Sorry I didn't answer sooner. I'm in the kitchen and couldn't get to the phone."

"Anything good on the menu?" he asks, his voice losing its urgency.

"I'm thinking about making cookies."

"Peanut butter?"

"Maybe," I reply, a small smile tugging at my mouth. Peanut butter cookies have always been Barry's favorite. On this day of utter insanity, it's nice being reminded of what *normal* usually means. "I haven't decided."

"Peanut butter gets my vote," he says.

"Duly noted," I assure him. Hearing Barry's voice helps me feel calmer. He's been checking in with me every day since DeAnna and the kids moved in. *Just calling to say hi,* he'd say, but it wasn't difficult to figure out that his daily phone calls were meant as a wellness check for Mom. He hadn't been thrilled by my decision to offer DeAnna and the kids a place to live. But what did he expect? Barry knew I'd never turn my back on them. It was my decision, one I made out of love and concern, as a mother, as a grandmother. I'd do the same for Barry and Holly if they ever needed my help. Which they don't, and probably never will. Barry and Holly are fully functional adults with college degrees and good jobs; he teaches science and technology at the same high school he and DeAnna attended, and Holly teaches Kindergarten in a nearby elementary.

And while Barry and his wife have managed to make a nice life for themselves, DeAnna continues to make a mess of things. At times, her behavior is no better than one of her kids. But LJ and Tiffany are children; eventually they'll grow up. DeAnna doesn't have that excuse. Hopefully, rehab will give her the insight to embrace the life lessons she needs to succeed.

Time is running out. If she doesn't learn them soon, it won't be too many years before DeAnna discovers that LJ and Tiffany have grown up and left their mother behind.

"So, what else is new?" Barry asks.

"Not much," I reply, stealing a glance at Lloyd's gun. Hopefully, Barry doesn't mention the kids or DeAnna, causing all hell to break loose. "What's for lunch at school today? Grilled cheese and tomato soup?"

"Mom, you crack me up," he says in a low chuckle. "You still miss the job, don't you?"

"What's wrong with that? I liked my job. It kept me busy." I'd been a lunch lady in the school cafeteria for years. Five other women worked alongside me. They started early, serving breakfast, while I came in later to help with the lunch shift. We all rotated jobs: working the cash register, dishing up food, refilling lunch trays. My favorite job was serving up the grilled cheese sandwiches I made every Friday. Very popular with the school kids, and the staff, too. But I'd quit my job earlier this fall, once DeAnna, LJ and Tiffany moved in with me. The school needed help, but my daughter and family needed me more. Now my days were spent at home, making grilled cheese sandwiches for LJ and Tiffany.

"Sounds like you miss the place. Hey, here's a thought: how about coming over and having lunch at school with me?"

"That's sweet, Barry, but not today."

"Tomorrow, then," he suggests. "We'll sit in the cafeteria together. It'll be like old times."

"We'll see."

"Come on, it's a date, Mom. You're not allowed to stand me up."

"All right," I promise reluctantly. "Tomorrow."

If I'm still alive.

He draws in a breath, and I hear him hesitate.

"Sure you're okay?" he finally asks. "You're taking care of yourself, not pushing yourself too hard? I don't want you getting stressed out. You're not getting any younger, you know."

"Thanks for that reminder, which I certainly didn't need to hear," I retort. "Listen, sweetheart, I know you mean well, but there's no need for you or anyone to worry about me. I'm perfectly capable of taking care of myself."

"Right. And while you're taking care of yourself, you're taking care of everybody else in the world, too." His voice edges tight. "You heard from DeAnna lately?"

"I couldn't say."

More like, I don't dare, I think, catching sight of the suspicious scowl growing on Lloyd's face.

"Hasn't she called?"

"Not recently," I carefully reply. It's not exactly a lie. *Recently* could mean anything: yesterday, last week, last month…or today. And if that's the case, then technically speaking, I haven't heard from DeAnna today.

"I thought you told me that she was supposed to get her phone privileges back a couple days ago."

"I did?" I say, shifting slightly in my chair so I won't catch sight of the surly reaction surely sitting on Lloyd's face. He's been listening to every word, and he isn't stupid. Sooner or later, he'll figure out what we're talking about, and there'll be hell to pay. "I'm not sure."

"These places have rules, Mom. Either DeAnna can call out, or she can't."

"I don't think it's that simple."

"If they won't let her call out," he presses, "then we should be able to put in a call to her. At the very least. There are kids involved."

Shut up, Barry! My stomach shifts into freefall, and I close my eyes, dreading what comes next. My gut is telling me that our conversation is about to derail.

"Kids get sick, they fall, they break an arm. I don't remember DeAnna giving you legal custody of her kids before she went off to rehab. What are you going to do if something happens to LJ or Tiffany? Or what if something happens to you? What are we supposed to do with the kids?"

I nod, eyes still shut.

"Holly and I would gladly take them, but I doubt the state would allow us to do that. Then again, it's not like any of us is going to call the prison and have a chat with Lloyd. Bad enough he's their dad. Why DeAnna got involved with such a lowlife like that guy, I'll never—"

"Hang up!" Lloyd hisses. He jumps to his feet, knocking over his chair in the process as he grabs the gun. He swipes it across his throat in a threatening motion. "Hang up! Now!"

My heart sinks as I realize the horrible turn things have taken. So much worse than I imagined.

"Barry, I'm sorry, I have to go. I love you, Barry."

"No, Mom, wait, I have to tell—"

I disconnect. Whatever he meant to say, it's too late. Much too late. Now I might never know.

Lloyd grabs the phone out of my hand, drops it back into his shirt pocket. The deadpan look on his face chills me to the bone. If ever I thought I knew this man, I was sorely mistaken. I don't know him at all. This is a man capable of anything.

"You been holding out on me, Marguerite." Lloyd's voice is low and smooth as he works the words. "Thought you'd be so smart, trying to pull a fast one on me. But it didn't work out that way, did it? Well, you can thank that loudmouth son of yours." He shakes his head in a long slow motion. "Always sticking his nose where it don't belong, shooting off his mouth. But this time, it backfired on him… *and* on you. Too bad, Marguerite. You should have told me Dee was in rehab."

"Lloyd, please, it's not what you think. Let me explain. You don't understand what—"

"Oh, I understand plenty."

"No, you don't. Please, let me tell you." I stumble over the words, desperately wanting to get my story straight. "I didn't mean to mislead you or—"

"It was a simple ask, Marguerite. I asked if you know where DeAnna and my kids were. Remember me asking you that?" His face darkens in an ugly shade of red, and his voice grows quieter, meaner. "I asked you *directly* if you knew where they were, and you said you didn't."

But he's wrong! I never said that! I've been extremely careful not to say anything that would give them away. But I'm not about to start arguing semantics. Lloyd has a weapon and I have nothing.

Absolutely nothing.

We've reached this impasse because of me. I made a mistake. Maybe the biggest mistake of my life. By not divulging what I knew, what he wanted to hear, I might have triggered the end. God help me.

"You made me a promise, and then you went and broke it by telling lies. Admit it, Marguerite. Looks like you're not as smart as you think. Whatdya have to say about that?"

I struggle to answer over the growing lump in my throat. My heart is flipflopping around inside my chest like a fish out of water. If my legs give out, I might flop right on the floor at his feet.

"Answer me, dammit!"

"All right! Yes, I lied to you," I admit. "I lied about DeAnna and the kids…but I only did it once." The truth is all I have left in my defense. "I was only trying to protect the kids."

"My kids!" he bellows, smashing the palm of his hand against the table, which rocks violently under the power delivered by his hand. "My kids, Marguerite!"

"Yes, they're your kids," I say softly. I'll grant him that much. But I refuse to apologize for what I did. LJ and Tiffany are barely more than babies, and none of this is their fault. I was only trying to keep them safe. Any grandmother would have done the same.

"So, for the record: Dee's in rehab, and you've got the kids."

I nod.

"Where are they now? School?"

I nod again.

"When do they get home?"

"The bus usually drops them off a little bit after three."

Lloyd glances at the clock, then turns back to me with a bone-chilling smile.

"Looks like we've got some time to kill."

Hopefully, he doesn't mean that literally. The word kill isn't conducive to friendly conversation. And for the two of us, the next three hours will be telling. Three hours, I note, watching as the train's little engine nears the top of the tracks and blows its noon whistle. Three hours to figure a way out of this mess, to fix things before they escalate further. It doesn't matter what happens to me, but I can't allow him near the kids. Not while he has that gun. I'd never forgive myself if anything were to happen to LJ or Tiffany. They are my heart. The same blood runs through us.

But they're his children, too. They share Lloyd's blood and his DNA.

He's done such damage to the family, to all of us, but especially to my grandchildren. They're still so young, and impressionable. How much did they see while their parents were together, before he left for prison? Will they remember the ranting, the raging, the hell Lloyd put their mother through?

What about DeAnna? My daughter is no saint.

Lloyd's right eye twitches, ramping up my anxiety yet another notch. I read somewhere that when a person purposely lies, all sorts of involuntary bodily functions (including facial tics) can be a direct result. Is that what's going on with him? He mentioned being on parole. It could be true. Then again, maybe not. For all I know, he's feeding me lies. For all I know, he escaped from prison, and he's on the run.

But putting aside the doubts and misgivings, I'm still left with one undeniable truth: Lloyd is armed and dangerous. He's held me at gunpoint for the past two hours, repeatedly threatening me with bodily harm if I don't do what he says or tell him what he wants to know. I doubt he's been involved in something like this before. No wonder he's acting all jumpy and edgy. If I was the one who'd broken out of prison and was holding someone hostage, wouldn't I be nervous?

Of course, I would. Anyone would.

Including Lloyd.

And with that, I suddenly realize what I've missed in this equation. Lloyd is scared. He keeps rubbing his eye, bouncing his leg up and down, tapping his boot against the floor. This whole situation has him just as unnerved as me; maybe more so.

The more I think about it, the more convinced I am that I've stumbled across the truth.

And there's one more truth I know: when I'm anxious or upset, food usually helps. Why not use it now? Whatever I can do to help him feel comfortable would work out for the good. Anything that benefits Lloyd will benefit me, too.

"It's nearly noon," I say. "Are you hungry? The two of us might as well have something to eat. The school bus won't be here for another three hours, so we have time. Besides, I never did eat breakfast."

I blink brightly, holding back sudden tears prickling behind my eyelids. I'm not sure I'll manage to get much food down, let alone keep it in my stomach. But I need to try. There's nothing left to do but try.

"Do you like tomato soup?"

Lloyd blinks. "Soup?"

"Tomato soup always tastes good…especially on a day like today, when it's so cold outside. It won't be long before winter's here."

I know I'm talking too much, but that's what happens when I get nervous. And with everything that's happened this morning—Lloyd breaking into my house, holding me hostage, threatening me with a loaded gun—today officially qualifies as the most nervous I've been in my entire life. Even more than when I was pregnant with Barry, scared out of my mind at the thought of giving birth. But that fear only lasted until I went into labor and nature took over. After that, the only thing I cared about was pushing the baby out of my body. I went into action and pushed aside my fear.

I can do that now. I can go into action and make us lunch. Maybe then things will get better and I won't feel so afraid.

"I'll put on some soup and make us sandwiches. Do you like grilled cheese? LJ and Tiffany say that I make the best grilled cheese in the world. Let's see if they're right."

Gritting my teeth, I turn my back on Lloyd and his gun and head for the refrigerator.

CHAPTER THIRTEEN

"**I** TRIED TO MAKE RESERVATIONS AT the CN tower, but they're closed for renovations," Alan said as we followed the Maître D to our table. "You would have loved it, Reet."

"But I'm loving this…and I love you!"

What a guy. He'd surprised me with a romantic weekend get-away for our twentieth wedding anniversary. *Pack your bags*, Alan told me. *The kids are old enough to look after themselves.* Before I could protest, we were on a train headed for Toronto. Two nights at the Royal York Hotel (Queen Elizabeth herself stayed here when she was in town!); tickets to *Phantom* with excellent seats center stage and close to the front; dinner to celebrate our anniversary at an elegant downtown restaurant.

"The CN Tower would have been perfect," he continued. "There's a restaurant at the top, and the dining room revolves in a rotating 360 view of the city. You can sit there and watch the world go by as you eat."

"It would have been nice, but this place is lovely, too," I told him as we were seated. "And I'm sure the food is excellent."

Not so excellent, however, was where they seated us. Our cozy table for two was shoved tight against a wall at the back of the restaurant, front and center on the edge of a busy traffic zone leading to and from the kitchen. Staff hurried back and forth through a door right beside us carrying heavy trays laden with delicious smelling foods.

"Maybe if I'd given the Maître D a better tip, he would have given us a better table," Alan said as yet another waiter zipped by us and headed for the kitchen with a tray full of dirty dishes.

"Don't worry, this is fine."

"The view at the CN tower would have been nicer," he added as we opened our menus. "I wanted this weekend to be perfect for you."

"But it is perfect," I insisted. "I'm sitting across from the man I love. The view doesn't get any better than that."

I knew my words sounded cheesy and schmaltzy, but I didn't care. Obviously, neither did Alan. Seeing his eyes light up, spotting the familiar crooked smile spread across his face, I felt just like that seventeen-year-old girl all over again, with the two of us on our first date rather than celebrating our twentieth anniversary.

Only a fool would marry him, my mother warned when she learned we were engaged. *That man will never amount to anything. Mark my words, girl: You'll be sorry.*

My mother was right about two things: Alan hadn't set the world on fire, financially. But he set my heart on fire, and that was enough for me. We had each other, and we got by. And as for her prediction about me being sorry? The only thing I was sorry about was that she was my mother.

The dinner menu was extensive, featuring elaborate entrées and four pages of wines. The listings were completely in French. The prices, however, were printed in a language I understood only too well.

"Alan!" I slapped the menu against my chest and grimaced. "Can we afford this?"

"Let me worry about that," he replied. "I've got some money saved up. Besides, this is our anniversary, remember? I'm taking my girl out on the town."

"I have no idea what I ordered," I confessed after we made our selections. "Do you?"

"Not a clue." His blue eyes sparkled. "Guess we'll be surprised."

He was right. We were definitely surprised once our dinners arrived, especially when we saw the food on our plates.

"The serving sizes are *très petite*," I said, salvaging a few words leftover in my brain from my one semester of high school French.

"I think they forgot to add the meat," he whispered. "All I see on my plate is pasta and…sauce." He raked his fork through a rich puddle of tomatoes, garlic, onions, mushrooms.

We'd ordered the same dish. I tasted mine. "The sauce is good."

"I still think the view at the CN Tower would have been better," he said as we finished our dinners. His eyebrows raised slightly as the waiter presented him with the bill. "Cheaper, too."

"A la carte adds up," I replied, remembering our plates of fresh asparagus, and the measly three stalks which counted as a serving. I could have eaten four more servings. Probably Alan could have, too. Both of us loved vegetables, but at these prices, we couldn't afford it.

"Thank you again, sweetheart," I told him as he reached for his wallet. "This whole day, this entire weekend, has been lovely. I'll never forget it."

"You're sure?" He hesitated. "I wanted tonight to be special."

A waiter bustled past us with a tray of dirty dishes, heading for the kitchen. Another waiter appeared from behind the door, carrying his own heavy tray. The two barely managed to avoid colliding with each other.

"*Merde*!" they exclaimed, glaring at each other.

"You wanted tonight to be special…I think you got your wish!" I said, dissolving into a fit of giggles as the waiters stormed off in opposite directions. "I'm never going to forget this dinner!"

Alan reached across the table and took my hand. Bringing it to his lips, he kissed each of my knuckles, then turned it over and kissed my wrist. "If only you knew how much I love you."

"Ditto," I whispered, and squeezed his hand in return. We were still holding hands as we left the restaurant.

"I'll call us a cab, if you like," he offered as we stood side by side on the busy street. It had been a lovely September day, but the air had cooled considerably as evening drew near.

"Why don't we walk? The hotel isn't far."

"Are you sure?"

"It's only a few blocks. We can do it." I pulled on his arm. "Besides, I'm still hungry. Maybe we'll find a fast-food place along the way."

"Now that you mention it, a burger and fries does sound great," he said with a laugh as we started the leisurely stroll back to our hotel.

We never did find that restaurant, but it was still a wonderful night. I was with my guy, and that was all that mattered. Alan wasn't perfect, but neither was I, and we'd made a wonderful life together. We had our ups and downs, but didn't everyone? Well, maybe not *everyone*. Some people had the luxury of having been born into a life of comfort and ease, knowing that whatever they wanted was theirs for the asking. Alan and I hadn't been as lucky as that. But we had each other, and then we had Barry, and eventually, DeAnna, too. We bought our little house, fixing it up over the years, making it into our home. Life in a small town in a small house wasn't always convenient and never thrilling, but it worked for us.

And living in the Midwest definitely had its benefits. A safe friendly neighborhood where our kids could grow up. Decent schools. Plenty of community services, including a local public library staffed by friendly people we knew on a first name basis. Churches, too; not that we were regulars by any means. Alan's family had been hardcore fundamentalists, in church twice on Sundays for both morning and evening services, plus every Wednesday night. My own parents were opposite with their casual approach to all things theological. Alan and I settled things between us by doing whatever we thought best on any given weekend.

Sometimes when he had a free weekend off from his job at the train yard, we'd throw the kids in the car and *go for a ride*. Living near cities such as Chicago, St. Louis, and Detroit, provided us with plenty of interesting adventures.

Massive underground caves in Kentucky and Virginia ripe for exploring. We were travelling through Northern Michigan on the day the World's Biggest Cherry Pie was baked. We spent some hours waiting for it to be served up to us and seven thousand other hungry bystanders, earning it a spot in the Guinness Book of Records. And while the World's Largest Ball of Twine wasn't as delicious as the cherry pie experience, our week-long trip to the Dakota Badlands was particularly memorable. Who could forget Devils Tower, or Wall Drug and all the highway signs proclaiming its claim to fame? Ice water never tasted so good. Best of all, it was free.

Our budget was tight. When the kids were little, I would sometimes take them down to the train yard so they could see where their daddy worked. Alan's title of apprentice engineer sounded grand, and the detailed work the company required him to perform more than qualified him as a certified engineer. But with no college diploma to back up his on-the-job expertise, his biweekly paycheck bordered on pathetic. If it had been me, I'd have given the company an earful, but Alan refused to complain. It took plenty of scrimping and saving, but somehow, at the end of each month, we always managed to pay our bills. It wasn't easy, and some months we held our breath. With two kids and a mortgage, anything could throw us off the deep end. And we were determined not to crash the budget.

A leisurely stroll through downtown Chicago didn't cost us a dime. We spent considerable time outside the Tribune Building gawking at its walls featuring stones from all around the world. The Great Wall of China. The Berlin Wall. When Alan pointed out a stone donated from one of the pyramids, even DeAnna seemed impressed.

"I'm gonna go there someday," she said.

"The pyramids are in Egypt, honey," Alan replied.

"I don't care," she scoffed. "When I grow up, I'll go wherever I want."

"Better start saving your money," thirteen-year-old Barry advised. He'd spent the summer working a daily paper route, quickly learning the value of a dollar. "Egypt is way across the ocean."

"I don't care!" DeAnna insisted, sticking out her tongue.

Where did we go wrong? Barry had been so easy, while DeAnna proved to be the exact opposite. Discovering that I was pregnant again (*it's a girl!*) had been a surprise. Another surprise was the difficult twenty-hour labor, which left me battered, bruised, and totally exhausted. If I ever discovered who was behind the ridiculous theory that second babies arrive faster than the first, I intended to give them a piece of my mind. But once DeAnna finally arrived, we poured all our love and attention into making sure our daughter was happy and healthy. She was our hearts' desire, and we tried to fulfill her every wish. Ditto for Barry, who loved his little sister. Like all siblings, they had their scuffles, but he never minded her tagging along.

Not that she tagged along. Not without some coaxing from us or Barry. DeAnna wasn't inclined to do anything except what *she* wanted to do.

"Give her a few years," Alan said in response to my grumbling one hot summer night as we lay in bed. "She'll grow out of it."

"What in the world am I going to do with her?" I replied. "Our daughter has a mind of her own."

Both our children were in their own beds, hopefully fast asleep. In this heat, I wouldn't have been surprised if they were awake. Our house had no air conditioning, and the noisy box fans in the bedroom windows barely managed to stir a breeze.

"Barry always did what he was told, even when he was a toddler. And he never talked back."

"You're worried about nothing. It will all be fine. DeAnna will grow up, and someday we'll look back at this and wonder why we made such a fuss."

"I hope you're right." I cuddled closer to Alan, resting my chin in the soft sweet-smelling nudge between his shoulder and neck. "Do you think we made a mistake? I mean, the way we're raising her? I know she's only five, but every year she gets harder to handle. Barry wasn't like this."

"Boys are different than girls." His words came slower.

"You should have seen her this afternoon," I said. "When I told her we were going shopping for school clothes, she threw a major hissy fit. She told me she wasn't going shopping, and she wasn't going to school, either. And when I said *oh yes, you are*, she said *oh, no, I'm not, and you can't make me!* Then she stamped her foot and stuck out her tongue at me."

"She did?" he asked through a wide yawn.

"Alan! Did you hear what I said?" I propped myself up on one elbow, staring at him through the darkness. I felt like shaking him wide awake. "She stuck her tongue out! At me! I'd appreciate some feedback."

"I suppose it wasn't very nice of her, was it?" he said with a soft chuckle.

"That's all you're going to say?" I punched him softly in the ribs.

"Ow."

"Alan, this isn't funny. What are we going to do? School starts next week, and she refuses to go. *Stupid old school, that's what she said.*"

"Maybe she's scared."

I paused, sifting through my memories, thinking back through the years to my first day of school. I'd been terrified, too, until I got there.

Maybe Alan was right. Maybe DeAnna's fussing was because she was afraid. Then I quickly dismissed the thought. DeAnna had never been afraid of anything in her life.

"How can she not want to go? I had so much fun in kindergarten. I loved every minute of it."

"She's not you, Reet."

"And don't I know it!"

Alan reached out and took my hand, gave it a gentle squeeze.

"You worry too much. It will all work out. Wait and see."

Alan sounded so sure of himself, and I longed to believe him. His voice was soft and dreamy, and I knew it wouldn't be long before I lost him to sleep. Would he remember our conversation when he woke up? Maybe I'd remind him as he ate his eggs and toast. I could urge him to talk to DeAnna. She was always more inclined to pay attention to him, and she normally did whatever her daddy said. Alan could encourage her, tell DeAnna how much fun she'd have at school.

And it worked. Long enough for me to take her shopping, to buy her new clothes, including a shiny pair of black patent leather shoes. *Our bestseller*! the shoe salesman beamed, throwing me back into long forgotten memories of my own pair of patent leather shoes, making my heart ache for Aunt Sis. How I missed her. She would have been full of helpful advice on what to do about DeAnna.

Early in September, when the calendar flipped and the big day arrived, Alan took the morning off and was right there beside me as we walked DeAnna up the school steps. She looked so pretty in her brand-new dress, despite the scowl on her face and the pair of scuffed up tennis shoes on her feet. *Choose your battles*, Alan cautioned, and so I quit arguing. And while I'd lost the battle over what shoes she wore, at least DeAnna had gone to school. Alan had been right all along.

He'd been such a good father. He'd always known what to say to keep his little girl in line, while DeAnna and I continued to be at odds. Now she was an adult, there were still times when she acted like that sulky child with the angelic face who consistently called attention to herself, and not always in a flattering way. She'd spent twelve years fighting her way through school, and somehow managed to graduate, despite falling in with the wrong crowd. Despite falling in love with Lloyd.

If only Alan was still around. He'd been the calm, sensible one of the two of us. If he were here, he'd know how to handle this slush pile of family troubles. Meanwhile, I was growing older by the minute, as my body constantly reminded me. Each day brought a fresh new assortment of aches and pains. Some days I simply ran out of energy, which was frustrating and scary. I was slowing down, and there was nothing I could do about it. No matter how much wishing and hoping I did, those days were gone.

If only Alan hadn't died. He might have been able to save DeAnna, and she wouldn't have ended up in rehab. LJ and Tiffany wouldn't have ended up living here with me.

Lloyd wouldn't be sitting at my kitchen table fiddling with a gun.

But Alan wasn't here to save me. No one was. Not Barry, not DeAnna, not even Millie.

The only one who would be able to rescue me, was me.

CHAPTER FOURTEEN

"ONE GRILLED CHEESE, MADE TO order." I set the luncheon plate next to his bowl of steaming soup, then add a few extra napkins. By the look of his shirt, Lloyd isn't currently in the running to win a Mr. Tidy contest.

"Got any ketchup?"

"Ketchup? You put ketchup in your soup?"

"Nope," he says, staring at me like I've suddenly qualified myself for Stupidest-Person-Of-The-Year award. He pokes the sandwich with a finger. "I dip it."

"One bottle of ketchup, coming right up." I head for the refrigerator. If he wants to spoil a perfectly delicious grilled cheese sandwich by smearing it with ketchup, who am I to complain? His sandwich, his taste buds. What do I know? I'm only the cook.

"Would you like anything else?" I call from the refrigerator. "Before I sit down?"

"How about pickles? They go good with grilled cheese."

I glance at the unopened jar of gourmet pickles I'd purchased at the grocery two days earlier. They were LJ's favorite, and nearly twice as expensive as the generic store brand I usually bought. But when LJ began to plead, I plucked them from the shelf and plunked them in my shopping cart.

When it comes to my grandchildren, cost be damned. God knows that little boy doesn't have much happiness in his life. If gourmet pickles will help keep him happy, then gourmet pickles it would be.

Do I really want to waste LJ's pickles on his dad?

I grab the pickles, the ketchup, and head back to the table, put everything in front of him. Lloyd doesn't say a word. Picking up the sandwich, he quickly devours it, plus wolfs down two pickles, as if it's the first food he's eaten in days.

"Well?" I say, hating myself for stooping so low as to fish for kudos from Lloyd.

He gives me a cold stare. "Whatdya want me to say? It's food, right?"

"Thank you," I say at the half-hearted compliment.

"You shoulda taught Dee how to cook," Lloyd says as he hunches over his soup. "She's got kids. She needs to know how to do this stuff."

"Believe it or not, I tried. Unfortunately, she wasn't interested. She seems to prefer being waited on, rather than the other way around."

"Tell me about it!" He busts out with a loud laugh. "I don't remember her ever cooking when we were living together."

Shacked up and living in sin, my mother would have said. But my mother is long gone and couples nowadays are free to live their lives the way they want to. There's no longer such a stigma when people live together or have children outside of marriage. My mother would have been appalled. But that's her problem, not mine. Besides, DeAnna and Lloyd have two children together. Would my mother have wished LJ and Tiffany had never been born? Two beautiful kids, and none of this is their fault. No one's fault.

Not even Lloyd's.

"So, who did all the cooking?" I ask.

"Who do you think? You're looking at him."

"You?" I say with a loud hoot.

"Laugh all you want," he says, looking mildly insulted but not angry, much to my relief. "I don't see what's so funny. I've been trained as a chef, and I know my way around a kitchen. Unlike your daughter," he adds with a hard stare.

"You're right," I quickly reply. I shouldn't have laughed. I don't want him thinking that I'm poking fun. "I'm sorry."

He reaches for another pickle. He's already scarfed down his sandwich, inhaled the soup. I try not to stare as he crunches his way through a fourth pickle. If he keeps this up, soon the jar will be empty, and I'll have to make another run to the grocery store.

If I survive this day.

"I guess you weren't kidding when you said you were hungry," I say.

"I didn't eat breakfast," he says.

I push away my own plate, ignore the sandwich I've barely touched.

"Would you like more soup? Maybe another sandwich? If you like, I'll make you one." My ask isn't courtesy as much as self-serving. I can't imagine him picking up that gun and shooting me while polishing off one of my grilled cheese sandwiches. Rich and gooey cheese, slathered in butter, a little bit of onion, some tomato slices, straight off the hot grill. The finest of comfort foods. The kind of food that puts a smile on your face, not murder in your heart.

"Naw," he says.

"You don't like grilled cheese?"

He shoots me a smug smile. "Mine are better."

"Oh." He's being purposely rude, and I am not impressed. I didn't have to make him lunch. In fact, I didn't have to do anything. I could have merely sat there, allowed him to point that stupid gun at me until he got tired of holding it.

And then what would Lloyd have done? Pulled the trigger?

"I bet I have something you'll like." Without waiting for a reply, I head for the counter, open the cookie jar, and stack a plate with some of the cookies I baked last night. It's a cobbled-together recipe I concocted on my own that earned me a five-star approval rating from LJ and Tiffany.

I put the heaping platter of peanut butter and butterscotch cookies directly in front of Lloyd.

"When Barry was still living at home, I baked cookies every day."

"Anything for good ole Barry," he mutters.

I take my seat across from Lloyd. "He had an afternoon paper route and was always starving by the time he finished. He'd come slamming in the back door and make a beeline for the cookie jar. I swear, if I hadn't stopped him, he probably would have polished off the whole jar by himself. Growing boys, right?"

Memories of Barry and his paper route put a smile on my face. Some things you don't forget. He'd worked that paper route of his all the way through high school. He'd found the two-mile route a rough go at first, but eventually he'd come to see the benefits of a part-time job. The ready flow of cash more than compensated for the occasional grouchy customer.

Barry had always been a go-getter. He knew what he wanted, and he went after it.

Lloyd snags a handful of cookies and drops them on his plate.

"He learned a lot, having that paper route. Plus, he always brought home a free paper. One of the perks of his job. I miss getting the paper delivered. Now everybody reads the news on their phones. Another few years, and they'll probably quit printing newspapers."

"Nothing but a bunch of stupid ads," he says through a mouthful of cookie crumbs.

"Not necessarily. The paper runs local stories, and other things, too."

Keeping up with the news of the world was a good thing. Meanwhile, if something extra happened to be included in the subscription, what was wrong with that? I like keeping up on the latest celebrity gossip and indulging myself with the daily advice columns and reader comments. I especially liked trying to figure out what answer I'd give before reading the scoop of what the experts had to say. I always got a little thrill when our answers matched. That wasn't the case when I first started doling out imaginary advice, but the longer I kept at it, the better I got.

"Millie and I go to a biweekly knitting class. I read about it years ago in the community announcements section of the paper. There's lots of good stuff in the community section. Plus, they print the local school news and daily horoscopes." I'm not about to confess my addiction to the advice colum-nists. "The sports coverage, stats, and scores. And, of course, the weather."

"Those weathermen got no clue what they're talking about," he says. "Save your money. Look out the window."

"You might be right," I say with a laugh as I reach for a cookie. In all the years I've known Lloyd, this is the longest conversation the two of us have ever had. Now that he's eaten, he seems more relaxed, and some of the things coming out of his mouth are borderline funny. It's obvious he's trying to carry his part of the conversation, and maybe even help alleviate some of the tension between us. Who knows? Maybe if I'd made more of an effort in the past, had tried to get to know him better, the two of us wouldn't be caught up in this crazy situation, sitting here at my kitchen table with a loaded gun between us.

"What about you? Did you have a paper route?"

He pauses mid-bite, then chokes out a short laugh.

"Do I look like a paper boy?"

Too bad for Lloyd. A paper route would have put some money in his pocket, and maybe helped him discover a few things such as how to deal with people.

Rule Number One: do not hold them hostage.

He reaches for another cookie.

"So, I guess you like the cookies?" I say, fishing for a compliment. I'm still rather miffed about him dissing my grilled cheese.

"They're okay. They kinda remind me of the ones Mags used to make."

"Mags?"

"My older sister." He wipes the crumbs from his mouth with the back of his sleeve. "She did most of the cooking."

"Your mother didn't like to cook?"

"My mom? Ha! She was never around long enough to figure out how the stove worked. She was usually out trying to sell a house."

"That's right, I do remember hearing something about that. Your father sold insurance and your mother sold real estate."

"She *tried*," he said with a dismissive smirk. "Put it this way: she didn't sell a lot of houses."

We sit there for a moment with his words between us.

"It must have been difficult, especially for you kids," I finally say. "I mean, your mother going off to work and the five of you left alone to fend for yourselves."

"Six. There were six of us kids."

"But DeAnna told me that—"

Lloyd turns away, stares out the window.

I stop myself from going any further. Every family has its drama, and obviously Lloyd doesn't want to talk about his.

"Sorry, I didn't mean to pry."

"Becky."

"Excuse me?"

"Becky, my other sister. Her name's Becky." He turns back to face me. "She's four years younger than me. She's Jimmy's twin. *Was*."

I gasp softly. "You mean…?"

He gives a quick shrug. "I've been gone a couple years. Anything coulda happened. Especially in that place they put her." A scowl slides across his face. "But whatever. At this point, if she *is* alive, she probably don't know where she is or what's going on. Not that any of them care…or that they'd bother telling me."

I'm left with more questions than when we first started talking. Was his sister involved in some kind of accident that left her paralyzed or mentally challenged? Did she suffer a stroke, or something that left her unable to speak or care for herself? His younger brother Jimmy is an adult. Becky, being his twin, would be an adult, too.

"I'm sorry, Lloyd. I didn't know."

"Whatever."

Though I'd like to hear more about Becky, it's probably better not to press him. He's loosened up considerably since barging his way into my house, but I don't want to jinx the situation. If he feels like sharing, then hopefully he will… eventually.

I can wait. It isn't as if the two of us are going anywhere or have something better to do.

I steal a glance at the clock and the little bubble of calm surrounding me pops. The little engine is chugging its way to one o'clock.

Time is running out.

I could dally in the kitchen, offer to make him another grilled cheese, serve him more cookies. But I'd only be stalling, trying to stop the inevitable.

No matter what I say or do, I can't stop time.

And I can't stop Lloyd. No matter how many cookies I feed him, he's a man on a mission. He wants his kids, and he's determined to wait for them, and wait me out.

In a little more than two hours, the school bus will show up at my house. LJ and Tiffany will tumble out and come bursting through the front door. They'll fling their backpacks in a heap, shouting for me as they run through the house, expecting hugs and kisses and cookies from their grandma.

But today, they'll find someone besides Grammie waiting for them, too.

CHAPTER FIFTEEN

THEY SHOWED UP ON MY doorstep without warning during one of those fierce late summer storms that arrive out of nowhere. Though it wasn't yet dinnertime, the skies had grown dark. Ugly and menacing, they were streaked with greens and browns. The smell of ozone hung in the air. I snapped on all the lights, tuned the TV to the local news station, then burrowed deep in the couch pillows and listened as an over-the-top-excited weatherman predicted doom and gloom with dangerous lightening and possible tornadoes.

"Help! Let us in!"

I caught the sound of wild cries and pounding from outside between loud claps of thunder. It sounded like someone was trying to kick down my front door. I jumped from the couch and hurried into the hallway. The rain had picked up and was beating hard against the roof. Who would be crazy enough to venture out in this storm?

I peeked through the peep hole and saw a woman and two children huddled on the porch, a wet bedraggled mess. Brilliant flashes of lightning illuminated LJ and Tiffany's faces streaked with tears and fear.

"Good grief!" I flung the door wide open. "Come in, come in!"

"Dammit, LJ, what's the matter with you? Get your butt in the house!" DeAnna shoved her son through the door, rushing them past me into the hallway.

"Grammie!" Tiffany broke loose and launched herself against me like a tiny tornado, grabbing me around the middle. "Yay!"

"Good grief, look at you!" I stroked Tiffany's wet hair. What in the world was DeAnna thinking? No mother in her right mind would venture out into a storm like this, let alone drag her kids along. It was times like this that had me wondering if all those years doing drugs had fried her brain cells. "How did you get so wet?"

"From the rain!" Tiffany shouted. "It's raining outside, Grammie! Don't you know that?"

"I see it is," I said with a laugh and hugged my granddaughter close. Despite the threat of tornadoes, any day was a good day when my grandkids came for a visit.

DeAnna wrung water from her own wet curls. Large puddles glistened on the hardwood floor as she shrugged a heavy canvas sack from her shoulder and flung it to the floor, followed by her purse. Kicking off her sandals, she stood there in bare feet, clinging t-shirt, and snug white shortie shorts, staring me down through dark eyes…almost as if she was sizing up the enemy, trying to decide if it was worth it to call a truce.

"I'm glad you're here," I said.

"I wasn't sure we'd be welcome," she said.

I heard the challenge in her voice. It was obvious the wound was still as fresh and deep as it had been a few weeks earlier. DeAnna's temper tantrum that day had left me heartsick and shaken. *All your fault*! she'd hurled accusations at me. *Give me some space!* She was sick and tired of my constant meddling, at me trying to interfere in their lives. *If you don't back off, I'll take the kids away*, she'd threatened. *You'll never see them again.*

"This is your home." I didn't know what else to say, so I went with the truth. "It's your home, and you're always welcome."

DeAnna dragged in a deep breath. "I didn't know where else to go."

It might be the closest thing to an apology I would ever hear from my daughter's mouth, but I'd take what I could get. Apologies were never easy, and for DeAnna they were torture. Something drastic must have happened to make her show up here tonight. Even as a little girl, she'd loathed having to admit when she was wrong; DeAnna never thought she was wrong. But none of that mattered. This was her home, and it always would be. And for tonight, at least, she'd remembered that, and brought the children with her.

She was here. They were here. They were home.

"I'm glad you came. You're always welcome," I repeated, and took a chance by leaning into my daughter's space to wrap my arms around her. DeAnna flinched but allowed a brief hug before pulling away.

I felt myself lightening up inside at the physical contact. Yes, it was minimal, but it was a start. That had to be a good thing.

LJ stomped his feet.

Tiffany, mimicking her brother, did the same. "We lost our house," she proclaimed, and used her feet to give an extra loud kick for emphasis.

I frowned. "What do you mean, *lost your house*? How can you lose a house?"

"That damn landlord locked us out again." DeAnna's scowl deepened. "Can you believe it? He's such a turd."

"That's not what you said." LJ snickered. "You called him a shithead."

"LJ said a dirty word!" Tiffany shouted. "Dirty word, dirty word! LJ is a dirty bird!"

"You shut up!" he hollered, making a lunge for his sister.

"That's enough!" DeAnna yelled. She grabbed his shoulder, gave him a little shake. "You've been acting up all day, and I'm sick of it, do you hear? Sick of it! You better get your act together, mister, and you better do it soon…or else!"

"Or else what?" He pulled away, beyond her reach. He jutted out his bottom lip, eyes gleaming as he glowered at his mother. "How you gonna make me?"

I sucked in a deep breath. Watching my ten-year-old grandson go toe-to-toe with his mother dragged me right back into the trenches of my long-ago wars with a pre-adolescent DeAnna.

"Don't you dare talk back to me," she hissed. "Don't you dare."

LJ kicked off his sandals, turned his back on his mother, turned to me.

"I'm hungry, Grammie. When do we eat?"

While I didn't want to ignore my grandson, I knew better than to get involved in their skirmish.

I looked to DeAnna for guidance. "It must be close to dinnertime. If you're hungry, we can eat. Or maybe get everyone into dry clothes first?"

"Whatever," she replied with a shrug.

"I'm hungry!" LJ insisted. "Let's eat!"

I made a rapid mental inventory of what food I had on hand that could be pulled from the refrigerator and cupboards. I hadn't been to the grocery in more than a week, but there was enough to feed the four of us. I smiled down at Tiffany. "I suppose you're hungry, too?"

"Yes!" she said with a vigorous nod as she shrugged off her sandals and kicked them onto the pile. "We didn't get lunch."

"No lunch?" I turned to DeAnna.

"Oh, for God sakes, yes, we ate lunch!" she snapped, rolling her eyes. "Don't go believing a word she says. This little miss has a nasty habit of telling lies. You can't trust a word out of her mouth."

"Tiffany's a liar!" LJ hollered. "Liar, liar!"

"Am not!" Tiffany cried.

"Liar, liar, pants on fire!" he taunted in a singsong voice and gave his little sister a shove. She sprang at him in quick attack.

"Take it back!"

"Stop it!" DeAnna yelled, stepping into the melee. She held each at arm's length, wedging her body between them as a barricade.

"Remember what I told you before we got here," she warned. "You'd better behave, or you'll be sorry."

"I'm not sorry!" Tiffany shouted. "LJ started it!"

"Liar! Liar!" he kept up his chant.

"That's enough! Do you hear me? Enough!" DeAnna tightened her grip on their arms. "The two of you better behave if you know what's good for you. Because, if you don't…" Her voice dropped low into dangerous territory. "If you don't, then Grammie will throw us out of her house, and it will be your fault. Is that what you want?"

"No!" Tiffany burst into tears. She did her best to squirm from her mother's grasp but couldn't quite manage. Her eyes held pure panic as she turned to me. "Are you going to do that, Grammie? Are you going to throw us out?"

I stood in stunned silence. How could my granddaughter think I would do such a thing?

"Welcome to my world." DeAnna spit the words in my direction. "You're seeing for yourself exactly what they're like. Maybe next time I complain about how horrible they're acting, you'll remember today and what little hellions they can be. And maybe, for once, you'll take my side."

But why did this have to be about choosing sides? Why couldn't we all simply get along and love each other? I'd thought that's what families were supposed to do. It's what I'd always wanted.

"Please, Grammie, don't throw us out!" Tiffany begged. She latched onto me, burying her face in my stomach.

"Get real," LJ said with a scornful glance at his sister. "You're so stupid. Why would she kick us out? She loves us."

"Do you, Grammie?" She lifted her head and gazed up at me. "Do you love us? Can we stay?"

"Of course, you can stay. And yes, of course, I love you. I love each one of you, very, very, much." I planted a kiss atop Tiffany's head and caught a whiff of a peculiar odor emanating from the top.

When was the last time her hair had been washed? The last time she'd had a bath?

For the first time that night, I took a good hard look at each one of them. My granddaughter wasn't the only one whose personal hygiene needed attention. The grubby state of their clothes, the sour smells lingering in the hallway was all the evidence needed. Thank goodness the upstairs bathroom shelves were stocked with bubble bath, soap, and shampoo. And seeing how I had no idea how long they'd be staying, it was probably best to lay in extra supplies. I'd make an emergency run to the grocery tomorrow, I decided. After breakfast would be soon enough. There was juice in the fridge, plus bread for toast, and some partially eaten boxes of their favorite cereals from their last visit. And coffee. DeAnna never ate breakfast, but she was a fanatic when it came to her coffee. I added it to the mental list rolling through my head.

This was the last thing I'd expected tonight. How was I going to manage?

But God help these little kids. And God help DeAnna.

God help us all.

And first things first, I thought to myself as I caught sight of LJ slinking down the hall headed toward the kitchen.

"Let's see about getting us some dinner, shall we?" I said to Tiffany. "And after dinner, maybe a bubble bath? What do you think? Does that sound good?"

Tiffany hugged me tighter. "I'm so happy we came to stay with you!"

"Me, too," I vowed, hugging her right back. Despite LJ's sullenness, DeAnna's all-too-frequent scowls, and Tiffany's gleeful tattling, I was glad they'd showed up. Where else were they supposed to go? They were my family, and I loved them all. Somehow, we'd get through this.

Dirty hair and all.

"Don't get me wrong. None of this is their fault. I know that. And it's not like I'm blaming them," DeAnna told me later that evening, once the business of dinner, baths, reading stories, and just-one-more-glass-of-water had been dispensed with, and the kids were finally tucked in bed and fast asleep. Burrowed deep in one corner of the couch, wine glass in hand, she stared at me. "They're just kids, right? And I'm the adult. I'm the one who's supposed to be in charge. But damn! Sometimes, it's just too much. And I know I take it out on them…but what am I supposed to do?"

"I don't know, honey," I replied from my chair near the couch. "I don't know."

"And that's the problem! No one knows! So how am I supposed to figure it out?" DeAnna's forehead twisted in a grimace. "You have no idea what my life is like, how hard it is. The older LJ is, the wilder he gets. You heard him tonight, shooting off his mouth at me like he did. It's not easy, trying to raise him by myself. His teacher at school is constantly giving me grief. She says he's a troublemaker, that he's always picking on kids. And Tiffany's no better than her brother. All she does is whine, whine, whine. She's always begging for what she can't have."

"Little kids are like that. Give them time. They'll grow up and—"

"I'm sick of waiting for them to grow up! And why should I have to? Why is it always me? Why am I the one who has to make all the sacrifices? There are times…" She sucked in a deep breath. "There are times when it gets to be too much, and then I get scared that if I don't get away, that

I'll totally lose it and end up doing something I'll regret. So, I get in the car and I drive around—"

"DeAnna, no! Please don't tell me that you leave them alone."

"Okay, fine, I won't tell you."

My stomach gave a nasty lurch sideways as I watched her lean forward and grab the bottle off the coffee table, pour herself more wine. She was the only one drinking. The bottle was nearly empty.

"I don't see why it's such a big deal." She glared at me. "It's not like they're babies. LJ's old enough to be left in charge. I'm never gone more than an hour, if that."

"DeAnna!" It's hard to keep the righteous indignation out of my voice. "He's only ten years old."

"He's old enough," she insisted. "Besides, it's not like I do it every night."

"You can't leave them alone by themselves," I say, disheartened at the way her face hardens. "I'm serious. You can't do that. I know you don't want to hear it, and I'm not trying to tell you what to do, but—"

"It sure as hell sounds like that's what you're doing!"

"LJ is only a little boy," I insisted on finishing. How can she sit there and blithely assume she's doing the right thing when she's dead wrong? Not to mention, the numerous charges she could be facing if Social Services found out she'd left her kids to fend for themselves. They'd yank LJ and Tiffany out of the house so fast, it would make DeAnna's head spin. "You can't leave them alone. If something were to happen," I added, "you'd never forgive yourself."

DeAnna's face morphed into a dark shade of crimson, and she looked like she wanted to spit.

At me.

I'd made her mad.

I also knew I was right.

"Nothing's going to happen," she retaliated. "It never has, and it probably never will. Meanwhile, what am I supposed to do? Am I supposed to stay put, sit around and get madder, and end up doing something awful to one of them? I'm doing the best I can, but all of us have our breaking point.

"You know how when you're a kid," she rambled, "and you think about how great it's going to be when you finally grow up? Adults have so much fun, and they get to do whatever they want, right?" Her voice was tinged with bitterness. "Talk about a bunch of shit. There's nothing fun about being an adult. It sucks. And it's totally not fair."

Life isn't fair. I'd grown up hearing my mother throwing those words in my face, and I'd swore I would *never, never, never* repeat them to my children. And I never have…until today. Today, I was tempted.

"You're in a tough situation," I agreed. "But it won't always be so hard. And it's—"

"Damn right it's hard! Why should I be the one who ends up having to deal with all this? Those kids have a father, too."

Listening to her rant, I didn't know whether to laugh or cry. The whole situation was so tragically ridiculous. Even before he was sent to prison, Lloyd was never up for Father-of-the-Year. Why would DeAnna think that he'd want to step up now and do the right thing for her and his kids? What made her think he'd suddenly want to do what he should have been doing all along? Parenting is difficult enough, without trying to manage things from inside a prison cell.

"Have you heard from Lloyd lately?"

"He called last week." DeAnna turned the wine bottle on end, making certain that every drop ended up in her glass. "Supposedly he's got a parole hearing coming up soon, but he said not to get my hopes up. I assume that means he won't be getting out anytime soon. And if he doesn't get out, where does that leave me? Stuck with the kids, as usual."

There was no denying she was in a difficult situation, but again, so much of it was of her own making. Not to mention, she wasn't making things any easier on herself. DeAnna, with her wild blonde curls and beautiful blue eyes the color of a summer's day. She looked so much like my mother. She had her looks, and the wicked tongue, too. I stared at her glass, suddenly wondering how much of tonight's poor-pity-me harangue had been fueled by alcohol. And where had she gotten the bottle? I didn't have any wine in the house. She must have brought it with her.

How much of the chaos in my daughter's life has resulted from bad choices that could be attributed to her drinking? As far as I knew, once she discovered she was pregnant, she'd quit doing drugs.

But she never stopped drinking.

"DeAnna, listen," I urged. "We'll help you get through this. You are not alone. You have a family, remember? Me, Barry, and Holly, too. We're here to help."

"You think those two are gonna help me?" DeAnna scoffed with a dramatic eyeroll. "What am I supposed to do? Go crawling on my knees, confess that I'm broke? Tell them that the landlord locked us out? *No big surprise*, that's what Barry will say. He never changes. My whole life, all he's ever done is wait for me to mess up. He think I'm a loser. Both of them do," she added darkly. "They think I'm such a loser."

"That's not true," I said firmly. "Your brother loves you, and so does Holly. And I love you, too. You're my daughter, DeAnna. I'll do whatever I can to help. And it goes without saying that I'll do anything for your kids. They're my grandchildren, and I love them dearly."

"Yeah, I figured you would say that," she shot back, though her gaze softened slightly. "You always say that. And I know you love us. But some things need more than love. Love is good…but right now, what I really need is money."

My heart sank even lower. The same old argument, over and over. If money was the answer, I'd be at the bank tomorrow morning three hours before they opened. The insurance settlement I'd received after Alan's death had left me with enough money to hopefully see me through for the rest of my life. *If* I was careful. But I'd gladly cash it all in if I thought it would fix things.

But it wouldn't.

"DeAnna, you know that I would do anything for you. I'd give you everything I have, and then some. You know that, right?"

"Seriously?" She stared at me, her face unreadable. "What I *know* is that it *sounds* like you're not going to help. I told you what I needed, but you're not going to help me. You're not going to give me any money. Am I right?" she demanded, challenging my silence with a defiant glare. "Fine. Never mind. Forget I even asked.

"I should have known you'd say *no*," she muttered with her next breath, pinching her nose, squeezing her eyes shut. "What a shitty life. I'm so sick of it."

And at that precise moment, I suddenly lost it. We'd had this conversation about money before. An intense family discussion following Alan's death between DeAnna, Barry and I; round and round about finances and property, mortgages and more. She knew the specifics. But, as usual, she wasn't listening.

"You're sick of it?" I heard the fury rising in my voice. "I'm sick and tired of listening to you complain. You complain about everything. No matter how much people try and help, no matter what they do for you, nothing is ever good enough. And it never will be…not if all you do is sit around and complain. Just like you're doing tonight: sitting there drinking yourself right into the *poor-pity-me*. Maybe it's time for you to shut up, quit drinking, and start trying to do something about your so-called *shitty life*."

"Excuse me?" She opened her eyes and stared at me as if seeing me for the very first time.

I dragged in a deep breath, trying to find some inner calm before I said something that would wreck our relationship forever.

"All I'm suggesting is that you take a good long look at what's going on around you," I finally said. "Is this what you want out of life? You said it wasn't. To me, I'm thinking that it sounds as if it might be the perfect starting point. Maybe this is the perfect time to figure out what you're going to do about it…before it ends up killing you."

"I have no f-ing clue what you're talking about."

"I think you do." Very few moments of utter honesty such as this have ever passed between us. But I might as well go for broke and say what I had to say before I lost my nerve.

"I think you're running scared. You've slowed down enough that you've finally realize what a mess your life is."

She started to protest but I held up a hand, cutting her off. "Don't get me wrong; not all of it is your fault. But some of it is. Your drinking, for instance. That isn't helping matters."

I struggled to continue, despite the high color staining her cheeks, the devil daggers her eyes are throwing at me.

"Maybe this is the best thing that could have happened. Maybe finally you've reached a turning point, and you're ready to take a good honest look at yourself. I hope that's what's happening. I hope and pray that's what's happening. But maybe I'm wrong. I don't know, DeAnna. You're the only one who can answer that."

"You think I'm not scared?" she demanded. "You think I don't lay awake at night thinking about things, wondering how the fuck my life ended up like this?"

"Do you?" It hurt like hell to see her in so much pain, but me getting upset wouldn't solve her problems.

"Of course, I do!" she screeched, arms flailing wildly through the air. "You think I want to live like this? You think I like it? You think I don't know what I'm doing? That I must be a horrible woman, dragging myself, my kids through hell? Is that what you think? You think I don't care?"

"No, I don't think that," I whispered. "I think you *do* care. You care about things so much. And that's part of the problem. You care about everything so much, and you want to do your best. But then you let it build and build, and it gets to the point where it's suddenly overwhelming. And then, when you can no longer cope, your subconscious brain goes into overdrive and figures out ways to sabotage yourself. That way, it doesn't hurt so much when things don't work out." I blew out a hard sigh. "That's what I think."

"And I think you're fucking crazy," she spit back at me.

"You might be right," I said. Acting casual was costing me plenty in emotional currency, and my heart ached something fierce. But I had to finish what I started. "Just know that whatever you decide, remember that I'm willing to help in any way I can. But it all starts with you. You have to make the first move to help yourself."

Hopefully, something I'd said tonight would touch a nerve or resonate with her deep down inside. Enough to make a difference. If not, I might have lost my daughter for good.

There was a long silence between us.

"I suppose you think I should go out and get a job," DeAnna finally said.

"I don't think a job is the answer."

"Then what the hell are you talking about?" she countered. "What am I supposed to do?"

"Get some professional help."

"Rehab." Her voice was flat. "You want me to go to rehab."

"What I want isn't important."

It wasn't my battle to wage. This was her life, and she had to make her own decisions. If DeAnna decided recovery was the answer, she would be faced with a long and difficult road ahead.

And it would be a road she would need to walk alone.

"Okay, I admit that maybe some of what you've said is true."

"Maybe?"

"*Most of it*," she acknowledged. "And yes, okay, I'll admit I drink too much. But the kids get so wild. All that screaming and shouting gets on my nerves. Drinking takes the edge off. But the weird thing about it…" DeAnna paused, frowned. "Drinking takes the edge off, but I think it makes me meaner, too."

"Oh, sweetheart." I wanted to reach out and take her in my arms, let her know how much she was loved, but I didn't move. *Just let her keep talking*, I thought. *Let her keep talking.*

"Sometimes I think about quitting. I've tried once or twice, believe it or not. But quitting isn't easy. If it was easy, I guess I would have already done it, right?"

"You don't have to do it alone."

"What about LJ and Tiffany? What am I supposed to do with them? It's not like rehab is going to let me bring them along. And don't go getting any stupid ideas, like me maybe asking Barry and Holly for help," she added darkly. "They stick their noses into things that are none of their business and end up making everything worse. Those two will never help me. They're way too wrapped up in themselves."

"I think you're wrong about that. I bet if you asked, you'd find them more than willing to help. Barry loves you very much, DeAnna. I think you'd be surprised if you knew how much. But that's neither here nor there. If you don't want to ask him, then don't. The kids can stay here with me."

"It wouldn't work. You have no clue what LJ and Tiffany are really like," she warned. "They're sneaky and selfish, and they're always fighting. They're experts at wearing you down. They'll make you choose sides, and you'll end up wanting to scream, or kick something and throw—"

"There won't be any screaming or kicking or shouting," I replied. "And no picking sides, either."

"If you say so," she said with a shrug.

What was I getting myself into? I adored my grandchildren, but I knew they were capable of acting like wild hooligans. I'd seen it with my own eyes tonight. Given half a chance, they would test my patience and tolerance, push me to my absolute limits. Did I really want to put myself through that?

Plus, I wasn't getting any younger. I'd grown accustomed to living alone, having the house all to myself. I finally was beginning to understand what they meant that living alone had its pleasures. Being accountable to no one. Sleeping till noon if I pleased, or choosing to get up at four am, moving through the house with no need to worry if I was making too much noise, disturbing someone's sleep. Living alone meant eating what I wanted, when I wanted, where I wanted; in front of the TV, or at the table with my nose buried in a book. And sometimes, on those rare occasions that I wasn't hungry, skipping a meal entirely.

But all of that would change if LJ and Tiffany came to live with me. I'd have to make sure they got to school on time. I'd have to plan nutritious meals; make sure they ate their vegetables. I'd be responsible for supervising their homework, watching over them as they brushed their teeth at night, assuring that they got enough sleep.

Could I do it? I wasn't *old-old*, and far from feeble. But I was closer to seventy than sixty, and the world was a much different place than it had been when my own children were little. What did I know about raising kids today? The thought of what I might have opened myself up to left me feeling as if someone had grabbed me, wired me up, plugged me in, and sent my heart surging into overdrive.

"We'll be fine," I replied confidently, though I knew I'd spoken just as much to reassure myself as I had for DeAnna.

Calm wasn't how I felt.

More like, *the calm before the storm.*

DeAnna finally shrugged. "If you want to put yourself through hell, be my guest."

"Does that mean you're going to rehab?"

She stared at me a long moment, then lifted one shoulder in a casual nod.

"Whatever."

I closed my eyes and flung a silent prayer of thanks heavenward. I had no doubt that what had happened here tonight was the direct result of a miraculous intervention. DeAnna had admitted she had a problem. She'd admitted it was too much for her. She was willing to go to rehab. She'd be taking those first crucial steps in getting herself some help.

If nothing else, it was a start.

And while DeAnna was off at rehab, hopefully Alan and the heavenly powers above would also be watching over LJ, Tiffany, and me.

I had a feeling we were going to need it.

CHAPTER SIXTEEN

ONE O'CLOCK AND ALL IS not well. Only two more hours before school ends, LJ and Tiffany climb on the bus, head for home. But instead of finding Grandma, they'll come face-to-face with the Big Bad Wolf.

Those poor little kids. They barely know their dad. He's been locked up for years. DeAnna's visits to prison were few and far between, and she rarely took the kids along. *Prison is a horrible place*, she'd said more than once. *I don't want to scare them*. But as of today, all bets are off. If they come home and find their dad here, especially if he's still holding me at gunpoint, they'll be terrified.

What has DeAnna told them about Lloyd? Children are always asking questions. Have they been taught to think of him as a good man, caught up in circumstances beyond his control? Or did they think of him as evil personified; a bad man who'd spent his life terrifying others and who deserved to be shut away in prison?

I couldn't recall a single time I'd heard DeAnna reference him in front of the kids. LJ and Tiffany rarely, if ever, mentioned him. It was almost as if he'd ceased to exist, that they didn't have a father.

But they do. Lloyd is their father, and he always will be. And there is nothing I can say or do that will change that. But there's an even greater truth involved, and he's sitting right here at my kitchen table. Lloyd is here, and he's waiting for them. If only I could stop him.

But I can't stop time. I can't stop the school bus.

I can't stop him from seeing his kids.

What if he decides to take them? He could spirit them away, travel across country, keep them from people who loved them.

But before he can do that, he'll have to go through me.

I won't make it easy for him. Lloyd is bigger, faster, and younger than I am, but he's underestimated the power and determination of a grandmother. If he thinks I'm going down without a fight, he's sorely mistaken. I'll kick and shout and do everything in my power to prevent him from taking the kids away from us. Would he use duct tape to shut my mouth, stop my screams? Would he tie me up, leave me writhing on the floor, helpless to stop him as he escapes with LJ and Tiffany?

Or maybe he won't want witnesses.

Maybe first, he'd turn the gun on me.

I can't let that happen.

I can't let LJ and Tiffany be witnesses to their grandmother's death.

I stare at the gun. There's a terrifying beauty to the weapon. The cold hard steel gleams in the sunlight. I have no idea what a silencer looks like, but I suspect Lloyd's gun doesn't have one. The same way I suspect he isn't about to jeopardize his chances of a safe getaway by shooting me. This is a quiet residential area. No one would be expecting to hear gunshots, especially on a Tuesday afternoon. If that gun goes off, someone will call 9-1-1.

It's obvious the situation has unnerved him, and I have a hunch he's trying to figure out his options. I caught him off guard when he showed up at my door. He came looking for DeAnna and the kids. He never expected to find me alone in the house. Maybe he will simply let me go.

Maybe. But maybe not.

Lloyd isn't stupid. Underestimating him will be my downfall.

I rack my brain for ideas on what to do next. All those tv shows I watch, some featuring FBI profilers dealing with hostage situations. Never in my wildest dreams did I ever imagine I'd be the one held hostage, and right here in my very own kitchen. I spent my career working in a school lunchroom. My specialty was serving up hot meals to hungry kids. I don't know anything about drug dealers and convicted felons. I have nothing in common with those kinds of people. They end up in prison, and with good reason. They're dangerous. Some are killers.

Lloyd spent years in prison. Has doing time turned him into a killer, too?

I don't know if he is. I don't know if he isn't. And I certainly don't know what kind of nasty scenarios he could be cooking up in his head.

But I love my grandchildren more than anything in the world, and I would do everything in my power to keep them safe.

Lloyd sprawls back in his chair, idly fingers the revolver, gives it a sudden spin. I watch in fascinated horror as it spins in aimless circles…around and around, two, three, four revolutions before it finally comes to rest. Pointed at the wall, not me.

I blow out a deep breath. Time is precious, and I can't afford to waste it. If Lloyd is stupid enough to play with a loaded weapon, there's no telling what he might do next. Abruptly I think of Alan, how he was always laughing at my ability to talk my way through things, how I regularly bested him in arguments. *You sure know how to get what you want*, he'd joke.

But this is no joke. I know exactly what I want to accomplish, and it's crucial that I get it right.

I nod at the gun. "Does your probation officer know about that?"

Lloyd snorts. "Yeah, like I'd tell him. You think I'm stupid?"

"Actually, I think you're much smarter than people give you credit for." I catch a breath. "Way smarter than I gave you credit for."

He flinches, and I realize my words have caught him by surprise.

"Big deal," he says, shrugging off my compliment. "What you want me to say? *Oh, thank you, Marguerite!*" he drones in a watery falsetto. "Like that's gonna happen. You never liked me, and I sure as hell don't like you. Guess you could say we hate each other's guts."

"You'd be right about that," I fire back without thinking.

"You think I give a damn what *you* think?" he snorts. "Dee always said you were a first-class bitch. Man, did she nail that, or what?"

"Don't you dare!" Fury erupts out of me from nowhere. "Don't you dare say another word about my daughter...or anyone else, either. You have no right to talk about me and my family. No right! Do you hear me!?"

"Oh, I got rights, Marguerite," he says, chuckling softly. "I got more rights than you realize."

He reaches out and picks up the gun.

That stupid gun. It's the only thing keeping me from lunging at him, spitting in his face, jamming my fingers into his eyeballs. I am not afraid of Lloyd Walsh. I've never been afraid of him. But I am afraid of his gun, and what it can do. If not for his gun, I'd find a way to take him out, put him back behind bars, where he belongs. Behind bars for the rest of his life. It would serve him right. He'd shrivel and whine and carry on about how he never meant to hurt me, never meant to put me or anyone else in danger.

As if anyone should believe him.

As if he deserved a free pass.

I've never hated anyone as much as I hate Lloyd. You're not supposed to hate people, but I don't care. I've hated him from the beginning, from that first day DeAnna brought him home to meet Alan and me. I've always hated seeing him swagger around DeAnna, acting like a big man, trying to impress her. He was always pushing…pushing, pushing, pushing; urging her to push back hard against Alan and me and our so-called rules. He would smirk in silent triumph at us behind DeAnna's back when she did his bidding. *See? She does what I want her to do.* I'd long suspected that Lloyd got his jollies at being the one calling the shots.

And here he is, goading me on, doing it again.

But I'll be damned if I'll give in, if I'll allow him to see just how much he's upset me. He wants to call me names? I've been called worse by DeAnna during some of our fights.

But just because I put up with it from her doesn't mean I'll put up with it from him. He and DeAnna aren't married, he isn't family, and he has no right to poke fun at me. Lloyd thinks he's such a big man, storming into my house, threatening me by waving a gun in my face. But I don't deserve to be treated like this. All his taunts and threats will not get the best of me. I'm determined that he will not take me down.

And if I'm careful and smart enough, I might take him down.

The gun gives him an advantage. Especially since I have no idea if he means to use it. But Lloyd underestimates me at his peril. If I have a chance, I intend to grab that gun and I won't hesitate to use it. If he forces my hand, I won't think twice about pulling the trigger.

And I wouldn't aim for his knees. I would aim to kill.

If someone ends up dead on my kitchen floor today, better him than me.

"On your feet." Lloyd motions me upward with a swoop of the pistol. "Let's go."

"Where are we going?" I eye him carefully as I rise and shove in my chair.

"What's up with you, always asking questions. You got problems, Marguerite, you know that? I'll bet you drove Alan batshit crazy."

"There's no reason to be so rude." Lloyd has no business dragging Alan's name into the conversation. He knows diddly-squat about the kind of relationship we had, and I doubt he has the slightest clue what it's like to be in love. People who truly love each other are always thinking of each other, putting their needs first. Lloyd has never done that with DeAnna. If he loved her, he would treat her better. He would have stood by her, done whatever he could to protect her and the kids. But instead, what did he do? What has he done?

Nothing. Absolutely nothing.

"All I did was ask a simple question," I say.

"I told you, quit asking questions."

He doesn't like all my questions? Too bad. I have no intention of stopping. This is my house, not his. Lloyd Walsh can go to hell.

And if I manage to get hold of his gun, I might send him there.

"Where are you taking me?"

"That's for me to know and you to find out."

I'll know soon enough. My house isn't large. A living and dining room, kitchen, and three bedrooms upstairs. Or maybe we're going outside. The sudden notion bursts through my mind like a ray of sunshine on a dreary day, and a surge of fresh hope floods through me. Outside, I might be able to break free and get away.

"Move." He urges me through the kitchen door and into the center hallway.

The living room is to our immediate left. Straight ahead is the front door, and freedom. If I move fast, I might be able to make it. I guesstimate my chances at fifty-fifty; so long as my right knee doesn't act up. It's been giving me trouble the past few months, sometimes seizing up without warning. But it's a risk I'm willing to take.

"Which way?" I ask, trying to keep my eyes off the front door.

Something cold, sharp, metallic, suddenly pokes me between my shoulder blades. I know exactly what it is.

"I gotta use the bathroom, and you're coming along. And don't go thinking up any bright ideas," he warns, "or you'll be sorry."

I'm not about to argue with him. *Keep the kids safe. Keep yourself safe.*

I will my feet to start moving. Down the hall we go.

Sideswiping me, Lloyd opens the door. "Ladies first."

He waves me in, but I don't budge.

"You go ahead. I'll wait out here." I have no intention of accompanying him inside, of being forced to stand meek and silent at his side watching him pee.

"I won't move," I add. "I promise."

"Yeah, right." He rolls his eyes.

"Swear to God, on my honor." I raise my right hand, dig in my heels. "Trust me, my word is good. I was a Girl Scout."

He shoves me toward the door.

I grab the door's handle and hang on as if my life depends on it. Which, in fact, it very well might.

"I mean it, Lloyd. You do your thing and I'll stand right here and wait. Keep the door open if you don't believe me," I suggest. "I won't run, and I won't watch, either."

He peers at me, then scowls.

"This door stays open," he warns. "And you better not move. You try leaving and the next thing you're gonna feel is a bullet in your back."

I have no doubt that he means every word. He stomps into the bathroom, and I lean against the wall, the back of my throat clutching tight with fear. There's no use taking a chance, trying to make a dash for the front door. It's too far from the bathroom and I'd never make it. He'd be after me in a heartbeat and make good on his threat. I close my eyes, trying to block out the sound of his stream hitting the toilet bowl. If I somehow manage to survive this day, I silently vow, one of the first things I'm going to do is hire a cleaning crew to come in and sanitize the house. Let them scrub away every trace of him. Whatever they charged, it would be worth every penny. Damn the cost.

I hear a flush and open my eyes to see him already back in the hallway beside me.

"Too much coffee," he says as he starts to zip up.

The shrill ring of the front door's bell catches both of us off guard.

"Yoo-hoo! Anybody home?" a woman's voice calls out.

"What the hell?" Lloyd hisses as three sharp raps on the front door knocker clang out. He grabs me and pushes me back against the wall.

"It's Millie," I stutter. "From next door."

He pushes himself against me, sticks his face right up into mine. I gag at the stench of his coffee breath, the stink of sweat coming off his clothes. But I get a whiff of something else, too: fear.

"Reet! It's Millie!"

"What the fuck is that old lady doing over here?"

"I…I don't know. She usually phones."

"Yeah? Well, guess what? This time she's at your front door!" He yanks my arm backward in a quick thrust, pins it behind me, forces it upward. "Your crazy neighbor is way too nosy for her own good. Get rid of her."

"Ow! You're hurting me!"

"Gonna be a lot more hurting going on if you don't get rid of her, and fast." He jams the revolver up against my ribcage.

Millie's finger on the doorbell doesn't let up. "Yoo-hoo! Reet!"

"What do you want me to do?" I whisper. "She knows I'm here. I told you she's always watching from her window. She knows when I come and go. She'll know I haven't left the house."

"That's your problem, not mine. You don't want that old bat hanging around causing trouble. Get rid of her. Now!"

Lloyd releases his grip on me, promptly shoves me toward the door.

I stumble down the hallway with him right behind me, racking my brain for something to say that will fly below Millie's radar. I don't want to rouse her suspicions and get her started asking even more questions, which could trigger Lloyd. I reach for the doorknob, then pause, somehow sensing something is different. I throw a desperate backward glance into an empty hallway. Lloyd is nowhere to be seen, but I know he's close by, watching and listening to whatever I say.

I open the front door.

"It's about time!" Millie says with a gleeful smile, her cap of white curls bouncing in a vigorous nod. "I *knew* you were home!"

I glance over the older woman's shoulder. Do I dare try? Two steps, maybe three, and I'd be out the door, on the porch and down the steps, on my way to freedom. I'd dash across the lawn, flag down a car, scream for help. Someone would help.

Someone.

Anyone.

The street is empty.

"I thought I might as well bring this over." Millie's gnarled hands hold a gaily wrapped package trimmed with pink ribbons and a large pink bow. "I know her birthday isn't until tomorrow, but I thought I'd bring it over so Tiffany would see it when she gets home from school."

My heart bottoms out at hearing my granddaughter's name.

"That's very sweet. Thank you, Millie." I reach out to take the gift.

"It's a paint-by-number set," she confides, hugging it tightly against her sweater. "I thought she might like it. You know how little girls around that age are, and how much they like doing art projects. I always did. I don't imagine things have changed that much since I was young."

"I'm sure Tiffany will love it. Thank you."

My heart hammers as we stand there making niceties. Millie still has hold of the package, and she doesn't seem interested in surrendering it. Somewhere behind me is Lloyd, lurking in the shadows. I need to get rid of Millie. For her own good, and mine.

I make another grab for the gift, but Millie isn't letting go.

"I had a hard time deciding between paints or a make-your-own-beaded-jewelry-set. But then I got to thinking that paints would probably be easier. A little clean-up involved, but other than that, they're simple to deal with. But the thought of her spilling all those beads? Not that she'd do it on purpose, but after all, accidents happen. You know how rambunctious kids can be. I didn't think you'd appreciate lots of tiny beads rolling around on your floors."

"You're right about that," I reply in a faint voice. "Paints were definitely the best choice."

"Exactly what I was thinking!" Millie says with a satisfied smile and starts across the threshold.

I hold up a hand, stop her from going any further. "I'm sorry, Millie, but now isn't a good time. Let's make it another day, okay?"

"Oh." My neighbor's face crinkles in dismay, then slowly morphs into something bordering on suspicion. She peers at me across the threshold. "Is something wrong? You're acting mighty funny, Reet."

Oh, God. What do I do now?

"Do you need help?"

Yes! Call 911!!! I silently shriek, abruptly wishing I could grab her shoulders, shake some sense into the silly old woman, scream a warning directly in her face. But I don't dare get her involved. There's no telling what Lloyd might do if he got his hands on her. Millie can be a pain, but she's not a bad sort and ultimately, she means well. I don't want the old woman to end up getting hurt…or worse.

"Everything's fine, thanks," I say, somehow managing to plaster a big smile on my face despite my swirling stomach and my jangling nerves. "Honestly, Millie, I'm super busy at the moment."

"Too busy for a cup of coffee? That doesn't sound like you, Reet. And plus, I wanted to ask you about that car." She shuffles round and points behind her toward the curb. "Do you know who it belongs to? I've never seen it around before, and it's been out there all morning. Do you think someone abandoned it? I wonder if we should call someone?"

Yes! Call 911!!! I swallow down the taste of vomit rising in the back of my throat.

"Sorry, Millie, but I don't know anything about the car. Someone will be back eventually, I suppose, and drive it away."

"Is that so?"

"Millie, honestly, I don't mean to be rude, but I'm super busy."

"Yes, I know. *I'm too busy, Millie.* You've told me that two or three times already. And you were too busy to talk with me earlier when I phoned. Remember?"

Millie steps back, straightens up, stretching her five-foot frame so that every inch bristles with indignation.

"Sorry to bother you. If I'd known you were so busy, I never would have come over. Obviously, I'm making a nuisance of myself. Rest assured I won't be doing it again."

I blow out a small sigh. I've offended her, and now she'll go away mad. But it can't be helped. Right now, Millie is the least of my problems.

"I'll make sure Tiffany gets your gift." I snatch the package out of her hands, slam the door in her face and throw the deadbolt.

And whip around to face Lloyd.

"I hope you're satisfied!" I throw him an angry glance, not even attempting to hide my annoyance. "Millie's furious with me, and it's all your fault."

"My fault? Ha!" He cackles with laughter and slaps his thigh. "You're the one who told her off."

"Yes, I did…but I wouldn't have, if it wasn't for you and your stupid gun."

I feel my face redden, my fury growing. I've had just about enough out of Lloyd Walsh. I take a step forward, getting up close and personal.

"Let me tell you something about Millie," I hiss softly. "You might think she's just some nice little old lady who lives next door to me. But when she gets mad, being *nice* flies right out the window. And something else: Millie holds grudges. After what happened today, there's no way she'll speak to me again without me first getting down on my knees and beg her forgiveness."

I glare at him. "Do you have any idea what kind of shape my knees are in? No, of course not. You're young, and you think your body is going to last forever. Well, I've got news for you, Lloyd…that is not the way things work. Ask anyone over the age of sixty, and they'll tell you the same thing: the older you get, the faster your body starts to fall apart. My eyes are crap, my knees are shot, and so are my nerves, after today.

"And for that," I say in a hot aside, "I *do* blame you. You've been here more than three hours, and you've done nothing to alleviate the stress I'm under. If I end up having a heart attack or a stroke, it will be your fault!"

I'm done trying to edit myself. I've tried being nice. I've done the things he's asked. I even made my famous grilled cheese sandwiches, *and* I let him eat all the gourmet pickles. And where has it gotten me? I'm standing in the hallway with that stupid gun of his aimed straight at my chest.

Forget that nonsense. From now on, I'm playing hardball.

"And one more thing," I add, feeling totally justified in my wrath. "You stand there and say all you want about Millie and her big mouth…but while you're doing that, I suggest you also give a thought as to why she came over here in the first place. She remembered that tomorrow is your daughter's birthday, and that's a hell of a lot more than you've done."

The gaily wrapped present is still in my hands, and I shake it in his face.

"Tiffany is going to love this paint set," I say. "She's turning out to be quite the little artist. But you don't know that. Do you?"

"Don't blame me," he says with a scowl. "It's not like I've had much time with her."

"And whose fault is that?" I'm on a roll, and I can't stop myself. "Nobody forced you to start dealing drugs. You knew it was wrong, but you did it anyway. You made some bad choices and you ended up getting caught and going to prison. What kind of message do you think that sends your kids? Think about that, Lloyd."

"You got no clue what you're talking about." His eyes narrow. "Who the hell do you think you are? You got no business judging me."

"Who am I? *Who am I?*" My voice trembles, my legs are wobbly, but I stare him down. I refuse to give in to fear. If I don't stand up to him now, I'll never find the courage again. "I'll tell you who I am: I'm that little girl's grandmother. I'm the one who's been taking care of her…and her brother, too, I might add, while you and DeAnna have been incommunicado. I think I've earned the right to speak my mind."

Instant rage flashes across his face, and I'm convinced he's about to raise his hand and strike me. I steel myself for the blow sure to come.

But, much to my surprise, nothing happens.

Maybe he's been listening after all.

"Lloyd." I huff out a small breath, praying for patience. "I'm sorry if you think I'm being unfair. But I'm only speaking the truth as I see it. Some things are hard to hear. And you don't get an automatic pass just because you were in prison. Kids need their parents. They need to know their parents love them. Whatever you've done…the good, the bad? It doesn't matter. Tiffany needs you. So does LJ. They'll always need you. You're their father. No one can take that away."

"You're talking shit," he throws back at me. "They might be my kids, but that doesn't mean I get to see them. I asked Dee to bring them around. Do you think she did? Not once." He spits out the words with a sour vengeance. "Other guys, their kids show up on Visitor's Day. But not mine. Never once did she bring them to see me. Got any idea how that makes a guy feel?"

"Pretty awful, I'd think," I venture a guess as I turn back toward the kitchen. I need to sit down.

"You got that straight," he says, following me. "And the times Dee did bother showing up, all she did was complain. Always whining about something. *Things are bad, I need money.* She harps about how she's stuck alone with the kids. She says they're growing up fast. *How long is it gonna be before you get out?* I told her I missed them, and I asked her, real nice, to bring them for a visit. I told her I was lonely. *Why should I bring them around,* she says, *when they don't remember you anyway?"*

It's difficult not to feel some sympathy for him. I know how it feels to be on the receiving end of DeAnna's brutal tongue lashings. I've been there more times than I care to admit, and some of which I probably deserved. But Lloyd made bad choices that put him behind bars. Locked up in a prison cell, shut away from society, from his family, his children. It was what he deserved.

But he's no longer in prison. Hasn't he paid the price?

How long will I continue kicking him, insisting he pay for his past mistakes? Kick a dog enough times and it's pretty much guaranteed he'll turn mean.

I sink into my chair, try to latch on to any stray bits of mercy and compassion floating around in my heart.

"You have a point," I say. "I suppose DeAnna thought she was protecting the kids. But I guess if I were in your shoes, I probably would have thought that nobody cared… that I didn't count."

"Right," he says with a scowl. "And know what she did then? Laughed in my face. Said it was my problem, not hers. *Serves you right*, she said. Told me I got what was coming to me. And maybe I did. But she didn't have to say it like that. Dee can be a real bitch."

I offer him a grim smile. "She certainly can."

He cocks his head and gives me a wide-eyed stare.

"Don't look so surprised," I reply. "We both know what she's capable of. DeAnna's said and done plenty of things she knew would hurt me."

"Yeah, but you're her…"

"Her mother?" I pick up where his voice trails off. "You'd think that would make a difference, right? Not necessarily. She's my daughter, and I'll always love her. But that doesn't mean I have to like the things she's done. DeAnna is no saint.

"See this?" I reach across the table, use two fingers to trace the edges of deep grooves carved into the wooden surface. "She did that with a pencil when she was little. She wanted to draw an apple tree."

Lloyd squints at the marred wood. "Dee trashed your table and you let her live? That's messed up."

"I was very angry when it happened," I admit. "But it happened long ago."

He pulls a grimace. "If Tiffany did something like that, Dee would whack her bottom good and hard."

"What good does spanking do?" I ask. "It doesn't change anything, except make kids more frightened than they already are. That's not something I want any part of. I don't want any children to be afraid of me. There's already way too much that they're scared about." I stare at the deep grooves in the tabletop. "Sometimes I wish I could go back and change things. But I can't. It's too late." I lift my shoulders, sigh. "Maybe DeAnna's right. I don't know. How do any of us know?"

"Sometimes, Marguerite, you don't make sense."

"You'll get no argument from me," I reply with a small smile. Some of the things I've said today, some of the accusations I've made against him, the criticisms I've lodged against DeAnna, have rushed out *sans* filter. And while I don't regret speaking the truth, every time I see and think about his gun, I'm reminded how fluid the situation is. The danger I'm in. How fast things could change.

And for both of us to make it through the next several hours, it's crucial that we think about something else. That we do something to take our minds off things.

Because if we don't, I'm going to end up completely stressed out, and Lloyd, all six-feet-whatever-inches of him, will need to pick me up off the floor.

I stand, and he abruptly jumps to his feet.

"How tall are you?" I look him up and down.

"What?" His eyes narrow. "What's that—"

"Never mind, it doesn't matter. You're tall enough."

"For what?"

Ignoring his question, I start for the dining room.

"Follow me," I call over my shoulder. "I'm putting you to work."

CHAPTER SEVENTEEN

"Sorry about bringing Lloyd along." DeAnna perched against the kitchen counter, watching as I stirred up my famous potato salad. "He showed up uninvited as we were walking out of the house."

"No problem," I replied, despite my growing reservations. DeAnna and Lloyd hadn't lived together for months and had been fighting non-stop. Why didn't she simply cut her losses, make a clean break from him? And what had she been thinking, dragging him along today? The last thing any of us wanted was having to referee another fighting match between them. Alan deserved a nice peaceful birthday, and I was determined that this afternoon should be extra special and drama-free. Lloyd being here substantially increased the chance that something would go wrong. So much already had. Hopefully that wouldn't include my potato salad, which Alan loved, and on his birthday especially needed to taste just right. I eyed the mixture of diced onions, olives, celery. It still looked too dry. I grabbed the mayonnaise jar and scooped a generous spoonful into the bowl, followed with another squirt of mustard.

"It's not like he gets to see the kids that often," DeAnna said. "Since he got his new job, Lloyd's always working."

"At least he's working," I said, immediately regretting it. Why did I always insist on throwing in my own two cents? It was an irritating habit I picked up from my mother; you'd think that knowing she's the source would be enough to stop me from opening my mouth in the first place. But still, I worried. And being DeAnna's mother, I had plenty to worry about. Especially since I usually didn't have the slightest clue as to what was going on. Especially when it came to anything Lloyd-related. DeAnna was always swift to make it clear that subject was off limits. What went on between the two of them was none of my business.

She was right. It was none of my business.

The potato salad still looked bland. I shot a few more squirts of mustard into the mix.

"Like I said, he showed up just as we were leaving. Totally unexpected." DeAnna sighed. "I had no choice but to bring him along."

"I said it was fine, didn't I?" I plopped another spoonful of mayonnaise on top of the mustard.

"*Yeeessss.*" DeAnna dragged out the word. "You said it…but did you mean it?"

"He's welcome here," I replied, hoping that I sounded properly enthusiastic, suspecting that I didn't. And what did it matter? In the grand scheme of things, DeAnna still wouldn't believe me. What a bust Alan's birthday party was turning out to be. I'd gathered the family together to celebrate his sixtieth, and the birthday boy was suffering from a miserable summer cold. He'd coughed his way through our well wishes, assuring us *I feel fine! Just fine!* Barry and Holly (with another of her migraine headaches). DeAnna and her kids. Baby Tiffany squawked and jabbered from inside her wheeled walker, beating a wooden spoon against its tray while four-year-old LJ tore through the house, out into the backyard, then back inside again. Constant and utter chaos, especially when Alan's older sister Mary showed up unexpected with her husband Burt in tow, then proceeded to needle poor Alan about what her baby brother should expect now his fifties were in the rearview mirror.

And Lloyd. If only Lloyd was nothing more than a blip in DeAnna's rearview mirror. A distant reminder from her past. If only she hadn't decided to drag him along today.

Poor Alan. What a disaster.

I eyed the bowl, grabbed the mayonnaise jar again. One more spoonful wouldn't hurt.

"Mother! Seriously?" DeAnna grabbed the jar out of my hand. "You're going to turn it into potato salad soup."

I stared down at the gloppy mess. Everything would have turned out fine, if only I'd been paying attention. If only Lloyd hadn't shown up. He'd spoiled things, as usual. Alan's birthday party. My potato salad. DeAnna's life, her future. Having Lloyd in our lives was the ultimate spoiler.

The spoon clanged against the counter as I grabbed the bowl away from her.

"What are you doing?" DeAnna stared as I headed for the trash.

"I'm going to dump it out and start over. You said it was ruined."

"I did not! Quit putting words in my mouth…and quit catastrophizing everything. You do that all the time, and it drives us all crazy." Whisking the bowl out of my hands, she headed out the door with it.

"Good Lord," I muttered under my breath and followed her into the dining room where everyone waited.

What a birthday bust. No surprise that my potato salad sat largely untouched. Alan honked and coughed his way through several spoonfuls before giving up, while DeAnna didn't even try. Mary used her age-old excuse of being on a diet. Holly shook her head and offered a wan smile, while Barry managed a few bites.

Lloyd, meanwhile, seemed oblivious to anything except the food on his plate. Including my potato salad, I noticed, watching as he gobbled up two generous portions, then went for the gusto with a third. Some things were beyond reasoning. I doubted he was trying to make a good impression. Maybe he was hungry. Maybe he liked soupy potato salad.

The same way he seemed to like my fried chicken, too. He'd scarfed down four pieces before finally pausing to sit back in his chair.

"Good chicken," he said to no one in general.

"Glad you like it," I replied, half-expecting to hear him let rip with a loud belch. How much fried chicken could a grown man eat? Not that I begrudged him enjoying his food. And there was plenty to go round; I'd fried up more than usual. Any leftovers would go inside Alan's lunch box next week.

"Think I'll have another piece," Lloyd said, using his fork to stab number five onto his plate.

"Reet's a great cook. You ever want a homecooked meal, you know where to find it." Alan offered Lloyd one of his customary smiles that anyone with a functioning set of eyeballs would recognize as genuine. "You're always welcome to join us, son."

Son? Lloyd isn't our son! I glared at Alan. Had he lost his freaking mind? All that nasty congestion swirling inside his head must have blocked some vital brain waves. There was no other explanation for why he'd be so accommodating to a lowlife like Lloyd.

Lloyd, who never made the slightest effort, who did absolutely nothing to help himself be liked.

What about you, Reet? You've done nothing to try and understand him or make him feel welcome.

The head talk was driving me crazy. I'd done nothing wrong, and I had no intention of changing up my behavior to suit him. Why should I? Lloyd wasn't worth the effort.

"Daddy, did you know that Lloyd has a new job? He's working at that brand new restaurant over on Fifth Street." DeAnna's gaze darted back and forth between Alan and Lloyd. "It opened last month. Lloyd, tell Daddy about your new job," she urged.

"Sounds like you already did," he said.

"Oh, you!" she joshed, and playfully tapped his hand. "Fine, if you won't tell them, then I will."

"Didn't say I wouldn't," he replied in a low aside, "just that I don't see no need to go bragging."

"It's not bragging if it's true," DeAnna retorted. "Lloyd is their new sous chef," she announced. "The owners are grooming him to take over the entire kitchen. Isn't that great?" She glanced around the table, her eyes shining bright. "I'm so proud of him."

"Good for you, Lloyd." Alan smiled. "Glad to hear things are working out for you."

"Congratulations," Mary said as she helped herself to a second slice of birthday cake.

"Sounds like a great opportunity," Barry said.

"Thanks," Lloyd mumbled.

"You in college, Lloyd?" Burt asked.

"Nope." He kept his head down, kept eating.

"He's not enrolled right now," DeAnna answered her uncle, "but he's planning on it. Aren't you, Lloyd?" she said in an aside that was more a statement of fact than a question.

"Lloyd, let me give you some advice," Burt said. "A good education, that's what you need. Get your diploma. Start with business school, some marketing classes. Those connections will be crucial, especially when the going gets rough. And it'll get rough, that I'll guarantee. It's a tough world out there. The economy's up, then it's down. You won't get far chopping carrots."

"Lloyd's super smart, Uncle Burt," DeAnna said. "Why should he have to go back to school simply to get a piece of paper? It shouldn't matter. Besides, if he wants to, he will."

"Having a diploma is like guaranteeing yourself to employers," Barry said. "It lets them know you were committed enough to wade through all the noise, work with the requirements, learn what was needed. You made a commitment and followed through. Going to college sets you up for success."

"College isn't for everyone," I reminded him. "Some people do fine without a degree."

"Ditch diggers, maybe," Barry joked. "Janitors. Garbage men."

When did my son turn into such a snob?

"I didn't go to college," I reminded him. I'd briefly toyed with the idea, only to nix the notion somewhere in my senior year of high school. My parents hadn't had the financial resources, and my grades hadn't been good enough to qualify me for a scholarship. When Aunt Sis stepped forward and volunteered to cover my tuition and expenses, it forced me to do some serious thinking. What did I want my future to look like? Did I really want to spend another four years stuck behind a desk in a classroom? A few of my girlfriends were headed off to university, intent on earning degrees in education, nursing, business and law. But I had no desire for a career. The only thing I wanted was to marry Alan, settle down with him and raise a family together. Happiness and true love didn't require a college degree.

"Your father didn't go to college either," I added, "and he does just fine."

"Sorry, Dad, no disrespect intended," Barry said.

"None taken," Alan assured him.

"Meanwhile," Burt added, "if you're stuck on this notion of trying to make it in the restaurant business, keep your resume updated. Especially in today's economy. You know, Lloyd, things can go sour, fast, and I don't mean milk or cottage cheese. The restaurant business can be brutal. I see it all the time."

"Uncle Burt's an accountant," DeAnna told Lloyd.

"Yeah, I know," he muttered. "It's not like you haven't mentioned it a thousand times."

Her eyes narrowed and she opened her mouth as if to hurl some snarky reply. Then suddenly seeming to think the better of it, she turned and plucked Tiffany from her highchair. She busied herself wiping down the baby's sticky fingers and drool from her mouth.

"I have a couple restaurants as clients," Burt continued. "The profit margin is minimal, and the overhead can kill you. Not to mention what could happen if the place gets some bad reviews. I remember this one restaurant we took on as a client. Two years ago, if memory serves correct. The place was doing okay, until their refrigerator broke. That's when everything started going south. Somebody called the health department, and when they showed up, they shut the place down. The refrigerator had to be repaired, plus they got tagged for a couple other minor infringements.

"Bottom line, having to take care of all that stuff meant the restaurant was closed for more than a week. Only one week, but that was plenty of time for the rumor mill to take off with a bunch of wild theories about why they'd shut down in the first place. People were saying all kinds of crazy stuff: they'd been serving spoiled food, switching out orders, inflating prices, stiffing the staff. A mice infestation? Bam! Within a month, the restaurant was out of business, shut down for good. It couldn't survive. My point is, even when things seem like they're going right, they can suddenly go wrong. The restaurant business is never a sure bet. And anyone who thinks so is a fool."

"I'm sure Lloyd appreciates the advice, Uncle Burt." DeAnna finished fussing with Tiffany and moved around the table, swiftly gathering dinner plates. "But you don't need to worry about him. He'll be fine. And so will his restaurant."

"Just telling it the way I see it," Burt called out as DeAnna disappeared into the kitchen. "Restaurants come and restaurants go. Flexibility is the name of the game."

Mary's husband was a pompous ass. Why didn't Burt do us all a favor and shut up? While I loved Alan's sister and was always glad to see her, I'd formed my opinion about my brother-in-law the day we met. Forty years later, my opinion hadn't changed.

"Personally, I like going out to dinner once in a while," I said. "It gives me a chance to try new foods. Plus, there's no cleanup involved. No dirty dishes."

"Pass me another slice of that birthday cake, Reet." Burt held out his plate. "It's dee-lish. You make it?"

"I did."

"You oughta see if Lloyd can get you hired as a pastry chef at that fancy restaurant of his," he quipped.

"Ha, ha. Very funny." I plopped another piece of cake on Burt's plate, then started for the kitchen. It was a mystery how Mary managed to put up with him. You'd think she'd get tired of the same old drivel coming out of her husband's mouth year after year.

I burst through the kitchen door with a stack of dirty dishes.

"DeAnna, swear to God, your uncle gets more obnoxious every—"

I stopped dead at the sight of my daughter at the sink. Glass in one hand, whiskey bottle in the other, she was pouring herself a shot.

"Oh, DeAnna." I'd had such high hopes that her drinking days were over. She'd quit during each of her pregnancies. I'd assumed she'd stayed stopped after Tiffany was born. "You're drinking again?"

"What's so wrong with that?"

"But why?"

"Why not?" She lifted her chin, eyes glittering with defiance. "Everybody else around here gets to do what they want. You. Daddy. Lloyd. Why not me? What's the big deal? It's only one drink."

But DeAnna couldn't stop at just one drink. DeAnna never stopped at just one drink. One drink was too many and a thousand was never enough.

And for that, I blamed Lloyd.

DeAnna fell in love with booze when she fell in love with Lloyd. With him as the catalyst, the alcohol quickly turned her into someone she wasn't meant to be. A daughter we did not recognize. A beautiful fifteen-year-old girl who, after only one drink, morphed into a mean ugly drunk. We struggled to keep her living in our house, attending high school. She'd graduated with a diploma clutched in one hand and a signed one-year lease in the other, for a one-bedroom apartment she and Lloyd intended to share. Alan and I weren't thrilled when we learned of her plans to move out of our house, to move in with Lloyd. Not to mention, their apartment was in the dumpy side of town. Somehow, we brokered a fragile peace, talked DeAnna into signing up for community college. Not that it did much good. With Lloyd in and out of her life, her classroom attendance was sporadic. Booze kept her company.

Then, DeAnna discovered she was pregnant.

Learning she was going to have a baby seemed to make enough difference and she cleaned up her act. Maybe there was hope for our daughter after all, Alan and I allowed ourselves to believe as the weeks and months tumbled by. By her seventh month, the apartment was long gone, and so was Lloyd. DeAnna was back living with us, lazing around the house, taking afternoon naps, cajoling her father to puh-leez! stop and pick up her favorite ice cream on his way home from work. It wouldn't always be like this, she'd promised. Things would be different once the baby was born. She'd go back to school, get a place of her own. As soon as the baby arrived, she'd make something of herself…until then, couldn't we give her some time? Surely it wasn't too much to ask that she be allowed the freedom to pamper herself in the last lingering weeks before she gave birth.

How could we say no? DeAnna needed us. She'd been abandoned by Lloyd. Of course, we would help. She would soon give birth to our grandchild. And so, we indulged her, allowing her time and freedom and space. We kept quiet as the days and weeks passed, as she lounged about the house, sleeping at all hours, reigning over the tv remote. Irritating, yes, but we were willing to do whatever it took to keep her happy and ensure that the baby was healthy.

And DeAnna had quit drinking. That was huge. A new beginning for us all.

Until one day when Lloyd showed up again and re-claimed his spot as the most important person in our daughter's life. Alan and I were forced to take a back seat. Years later, with another baby on the way and Lloyd once again bopping in and out of the picture, DeAnna turned to an old friend. But seeking comfort in a whiskey bottle was never going to be the way out or provide her with the things she longed for. Would she ever learn?

"Talk about an ass." DeAnna said with a quick scowl as she nodded toward the dining room. One of Burt's loud guf-faws could be heard through the door. "Why does he have to be like that?"

"Because your uncle *is* an ass," I agreed. "It's a miracle Aunt Mary has stayed married to him all these years."

"Not Uncle Burt," she muttered. "I'm talking about Lloyd. He's driving me nuts! Didn't you hear him? Acting the way he does, pretending like everyone should feel *soooo sorry* for him. *Poor Lloyd*, he has to carry the whole load. *Poor Lloyd*, his life is so hard. *Poor Lloyd*, right? As if he actually has something to bitch about." Her eyes narrowed. "You know what I'd really like? For once, I'd like to see him try and take care of the kids. After all, they're his kids, too. Why is it always *me* who gets stuck doing all the work? He's always ragging on me about the way I handle them, how I'm doing it wrong. I'd like to see him try!"

The last thing I wanted was to get involved in the middle of yet one more of their fights or whatever was going on between them. But it was hard to keep my mouth shut.

"I know he's not around as much as you'd like but try not to let it get you down," I said. "We all know you're doing the best you can."

"Damn right I am! And by the way," she said, with a sharp look for me, "what did you mean, making that little crack about him not being smart enough for college?"

Her words pulled me up short. I couldn't recall having said any such thing.

"I don't know what you mean."

"Don't go acting all innocent," she warned. "Everyone heard you. When it comes to Lloyd, you never let up, do you? You're always after him about something. His hair, his clothes. The things he says, what he does…and what he doesn't do."

"You're not being fair." Why was she suddenly picking on me? "I've never said a word against Lloyd, and I never will."

Not to her, at least. All these years I'd held my tongue, careful not to speak out against him to anyone but Alan. He knew how I felt about Lloyd, and we agreed when it came to DeAnna, Lloyd was toxic. What in the world did she see in him? Why would she choose to be with a man like that?

"He'll never be good enough in your eyes, will he?" DeAnna's voice was low and lethal. "No matter what he does, he'll never be good enough."

"You're wrong," I insisted. "Did I ever once say anything—"

"You didn't have to. It was obvious." The sneer stretched all the way across her face. "Thanks a lot, Mother. Lloyd and I appreciate your support."

Off she flounced, the kitchen's screen door slamming behind her, leaving me standing alone in the kitchen to ponder how, when and why our mother/daughter relationship once again had ended up in such a dramatic downward spiral.

It was some minutes later before I realized that not only had DeAnna disappeared, but she'd taken the whiskey bottle with her.

CHAPTER EIGHTEEN

"You complain no one treats you right, that you never get a break. Okay, Lloyd, I'm giving you one right now."

I do my best to wrap myself in confidence as I confront him in my kitchen. Despite my bluster and bravado, my attempts to one-up him, he must know I'm running scared. No doubt he can smell the fear radiating off me. And he'd be right…I am scared. Not so much because of him, but the gun he holds in his hand and what he'll ultimately decide to do with it.

But one good thing has come out of the situation: Lloyd's gun has helped steel my resolve. I might be scared, but I'm equally determined not to give in. Just because he has a weapon capable of deadly force doesn't mean that he gets to make the rules and have everything go his way. I intend to do whatever I have to do to protect LJ and Tiffany. My grandchildren deserve to live, and I'll do anything to make sure they do. Even if it means sacrificing myself.

Over my dead body might end up being my legacy as a grandmother.

"I could use some help. And since you're here, I guess you're elected. Besides," I add, "it's not as if you have something better to do, right? You're hanging around, killing time."

Killing time? Am I crazy? The last thing I want is to encourage him to think about killing something.

Killing time, killing me.

His eyebrows vex into a frown. "Help with what?"

"We're going to decorate the dining room. I'm throwing a surprise party tonight."

His eyes and mouth harden with suspicion.

"Tomorrow is your daughter's birthday," I remind him. "Tiffany will be six years old. I think we can agree that a little girl turning six deserves to have a birthday party. Balloons, party hats and games. Have you ever played Pin the Tail on the Donkey?"

Lloyd stares at me, his eyes popping wide as if two long donkey ears have suddenly sprouted from the top of my head.

"There's no party. You're making this up," he accuses.

"I'm not."

"You said it's a surprise."

"And it *will* be," I insist, my thoughts flying fast and furious. "She'll be expecting the party on her birthday tomorrow…not tonight."

"Quit messing with me, Marguerite. I know what you're trying to do."

"What I'm *trying* to do is get the party organized." Originally I'd planned to tackle the decorating tonight, once LJ and Tiffany were fast asleep. But who knows what will happen in the next few hours? Given the circumstances, there's no time like the present. "I've been planning this party for weeks."

Lloyd snorts. "I don't believe you."

"See for yourself." I move to the pantry, throw open the door, wave a hand at the sacks covering the floor. "Streamers, balloons, party favors…the whole shebang. I bought this stuff last week, and I've been hiding it from the kids. Look, I even got the stepladder out to help with the streamers. Will you hang them for me?"

"How about you take a flying fuck, Marguerite."

"Why are you being so stubborn?" I stand my ground, ignoring his language, eyeing him dead on. Let him swear. I don't care. I'm too busy worrying about my heart and the way it's doing jumping jacks inside my chest. "Do you seriously think a woman my age should be climbing ladders? I don't think so. But you're young, you're tall. You're perfect."

"Yeah?" he says with a sneer. He jams his face close to mine, his eyes gleaming in a not-so-nice way. "And why should I?"

"How about because it's the right thing to do?" I challenge. "How about you do it because you love your little girl, and you want to see her happy? You *do* love her, don't you?"

He shifts on his feet, and I have the quick satisfaction of seeing his face flush. My words have hit a nerve. And while I know he loves his kids, that doesn't mean Lloyd can be trusted to be the adult and do what's best for them.

"Think back to when you were a little boy," I urge. "Remember how much fun it was when your birthday rolled around? The parties, all the presents, the cake."

"I never had a party."

"I find that hard to believe," I say without thinking.

Lloyd doesn't answer.

"Maybe you just don't remember," I suggest.

His chin tilts upward. "You calling me a liar?"

"No, of course not." I don't want to set him off into doing God-knows-what. A person can only handle so much, and I'm not sure how far I've pushed him. Usually, I pick up on people's emotions fairly quickly; what they're like, the things they care about. But not with Lloyd. It's as if his feelings are hidden away inside multiple layers of bubble-wrap, and any questions about his family, his life, and/or the things people would normally ask of their daughter's boyfriend, are protected with quick one-word answers. He'd seemed determined not to fit in, as if he suspected our interest in him was not genuine. After a while, we quit asking. There was no point in asking. We already knew he wouldn't answer. He had no desire to know us.

Now I find myself suddenly questioning that very thing. I'd always assumed he'd taken offense specifically with us. But what if he'd never meant for us to take things person-ally? What if Lloyd was like that with everyone?

His parents had never thrown him a birthday party.

Never?

The word isn't in my vocabulary. Year after year I'd knocked myself out throwing birthday parties for Barry and DeAnna. Not elaborate parties, but still, plenty of work had been involved. And every year, once the parties were over and I ended up collapsed on the couch, I'd swear to Alan that we'd thrown our last party, that we wouldn't be putting our-selves through that again. Yet inevitably, when the next year rolled around, there we were again, blowing up balloons, setting out party favors, serving up cake and ice cream. It was exhausting and time-consuming but totally worth it, and wasn't that the point? Our children knew how much they were loved.

I was beginning to doubt that Lloyd could say the same.

You never knew about some people. We'd never seen much of Donald and Margo. Maybe it was by happenstance…or was it design? There'd been that one awkward time at their family barbecue, and a Mother's Day incident years ago when Margo had been drinking. Some of the things she'd said that day would have been better off left unspoken. I'd heard other things, too, throughout the years and some today, straight out of Lloyd's mouth.

Children left to fend for themselves.

A daughter no one acknowledged or spoke of.

A son who claimed to have never had a birthday party.

Growing up in a family like that, with parents like that, was it any wonder Lloyd had turned out the way he did?

All of this would be so much easier if only I could be sure that I could trust him. I want to trust him. I want to believe him. He said he's out on parole, that he was released only yesterday. But there's no way of knowing if that is true. He could simply be spouting nonsense, laughing behind my back as he feeds me lie after lie. Maybe he wasn't paroled. Maybe he busted out, spent the night hiding at a buddy's house, staying out of sight and biding his time until he figured out what he wanted.

DeAnna and the kids. The answer is obvious. Only two questions remain.

How determined is he?

How far is Lloyd willing to go to get what he wants?

I force a deep breath. If I don't stop the catastrophizing, I'll drive myself crazy. The odds are slim that he risked an escape or we would have heard about it by now. The prison authorities would have tried to contact DeAnna, to warn her to be on the lookout, that he was armed and dangerous. And if they couldn't reach her on her cell, surely they would have called here, her last known address.

No, I had to trust that Lloyd was telling the truth about having received an early parole. He deserved the benefit of the doubt. The right thing to do was for me to step up and offer to help him. Lloyd would need help. Now more than ever. He mentioned he was staying with friends. Which friends? He hadn't exactly proved himself to be the best judge of character. Had he fallen back in with the usual crowd? The people who'd been responsible for him being sent to prison in the first place?

I need a moment. I can't remember when I've ever felt as tired, not even during those horrible first days and weeks after Alan died. This is different. I feel myself fading. I need to sit down.

I don't dare.

I shoot a glance at the clock. The little engine is headed straight toward the one-thirty mark. While I suspect my poking and prodding, all my incessant questions have pushed him closer to the edge, Lloyd still hasn't reacted with violence. The gun is pointed at me, but he hasn't pulled the trigger. I chance a closer look. His index finger isn't even sitting on the trigger.

Not yet.

The most important thing I can do right now is to keep myself involved. Keep my mind alert. Keep both of us moving.

"Let's get busy." I grab a sack of streamers, and a separate sack of balloons, shove them into his hands. "Let's get this place decorated before LJ and Tiffany get home. The school bus will be here sooner than you think."

"Sooner than *you* think," he agrees. "And then we'll see what's what."

I don't dare allow myself to wonder what his words might mean. I'm pinning everything on the next two hours. Maybe I'm a fool, thinking that I'll be able to talk him out of whatever he's planning. What makes me think I'm smart enough? How naïve, allowing myself to think that common sense will prevail. Common sense has flown out the window.

I am on my own.

CHAPTER NINETEEN

"T HIS IS GOING TO BE so much fun!" DeAnna burbled as we headed through the restaurant door.

"I've been looking forward to it," I heard myself say, amazed how easily the lie slid off my tongue. Since I was a little girl, I've dreaded anything that had to do with Mother's Day. The house where I grew up hadn't been filled with Hallmark moments, but not for lack of trying. My father and I had done our best to pamper my mother. Flowers from him (lush pink roses) and my attempts to serve her up a delicious breakfast in bed. Granted, the eggs were often runny and sometimes I burned the toast. Once I accidently spilled a full glass of orange juice all over her bed as I set down the tray. That hadn't been the most pleasant of Mother's Day breakfasts. But at least we tried. My father and I always tried. And we remembered the chocolate, too. Woe to us both if the obligatory box of chocolates failed to appear. And further woe and a hex upon our heads if either of us dared to sample a bite without an invitation to do so. *This is my day! I'm not sharing!*

Long before her mental illness was officially diagnosed, I'd already concluded that my mother was not the nicest of women. It took me years before I was finally able to admit that she wasn't nice at all. But she was still my mother, and I couldn't let go of that. Even after Aunt Sis succumbed to breast cancer shortly after I graduated from high school, and even after my father died, I refused to abandon the woman who'd given me birth. Ironic, that at the end of her life, it came down to just my mother and me. She was the only family I had left, and I was all she had left. And though she no longer recognized me, I made sure to remember every Mother's Day with a card, flowers, and a box of chocolates and a personal visit to the long-term care facility where she lived until the day she died at the ripe old age of ninety-two.

Good riddance is what I thought then and still thought today. Given my preference as to Mother's Day outings, what I'd prefer to do is forget the whole thing. Which is why I'd been inclined to pooh-pooh DeAnna's invitation to celebrate with a Girls-Day-Out-Brunch. A person could only take so much, and my mother had spoiled the day forever. But after a little prodding from Alan and after further reflection on my part, I agreed to go. Who knew? This year might be different, and I might actually end up having fun. Plus, LJ had been invited to tag along, and I wasn't about to say no to anything involving my grandson. Hearing that Lloyd's mother Margo had also been invited? The more, the merrier, I decided. And while I had some misgivings about DeAnna treating us with money she probably found hard to come by, I didn't want to discourage her, either. Something had hijacked my daughter's psyche of late and I much preferred this quieter, gentler version. For once in her life, she was pleasant to be around. Perhaps it was the hormones, seeing as how DeAnna was pregnant again. But whatever reasons behind her latest metamorphosis, I was keeping my fingers crossed that the new and improved DeAnna 2.0 stuck around long after her November due date.

The hostess ushered us through the restaurant and seated us at a round table with a window view. Margo joined us ten minutes later, huffing and puffing about the traffic, then fussing over her seat.

"I hate sitting with my back to the window. You can't even see the view."

"Sorry about that. Do you want to trade places?" DeAnna asked.

"What I *want* is a drink. Where is that waitress?" Margo demanded.

I kept my head down, studied the menu, determined to have a good time. This would be fun. And it was.

Until it wasn't.

Margo lobbed her first bombshell as our food was delivered.

"I'm curious. Tell me: whose brilliant idea was it to have another baby?" Margo served a pointed stare at DeAnna. "I assume it was yours."

DeAnna's face reddened.

"I can't believe you're pregnant again. Do you have any idea how difficult it will be when the new baby comes? You already have one child you can barely take care of." Margo spared a frown for LJ, seated next to his mother. Happily humming to himself, he picked his way through a mountain of French fries and a puddle of ketchup. "The two of you are barely managing to keep your heads above water as it is. Two children will make things so much worse. My son isn't made of money, you know."

I nearly choked on my pasta. Was Margo's verbal attack purposely planned to coincide with our mouths being full? Or were her words courtesy of the two Manhattans she'd drained before lunch, brunch, or whatever. Drinking liquor on an empty stomach was asking for trouble.

"You're being rather harsh, don't you think?" I said, wading into the thick of it. I wasn't accustomed to fighting DeAnna's battles, but she didn't look capable of defending herself. She'd gone pale, with a vague shellshocked look covering her face. And besides, she *was* pregnant. Someone should step up and speak out in her defense. Who better than me? I was her mother.

"Margo, I don't think this is anything we should be worried about," I said. "DeAnna and Lloyd can take care of themselves, and they'll be able to take care of LJ, and the new baby, too."

"Is that so?"

I nodded. "Trust me, they'll be fine."

"Trust you?" Margo shifted her attention to me. "Why should I trust you? Obviously, you know nothing about the money."

I hesitated. Money? What money?

"I didn't think you knew." A thin smile slid across her lips. "Lloyd and your daughter want to borrow fifty thousand dollars from us."

My eyes popped. Fifty thousand dollars?

"Mama, more ketchup," LJ squirmed in his seat, pointing at his plate.

"You don't need more ketchup," DeAnna replied, even as she shot a generous squirt onto his plate. She threw a guarded glance at Margo. "The money was Lloyd's idea. I told him I didn't think—"

"Oh, yes, I know, it's never your fault." Margo quickly cut her off, then eyeballed me. "As usual, your daughter is trying to put the blame on my son. This isn't the first time they've come sniffing around for money. Did you know that they hit us up for five thousand dollars when LJ was born?"

"We did not!" DeAnna cried.

"You most certainly did," Margo replied.

"No!"

"Dear girl, there's nothing wrong with my memory, or the balance in my checking account, either," she said cooly. "You wanted money and we gave it to you."

"But it wasn't like that," DeAnna said softly.

"Did you take our money?" Margo demanded. "Did we give you five thousand dollars?"

DeAnna hesitated, then finally nodded. "Yes, we took it. But Lloyd said it was a gift."

"A gift?" Margo gave her an open stare filled with contempt. "How stupid do you think we are?"

"Lloyd told me that you gave us the money." DeAnna's face flushed the same shade of red as the ketchup drenching LJ's French fries. "He said that you insisted we take it, that it was a gift in honor of LJ, your first grandson."

"Oh, yes, LJ, our grandson. Isn't he just a peach?" Margo cast a withering glance at our mutual grandson. The little boy's head snapped up as he heard his name, and he gave us all a happy little wave, his fingers smeared with ketchup. "Look at him," she added. "Doesn't he do us all proud?"

"Margo, you're not being fair," I said. "Who cares if he's messy? He's only a little boy."

"He's four years old," DeAnna said. "He doesn't know better. Do you, LJ?"

LJ vigorously saluted us with a messy grin and a fistful of ketchup-covered-French-fries that promptly deposited a glob of tomatoey-goop across his eyebrows.

"Your son might not be old enough to know better, DeAnna, but that doesn't excuse you," Margo said over LJ's howls as DeAnna grabbed him, hurriedly cleaned his face with a napkin dunked in her water glass. "You're old enough to know how all this works. There's no reason that you should expect people to constantly bail you out. Perhaps you have the wrong idea. This is not a matter of *ask and you shall receive*. That might be well and good for the Bible crowd, but the rest of us live in the real world. Life holds consequences, which you must be willing to pay. And I don't see you paying us back. First it was five thousand dollars, then it turned into ten. Now you come begging for fifty. When does it stop, DeAnna? That's what I want to know. When does it stop? My husband and I are not made of money."

"But I already said I—"

"Yes, you've said plenty," Margo cut her off. "You've said plenty, and now it's my turn. Shall we start with the horrible things you've been telling my son about his father and me?" Her eyes narrowed. "Don't think for one minute that we don't know what you've been saying. We know what you're trying to do, how you're trying to turn him against us. You want Lloyd to believe that we haven't always had his best interests at heart. But we have, DeAnna. We do. He's our son, and you can't change that, no matter how hard you try. We know who you are, DeAnna. You're the reason behind his problems."

"Mama? Why you crying?" LJ lifted a pudgy hand to finger the hot tears streaming down DeAnna's cheeks. "Mama, you sad?"

I've never considered myself a violent person, but the thought of slapping Lloyd's mother suddenly seemed immensely appealing.

"Margo," I warned, reaching over to clamp my hand on her arm. "I suggest you stop this nonsense before—"

"I suggest you keep your hands to yourself." She shook off my grasp. "That goes for your opinions, too. This is none of your business."

"Of course, it's my business! DeAnna is my daughter!"

"And Lloyd is my son!" Margo pointed her finger directly at DeAnna. "*You* are the problem. If my son hadn't met you, he wouldn't be the mess he is today. You knew what you were doing, manipulating him, leading him on."

"But I didn't!" she cried. "I didn't!"

"Don't go giving us that same sob story. It won't work. Not this time, and certainly not with me. You told Lloyd what he wanted to hear, didn't you? The only reason the two of you are in this mess is because you encouraged him. What you should have been doing was telling him *no*…which you obviously didn't, and now you have only yourself to blame."

"*No?* I should have been telling him *no*?" DeAnna's face scrunched in confusion. "What are you talking about? *No* to what?"

"Sex." Margo's mouth pinched tight. "He'd never be in this horrible mess if you'd done what any decent girl should do and kept your legs shut."

DeAnna threw down her napkin and staggered to her feet.

"That's it," she cried, pushing in her chair. "I've heard enough."

"Where are you going?" I asked.

"The bathroom. If I sit here listening to her any longer, I'll vomit!" She rubbed her hands across her belly's baby bump as she glared at Lloyd's mother.

"Spare us the theatrics," Margo advised. "If anyone's leaving, it will be me."

Draining her Manhattan, she rose to her feet and threw a crumpled twenty-dollar bill on the table.

"That should cover my drinks," she said. "If not, deduct it from the money you already owe us."

Margo headed for the exit, DeAnna bolted for the bathroom, leaving me to sit and stare at my luncheon plate of congealed fettuccini. I pushed it away. I'd lost my appetite.

"What a mess," I muttered. Thank God DeAnna and Lloyd weren't married. At least DeAnna didn't have that horrible woman as her mother-in-law.

"Grammie! Grammie!"

I glanced at my grandson. LJ's face wore a grubby grin, and his hand held a ketchup-drenched French fry which he offered out to me.

"I share," he said.

I offered him a faint smile. My appetite was gone, but my love for this little guy would never desert me. I nibbled one edge of the fry. The potato was cold and greasy, with way too much ketchup. But it was from my grandson, and that made it perfect.

"Very tasty. Thank you, LJ."

He grinned and pointedly stared at the ketchup bottle across the table from him, beyond his reach. His eyes lit up as I squirted a generous dollop on his plate.

"Is that enough? Or do we need more?"

He nodded, rewarding me with a devilish grin.

I added another squirt. Anything for this little guy.

"Don't tell Mama," he said in a loud whisper.

I held up one hand in mock salute. "I swear, I won't say a word."

"No, Grammie! No! Don't do that!"

"Don't do what?"

"Swearing is bad." His eyes were wide as he paused mid-ketchup-bite. "Mama says we can't swear."

"You know what? She's right. People shouldn't swear. I forgot. I'm sorry."

"It's okay, Grammie." Reaching out, he patted my fore-arm. "But don't do it again."

I nodded solemnly. "I promise."

"You want more French fries?" He shoved the plate closer between us.

"Thank you, sweetie."

Maybe all wasn't lost. For once in her life, despite an uncomfortable pregnancy in tremendously difficult circum-stances (was it true that she and Lloyd were really having money problems?), especially under the eyes of that cold hardhearted woman who passed as Lloyd's mother, DeAnna seemed to be trying her best. She was teaching LJ manners, raising her son to be thoughtful and caring. A good mother teaches her children, passes along the things she herself learned as a child. A good mother helps her children understand that while doing the right thing isn't always easy, it is always better to try.

After all, wasn't that the point?

Maybe Mother's Day wasn't ruined after all.

CHAPTER TWENTY

I PAUSE, STEP BACK TO ADMIRE our efforts. Ribbons and banners swirled from the dining room chandelier. Pink and white balloons danced above each chair. Glitzy beads were draped around the table, and toy noise makers and mint candies in foil cups were at each place setting. Pink paper plates topped with colorful napkins brought it all together.

"It looks nice, doesn't it?" I say. "Tiffany will be thrilled."

"Whatever." Lloyd shrugs.

I suppose it would be asking too much to expect a grown man to express enthusiasm at a little girl's birthday party. Then again, that little girl is his daughter. A daughter whom he hasn't seen in months…perhaps years.

And if he'd been telling me the truth, DeAnna had refused him access to the children while he was in prison. She'd never taken them to visit, not even once.

"Thanks again for helping me, Lloyd."

"Not like you gave me much choice."

"Oh, come on, you did a great job," I josh. "Tiffany will be so surprised when she sees what you've done. She'll love it."

Once I coaxed him into it, he turned into a semi-willing participant, taking directions from me. He asked where the balloons should go, how and where I wanted the streamers hung. But I knew how I wanted things to look, and he didn't. How could he? Lloyd had been absent from their lives such a long time. He had no idea how his children celebrated their birthdays. Such a sad fact of life for all of them.

What a sad, little boy he must have been, especially if what he'd said was true about the way he'd grown up. No birthday party? What else had he missed out on? No wonder Lloyd turned out the way he did. Easily offended, fueled by anger and resentment at what others have, and what he doesn't.

Constantly feeling sorry for himself.

I draw in a quick breath, abruptly pulling myself up with a start. I must be crazy, to suddenly be thinking this way. Lloyd doesn't deserve my pity or compassion. He hasn't done anything to earn my trust. Why should I show him mercy? He wouldn't do the same for me.

I start for the kitchen.

"Where do you think you're going?"

"Ow! You're hurting me!" I glare at his hand now tightly wrapped around my forearm, preventing me from moving. "Seriously, Lloyd? This isn't necessary. I was going to make myself a cup of tea."

"Let's get something straight, Marguerite. You don't go anywhere without my say-so." His eyes gleam with suspicion, and though he doesn't let go, he relaxes his grip somewhat. "You got that?"

"Yes, I got it."

Don't let your guard down, I remind myself. Lloyd is dangerous, and I can't allow myself to think otherwise…the minute I do, I'll be a goner. No matter how bad I might feel for him, and for the things he might have suffered, I can't let it alter the way I act. Most likely he was neglected as a child, but that was long ago. He's an adult now and knows what he's doing. He's not a victim, he's a veteran of the prison system. He's done hard time, with hard men. No doubt he's witnessed people doing dreadful things to each other. Cruel, evil things. Things that would scare the bejesus out of normal people like me.

But after today, I doubt I'll ever feel normal again.

And tired. I can't remember ever feeling so tired. It's difficult to catch a breath, especially given how my heart is doing funny little flip-flops deep inside my rib cage. I've never experienced anything like it before, which is only adding to my anxiety.

"I need to sit down and rest. All this decorating has worn me out." I don't care if it makes him mad, but I don't think I can put up with much more. "Let's go into the kitchen. I'll make us some tea."

He thinks for a minute, then grunts and drops his hold on me. I rub my arm. I suspect I'll be sporting some fresh bruises by morning.

If I make it till tomorrow.

Dear God, I need help. As we start for the kitchen, I fling a silent prayer to heaven. *Please help me out of this mess. Help me find the courage to do the right thing and keep LJ and Tiffany safe. And please, dear God, help Lloyd do the right thing.*

"What you mumbling about?"

I stumble, catching myself just as I begin to fall. I stand there a minute, clinging to the edge of the counter, hanging on for strength and balance.

"I was saying a prayer," I say.

"Ha! Good luck with that," he comments in a dry voice.

The kettle simmers on the back burner.

"I hope you like mint tea. It's all I have."

I reach for two mugs, place them side by side, then turn back toward him.

"You know, Lloyd, lots of people talk to God."

He lounges against the counter, watching as I fill our mugs.

"Got any sugar?"

I add two heaping spoonfuls into his mug and my own, too. Calories be damned. I carry the mugs to the table and once again take a seat across from him.

"Have you ever tried it?" I blow gently on the tea, waiting for it to cool.

"Tea's not high on my list."

"I'm talking about praying."

"Praying?" He throws me a hard stare. "Why would I do that?"

"Why wouldn't you?" I counter.

"A waste of time." Lloyd rolls his eyes. "Organized religion is nothing but a bunch of do-gooders spouting self-righteous bullshit. They've seen the light, hallelujah! And now they're going to show us the way, going to force it down our throats. We'll sing and pray, and we'll shout together, hallelujah! We'll be so involved, we won't know what's happening. They'll have us scrambling to fall in line, like a herd of sheep. Stupid sheep. Stupid people. They deserve what they get."

"Believe it or not, I actually agree with some of what you just said." I take a careful sip from my mug, find the tea is only lukewarm. The kettle didn't catch a good simmer. "I think things take a wrong turn when people equate practicing their religious beliefs with living a spiritual life. The two things aren't necessarily the same."

"Whatever."

Lloyd doesn't seem interested in discussing it further.

"Do you think that prayers don't matter?" I ask, hoping that my prayers are being heard.

"Nobody gives a shit what I think. Why should you?"

I pause, trying to herd my thoughts into a sort of cohesive order that will make sense to both of us.

"I think, whether they realize it or not, there's always a reason why people say and do the things they do. That tattoo of yours, for instance." I point to the inky image of the snake slithering from under his shirt collar up the side of his neck. "What made you decide to get it?"

"You ask too many questions."

"No, I'm curious." I hunch closer for a better look at the design. With its multi-colored hues of blues and greens, it's an elaborate display of body art. "You know, I've always wondered what it would feel like to get a tattoo. And right there, on the fleshy side of your neck? Ouch!" I pull back, grimace. I've always had a fear of needles. "It must have hurt like hell."

"Ha! Didn't feel too great, that's for damn sure."

"How long did it take? I mean, for them to ink the whole thing?"

"Couple hours," he says. "Not that I was keeping track."

"You're braver than me."

"You do what you gotta do."

Briefly I think about following up, asking why he'd gone through with it. Vanity? Boredom? Was he trying to show allegiance to a gang? Or maybe it was meant as a warning to others that they should think twice before messing with him. Lloyd is a big guy; bigger than most men. The judicial system labelled him as dangerous. He *is* dangerous. But there's also a private side to him. Who he is as a man. DeAnna's partner. LJ's and Tiffany's father. And if I'm being honest, I'll admit that he was a big help with the party decorations. He followed my directions and didn't grouse when it came to blowing up balloons and stringing up party favors. There's some goodness locked away inside him, no matter how fiercely he fights against me and the rest of the world thinking otherwise.

I drain my cup and stand. Lloyd's head jerks up.

"Don't worry, I just want to heat up more water," I say. As long as I'm honest and tell him what I'm planning, I doubt he'll object. I move to the stove, refill the kettle, turn the heat on high.

"Can I ask you another question?" I say, rejoining him at the table.

"Here we go again," he replies with a dramatic eyeroll. "What if I say *no*? Like, that's gonna stop you, right?"

I ignore his snide remark. "It's about prison. I'm curious."

"Go figure," he drawls.

"The thing is, I've always wondered what prison must be like—"

"What the hell do you think it's like? It's prison! Talk about a stupid question."

"You told me I could ask," I remind him. "Besides, how would I know? I've never been in prison."

"Lucky you." He drains his tea in one long gulp.

"You know what I mean. When I watch some of the movies and tv shows, they—"

"Forget that shit," he growls. "Prison's nothing like the crap on tv. For starters, nobody's acting. And nobody gets to go home at night, either. When those bars slam behind you, you're locked in and you're not going anywhere. Things can turn ugly, real fast. Doing time is real. The stink is real; the blood is real."

"Blood?"

"Yeah, blood. Lots of blood." He smirks, almost as if taking pleasure in watching me squirm. "You learn fast to watch your back. Sooner or later, somebody jumps you."

"What about the guards? Isn't it their job to keep things under control, to make sure no one gets hurt?"

"Damn hard to see much with their backs turned," he notes.

"But not all of them," I insist. "I mean, surely there must be some guards who try to…to do the best they can to keep everyone safe."

"Guards, most of them, got their own agenda. You learn real fast not to trust them. Meanwhile, get a bunch of violent guys locked up together, some of 'em in for twenty years or more, and shit's gonna happen."

"I suppose," I say doubtfully.

"What have they got to lose?" he continues. "Guys like that, they're not looking for an excuse. When you're locked up, anything goes. Anything to break the monotony." His voice tightens. "You wanna know what prison is like, Marguerite? You're always behind a locked door. Think about that. And if you wanna get out alive, you learn to keep your mouth shut and keep your eyes to yourself. Look the wrong way, and there'll be hell to pay."

Had it been hell for Lloyd?

"Why would someone do something like that?" I press.

"How the hell do I know? Maybe they were having a bad day. It happened, okay?! It's not like I asked."

I draw in a small breath, try to process what he said. I don't think I misunderstood.

"Something happened to you, didn't it?" I ask after a moment. "Someone went after you but the guards did nothing."

Lloyd's face flushes a dark angry red.

"Don't go thinking I deserved it," he says, "because I sure as hell didn't."

I wrap my sweater tightly around my shoulders, shivering at the thought of him being targeted, attacked, beaten up, or even something worse while in prison. I'm not so naïve that I believe evil doesn't exist. Of course, it does. The world can be a dangerous place, and being incarcerated dramatically increases the odds. Lloyd did some very bad things. Anyone involved in dealing drugs isn't searching for happily-ever-after. But in all the years I've known him, I've never thought of him as evil. He's made some bad choices throughout his life, but he's not all bad. DeAnna has never shown any fear of him. She trusts him. He isn't perfect. Far from it. He can be sullen, nasty, and his uneven temper doesn't do him any favors. But if Lloyd Walsh is the worst kind of evil that I encounter, then when all of this is over, I intend to get down on my knees and thank God that things hadn't been worse, that Lloyd had done the right thing and decided—

But will he? And what if he doesn't? I'm yanked right back into a cold brooding reality. What if I'm wrong and Lloyd is no longer the man I thought I knew? What if his four years in prison have turned him into someone else?

A man prone to violence. A man who knows what he wants, and who's willing to do anything to get it.

Including murder.

My heart thuds to a stop. So much for all those coins I've dropped in the Salvation Army Christmas kettles. If Lloyd intends to get rid of me, my goose was cooked the minute he shoved his way through my front door. No amount of heavenly good will can stop that.

"When you showed up at my house this morning…"

"What about it?"

I take a deep breath. I'm running out of time. Sooner or later, the school bus will come rumbling down our street, open its door, and LJ and Tiffany will tumble out. They'll tear up the sidewalk, fly through the front door.

All hell will break loose.

I have to know. I have to ask.

"You said you were paroled, that they gave you an early release. Are you telling the truth?" I croak out the words. "Which is it, Lloyd? Were you paroled…or did you escape?"

CHAPTER TWENTY-ONE

TEENAGE GIRLS ARE NOTORIOUS WHEN it comes to their privacy. They also tend to be overly dramatic, and DeAnna was queen bee when it came to dissing drama with her girlfriends. I never intended to purposely eavesdrop on my fifteen-year-old daughter's telephone conversation. But once I realized what she and Suzy were discussing, I was helpless to stop myself. I stood there, just inside the kitchen doorway, my maternal radar siren blaring as I absorbed my daughter's words.

"Suzy, you should hear him. I mean, all that stuff Lloyd rambles on about? Some of it—lots of it!—is over-the-top crazy. Institutions, bureaucracy, the federal reserve. Politics? Who cares about that stuff? Not me, that's for sure! Most of the time, I don't pay attention. It's easier to zone out and think about other stuff. Sometimes, I even think about breaking up with him.

"But oh, Suzy, when he starts kissing me? All those thoughts fly right out of my head! I mean, how can I walk away from him? And why would I want to? I'm crazy in love with him! But I don't know what to do. It's like, when we're together and he touches me, I feel myself getting lost in him, and I can't find my way out. I've never felt this way about a boy before. Never! Then again, Lloyd's not a boy.

He's a man. A man who's in love with me! And I'm in love with him. Being with him is crazy and exciting and scary… sometimes I can't breathe."

I myself was finding it hard to breathe, listening to her excited rambling. DeAnna was only fifteen years old, a sophomore in high school. Lloyd Walsh was eighteen, and much too old to be hanging around her.

I edged closer to the kitchen door. How far had things gone? Were they sleeping together? Had he threatened her with violence if she didn't give in to him? Or, even worse, had he taken what he wanted despite her saying no? The very idea that he might have forced her was mind-boggling. DeAnna wasn't the kind of girl who'd allow a man to push her around. But Lloyd was bigger than her, older than her. And if he'd touched even one hair on my daughter's head, if he'd hurt or abused her in any way, then he'd better be prepared to face the consequences. I was DeAnna's mother, and it was my job to protect her, no matter how much she fussed and fought me over my so-called intrusions into her personal life. But DeAnna had no idea what the real world was like and she had no business getting involved with somebody like Lloyd. A boy, a man-child, who'd dropped out of high school and flipped burgers for a living.

Lloyd had no business sniffing around DeAnna, filling her head with nonsense.

And wait till Alan found out what was going on. Normally my husband was even tempered, with a gentle way about him that I'd always found endearing. But all bets were off when it came to his daughter. And if someone threatened or harmed her? Lloyd would be amazed at how quickly a father's outrage could reach the failsafe point.

Lloyd would have only himself to blame.

"What's going on?" a voice whispered in my ear.

I muffled a shriek of surprise and whirled around to face my son.

"Barry!" I hissed as I rapped him on the arm. "Good Lord! I almost had a heart attack!"

"Sorry, I thought you heard me come in the back door." He nodded toward the other room. "What's up?"

"Shh," I warned. "Your sister's on the phone with Suzy."

"And you're spying on them?" His eyes widened. "Careful, Mom. If DeAnna catches you, there'll be hell to pay."

"I'm *not* spying on her," I insisted, pulling him away from the doorway into the safety of the kitchen.

"Whatever you say."

He planted a kiss on my cheek, then slung his backpack on a nearby kitchen chair and shrugged out of his jacket. I smelled the frosty nip of gathering winter clinging to his clothes and hair. Seeing his face covered with a dark shadowy fuzz tugged at my heart. My boy was growing up. A college freshman at Illinois State, he'd decided to commute to and from school while continuing to live at home in order to save money. Alan had signed off on the idea, and naturally I was thrilled by Barry's choice to stay close. What mother wouldn't be? I loved my son. Soon enough, he'd be gone for good.

"You need a haircut," I said, fingering the shaggy hair brushing his collar.

Barry rolled his eyes.

"You should get one soon," I advised. "Your aunt and uncle are coming for Christmas, and you know how your

Uncle Burt loves bringing his camera along. I don't want our holiday pictures to end up with you looking like King Kong straight out of the jungle."

"Some women have told me that they actually prefer the look," he replied with a cocky grin.

"Not this woman," I volleyed back, reaching up a hand to cluck him softly on the cheek. Barry had sprouted a few extra inches while I hadn't been looking. He was now taller than Alan. "And seeing as how I'm your mother, and I'm *also* the one who does your laundry, and cooks your meals, and keeps you—"

"Okay, okay! You made your point. I'll get a haircut." He nodded toward the other room. "So, what's up with the kiddo and her friend? Did you hear anything interesting?"

DeAnna's chatter was still weighing on my mind, but some things were not meant to be shared, especially when it came to big brothers and their little sisters. Sexuality. Violence against women. Domestic abuse. Not that these things had happened to her, but the word *yet* flitted through my mind. Bad enough I'd be discussing it all with Alan. Barry didn't need to hear about it.

"Never mind," I told him as DeAnna, empty popcorn bowl in hand, sailed into the kitchen and ended in a dead stop.

"What?" she asked with a stony stare back and forth between us. "What's wrong?"

"Not a thing," I replied. "We were merely talking."

"About me?" Her eyes narrowed. "Were you spying on me?"

"Don't look at me. I just got home," Barry said, and headed for the cookie jar.

If my son hadn't already thrown me under the bus, my face was a dead giveaway.

"You were listening to Suzy and me? Mother, I cannot believe you!" DeAnna slammed the popcorn bowl into the sink. "That was a private conversation! You *knew* that!"

"Yes, but—"

"Private!" she shrieked. "Do you know the meaning of the word? *Private* means *private*! I was having a *private* conversation with a friend, and you had no business listening!" She rolled her eyes, heaving a mighty sigh indicative of the highest level of teenage drama. "Ohmigod, I can't *wait* until I'm old enough to move out! I *hate!-hate!-hate!* living in this stupid little house. Bad enough that I'm forced to share a bathroom with everybody. But people shouldn't go snooping around and spying on me! Which is another reason why I need my own phone!" Her face dissolved into an ugly scowl. "It's so unfair! All my friends have phones. Why not me?"

"We've talked about this before. You know how your father and I feel," I replied, hoping to shut things down fast. I didn't have the energy for yet another round of this particular conversation. "Having your own phone is a privilege. Maybe next year. You're only fifteen."

"I'll be sixteen soon." DeAnna's words marched across the room more as a threat than a reminder. "And plus, I have a job. I'm making my own money. I don't see why I can't have a phone!"

"That money isn't meant to pay for a phone," I reminded her. We were living in a much different world than the one I grew up in. Starting with the fact that I never would have dared argue with my mother. Personal opinions were not encouraged. And even had I ventured to speak up for myself, she promptly would have shut me down. End of discussion. But not for DeAnna, who always insisted on having the last word.

I loved my daughter, but there were times I didn't like her. Why did she have to be so disagreeable?

"When we agreed to let you get a job, you agreed to put aside the money you earned," I reminded her. "You promised to use it for clothes and incidentals."

"I don't see why a phone doesn't qualify as an incidental!" She pouted. "And besides, it shouldn't matter! I'm the one with the job. Why shouldn't I get to decide what to do with the money? It's *my money*!"

"Way to go, sis…keep on keeping on," Barry calmly noted. "You're digging yourself deeper and deeper."

"Oh, shut up," DeAnna retorted. She turned her back on him, then suddenly thought the better of it. Whirling around, she scowled at me as she pointed at him.

"What about him?" she demanded. "He gets to have his own phone. What makes him so special? How come he gets to have a phone, and I don't?"

"You need to make a call? No problem." Barry, lounging against the counter calmly eating a cookie, whipped out his phone and offered it to her. "What's mine is yours, sis. Lemme give you my number."

"Oh, I've got your number," DeAnna cried, lunging at him.

"Enough!" I insisted, stepping in between them the way I'd been doing since they were children. "Stop it right now. Both of you!"

I wagged a finger at Barry. "What is wrong with you? You're older than she is. You should know better than to tease your sister."

"Ha! Guess she told you, and it serves you right!" DeAnna sneered in his face.

"And as for you…" I whipped around to face my daughter. "I suggest you wipe that smirk off your face. You know perfectly well why your brother has a phone. He's in college and he needs it—"

"To call his girlfriend," DeAnna taunted, sticking her tongue out at Barry. "How many times did you and Holly talk today?"

"None of your business," he shot back.

I glared at them both. My children were nearly adults, but the way they were squabbling sounded as if they were both still in kindergarten. "Your bother has a phone because of all the driving he does back and forth to school."

"Fifty miles, round trip, every day," Barry reminded us. "Through snow, and rain, and gloom of night, just like the U.S. mail—"

I shot him one of my best if-you-know-what's-good-for-you-you'll-shut-up-right-now-mother-on-the-warpath looks.

"Sorry," he muttered.

"This family is so pathetic!" DeAnna shouted. "I hate all of you!"

Barry and I watched as she flounced out of the kitchen.

"She sounded annoyed," he deadpanned.

"Don't start," I warned. "Besides, it was mostly your fault. You know better than to tease her."

He shrugged, popped the last cookie in his mouth.

"She's an easy target," he replied through a mouthful of crumbs. "Especially since she started hanging out with that guy. What's his name again?"

"Lloyd?"

Barry nodded.

"Yep, that's him…Lloyd the loser. DeAnna's got problems, and he's the biggest one of all. What a creep. Hope she dumps him soon. She deserves better than that." He leaned forward and planted another kiss on my cheek. "Big test tomorrow, gotta go study. Thanks again for the cookies. You're the best."

I checked the cookie jar after he strolled out of the kitchen. I lifted the lid, peered inside. Empty, as usual. How my boy managed to put away so much food without gaining weight was something I'd never understand. Meanwhile, I might as well get busy. Alan wouldn't be home for at least another hour, which meant I had enough time to bake a fresh batch of cookies before putting dinner in the oven. Pot roast tonight, I'd already decided. One of Alan's favorites. I could always count on pot roast to put him in a good mood. And seeing as how I planned to bring up the subject of DeAnna and Lloyd after dinner, it wouldn't hurt to soften him up in advance.

But DeAnna had raised some valid points. She was a teenager, and she deserved some privacy. But should that equate into having her own phone? Meanwhile, she was right about one thing: our landline didn't offer any of us much privacy. Maybe it would be a good idea to dump the landline, invest in a family plan that offered multiple cell phone lines. Just the other day, Millie had mentioned something about being on a family plan with her daughter, who lived three thousand miles away. No more long-distance charges, Millie had crowed in delight.

But our situation was nothing like my neighbor's. Our family was relatively small, and most of them lived within our local area code. Still, it wouldn't hurt to discuss the idea with Alan. Not only was he smart, but he had an uncanny ability to deduce the pros and cons of any situation and pull it all together in a clear, logical way that made sense.

Who knew? Maybe Alan would think getting rid of our landline and signing up for a family cell phone plan was a good idea. The more I thought about it, the more I decided that DeAnna might be right. Maybe it *was* time she had her own phone. Maybe it was time we all had our own phones. Including me.

And maybe it was a good idea to make another of Alan's favorites for dinner tonight. Garlic mashed potatoes would go perfect with that yummy pot roast. Certainly couldn't hurt.

I opened the cupboard and grabbed my biggest saucepan.

CHAPTER TWENTY-TWO

"I TOLD YOU I WAS PAROLED," Lloyd says. "I shoulda figured you wouldn't believe me. You never believe me."

Paroled or escaped? There's no way of knowing which is true. But there's also no point in arguing about it. Whatever I said, he would only end up tearing into me, ripping my words apart.

Lloyd was no longer listening.

Had he ever been listening?

"I think I have a right to know," I say, trying to shrug off the weariness I feel settling in on me. With everything that's happened, I'm not sure how much energy I have left. Maybe if I were twenty years younger, I'd be able to handle this better. But my forties are long gone, as are my fifties, and I've nearly maxed out my sixties, too. A person can only suffer so much before they finally give up the ghost.

Lloyd's gun isn't helping matters.

"I think I have a right to know," I repeat as the tea kettle begins to shriek.

"You trying to piss me off?"

"Why would I want to do that?" I lumber to my feet, move to the stove, snap off the burner. "All I have to go by is what you've told me. But if past experience means anything, I'm not sure what to believe."

"You sure love hanging on to shit, don't you?" he spit. "Give it up, Marguerite."

"Trust me, Lloyd, I'd love nothing more than to believe you. And in a perfect world, I would."

"No such thing as a perfect world. But that's just not good enough for you, right?" He shakes his head. "I'm sick of all your preaching. You're always telling people what they oughta be doing, how they should live their lives. You think you're so much better than the rest of us. Better than Dee. Better than me."

"I never said I was perfect." I struggle to push aside my growing resentment, to keep it from creeping into my voice. Lloyd has a way of pushing my buttons, and I'm sick and tired of it. In fact, I'm sick and tired, period. "I'm not perfect. Far from it."

He busts into loud laughter, and now I'm the one left scowling.

"I fail to see why you think that's so funny."

"You're such an easy target, Marguerite."

"Well, Lloyd, that makes two of us. Unless you think you're better than me. You're very quick to flip flop that attitude of yours when you think it suits your purpose."

The smile drops from his face.

"You don't like people making fun of you?" I continue. "Well, guess what? Join the crowd. No one likes being the butt of a joke. It hurts…having people laugh at you. I should know. Plenty of people have poked fun at me. But I've never done that to you, Lloyd. I've never laughed at you. Not once, despite the fact you've been doing that to me since the day we met. And I'm tired of it. Sick and tired of it. And I've had enough.

"Enough. Do you hear me?" I drag in a shallow breath and lean against the counter, allow it to take my sagging weight. "No more laughing at me."

"Goes both ways, Marguerite. You talk about me making fun of you? You been doing that to me since that first day Dee brought me over to meet you guys. You think I don't know how you felt? That I didn't see it right there on your face? You and that whole damn family of yours. You hated me from the start."

"I...I..." I can't find the words to refute him. He's caught me off guard.

"Yes!" He punches the air with a fist bump. "That's what I'm talking about."

What a big baby he is, always trying to make things all about him.

"I don't hate you," I spark back at him. "I don't like you very much, that I'll admit...but I don't hate you. I just think you're not the right man for my daughter. You and DeAnna are dangerous together. You play off each other like you're matches held up to super dry kindling that sparks a fire and burns down the house. That house is my family, Lloyd. I don't want to see it destroyed."

"You think I do?" he demands.

"No, probably not. But that doesn't mean it's not on fire. Maybe you just don't see it yet, but it's there. There's already been so much damage."

"I love Dee," he says. "She's the woman for me."

"But are you the right man for her?" I ask softly.

He hisses a soft breath through his teeth.

"Who do you think you are," he asks, "calling us a mistake?"

I've insulted him, I abruptly realize. Hearing him call me out shakes me to my core.

Realizing he isn't far off the truth strikes like the final nail.

Obviously, Lloyd doesn't like me any more than I like him. But no matter how much anger and resentment either of us holds against the other, neither of us can claim vengeance. Lloyd and I are both at fault. I think long and hard about those close-held opinions he's accused me of harboring against him. My judgmental attitude; my unforgiving nature; my belief that he might be capable of the worst.

But if I think Lloyd is capable of the very worst, what does that say about me?

It means that I'm capable, too. And I'm proving it to myself right now.

"I didn't mean to offend you," I finally say. "I thought we were being honest with each other."

"Yeah, like you know what that's all about."

"I've made plenty of mistakes in my life. But here's the thing, Lloyd: at the time, I didn't realize that's what they were. I made mistakes, but I made them while I was trying to do what I thought was right. And if you think about it, isn't that all a person can ask of themself? To try and do your best, with what you have, at any given moment?"

"There you go again, Marguerite, preaching at me. You always have to make sure you're right, don't you? You're so goddamn sure you did your best, yeah?" He throws me a hard stare. "But how 'bout this? What if I did, too?"

His answer catches me off guard. I'm not used to being called out, of being accused of smug self-righteousness. But he does have a point. What makes me so certain that I'm right and he's wrong? I'm constantly passing judgment on people. I play at being judge and jury every night when I watch the national news with its endless parade of countless victims, most of whom have only themselves to blame. If they were smart, they'd have known better than to be in the wrong place at the wrong time, I think, watching and judging. I've never been one to show mercy.

What about Lloyd? When have I ever shown him mercy?

Don't trust him! a little voice shrieks inside my head. *Don't be stupid!* But what choice do I have? Everything is riding on what happens between us in the next several minutes. I can't let fear stop me. Someone has to make the first move. Someone needs to be the grown-up in the room.

Seeing as how I've got thirty-plus years on him, it appears that someone will have to be me.

"Lloyd, listen, I have—"

"I'm sick of listening to you," he says. "That's all you do, Marguerite: talk. You talk and talk and talk…"

"You're right," I agree. "Talking too much has always been one of my biggest faults. When I was a little girl, my mother told people that I never talked before I was two, and she was worried I'd never have anything to say…but one day I did start talking, and then I never shut up."

"Smart woman, your mother," he says.

"Anyway, I guess that's the way I am. I've always talked a lot, and I doubt that's going to change. Especially since I'm getting older. It's hard to make changes after so many years of doing it the easy way. But the easy way isn't necessarily the right way, is it? And that's something else I'll admit. I'm not always proud of the way I've acted. Sometimes I'm not a nice person."

"Ha!" He slaps his hand against his thigh as his face fills with glee. "You can say that again!"

I sink back against the counter, bite my tongue. I'm doing my best to be honest with him. I'm sharing personal details that I've never even admitted to myself, let alone to anyone else. And this isn't easy. Ticking off my character defects one by one is downright humiliating. The least he could do is cut me some slack.

But this isn't about him, I remind myself. This is about me. I need to keep the focus on myself, or I'll get caught up ticking off his faults, which will surely drag us down a dangerous road.

"I'm just as mean and nasty as anyone else," I say, "especially when I put my mind to it. Especially when it comes to certain people." I draw a deep breath. "People like you, Lloyd."

Any trace of mirth disappears from his face.

"I'm not trying to make you mad, I'm just trying to be honest," I remind him. "The way I've acted around you, and all the things I've said? I owe you an apology." While I long to look away, I force my eyes to keep trained on his. "I'm sorry, Lloyd, and I hope you'll forgive me."

He stays silent for a long moment, as if he's digesting my words, trying to work things out in his mind. Then abruptly, a knowing smile begins to spread across his face.

"You're a real piece of work, Marguerite, you know that? You sit there, apologizing like you think it's gonna make a difference, and we'll have ourselves a nice little kumbaya moment. And if that's what you want, go right ahead and keep on apologizing. I kinda like hearing it. I like hearing you grovel. Not that it's gonna make a difference. Nothing you say is gonna change anything. Not one damn thing."

"I'm not saying these things merely for your benefit."

"No? Who then? Nobody here but us." He glances around the room. "Or maybe you're talking to a ghost?"

"Has it occurred to you that I might be talking about myself?" I plop a fresh tea bag into my mug, stir in steaming water, turn back to face him. "You called me a bitch a while ago. And you were right. I *can* be a bitch. Obviously, not all the time. I can be nice enough…when and if I want to be. But we all have our moments, and that goes for me, too." I offer him a smile as I start across the room. "I'm quite good at being bitchy, if you want to know the truth."

Lloyd peers across at me as I near the table.

"You're talking crazy."

"I've never been more serious in my life."

"You expect me to believe you?" he says with a snort.

"Believe whatever you want. I wouldn't say it if it wasn't true."

I reach across the table to set my mug down when my toe suddenly tangles in the heavy fringe around the throw rug. My hand catches, knocking over the cup, sending a rush of scalding hot water pouring across the table.

"Shit!" Lloyd jerks away with a violent shove to escape being burned. His chair tips sideways, spilling him onto the floor. The gun, however, remains on the table.

He scrambles to his feet, but he's not fast enough. I manage to grab it first.

"Don't you move," I warn in a trembling voice as my fingers wrap around the cold hard steel. "Don't you dare move."

Heart pounding, I point the gun directly at his chest.

CHAPTER TWENTY-THREE

"GREAT," LLOYD MUTTERS. "JUST GREAT."

Not so great, I reflect silently as I take in the unexpected sight of Lloyd sprawled flat on his back on the kitchen floor. Then I shift my gaze to the equally unexpected sight of his gun which now rests in my hands. I swallow down a rush of sour bile surging in the back of my throat. I've never held a gun before, and its hefty weight catches me by surprise. No wonder they call it *deadly force*, for it's a lethal weapon with the power to kill. And until this moment, Lloyd was the one holding the power. I hold it now, and I have a kill shot. Everything will be over if or when I pull the trigger.

If.

I shift my stance, affording myself better balance. If he decides to lunge, make a sudden grab for the gun, it wouldn't take much for him to wrestle the pistol out of my hands. And if that were to happen, I have no doubt as to what would come next. While I might hesitate at pulling the trigger, Lloyd never would. Not in a heartbeat. He'd take aim and shoot me dead.

"Don't you dare move," I warn. "Don't you move. Not one inch."

"Easy, Marguerite," he cautions. "That's a loaded gun, remember?"

"I am very much aware of that fact." My eyes are trained on him. I'm not about to give him a chance to take me down.

"Put your hands up," I order. "Both hands."

"Come on, Marguerite, put the gun down. You don't want to fool around." His voice sounds strained and any earlier bravado on his face has disappeared.

"I guarantee you, Lloyd, I'm not fooling. I'm deadly serious." I feel the sweat beading on my forehead as I tighten my grip on the gun.

"Put your hands up, where I can see them."

He lifts them high, palms extended outward.

"That thing has a mean kick," he cautions. "Don't go getting trigger happy, or one of us might get hurt."

"Don't worry about me," I assure him. "I know what I'm doing."

But his words trigger a fresh rush of fear. The truth is, I *don't* know what I'm doing. I've never held a gun before today, let alone pulled the trigger and shot someone. Deliberately or accidentally. God help us both if I make a wrong move and it suddenly goes off. The thought of his face exploding, spewing bones and blood all over my kitchen floor…

My stomach yawns. My hands begin to tremble, and the gun slips slightly in my sweaty grasp.

"Steady there," he says, never taking his eyes off the weapon.

I need to act now. This might be my only chance. I open my mouth, but no words come. All my spit is gone. I swallow hard, suck a deep breath into my lungs, reposition my fingers once more around the cold hard steel.

Lloyd slowly shifts his gaze from the gun to my face.

"Okay, Marguerite, you got me where you want me." His voice is low and steady. "Now what?"

"Now you answer my questions." This time, I find my words. "Were you paroled, or did you escape?"

"I already told you: I got an early parole. But you don't believe me, right?"

"When it comes to the truth, you don't have the best track record."

"That's supposed to be *my* fault?"

"It's certainly not mine," I retort. "You're the one who sold the drugs, remember? They caught you in the act. Actions have consequences, Lloyd."

"Damn straight," he says as he rightens himself to a sitting position. "But how about when the system is rigged against you? Those guys I worked for, they knew the police were watching. They'd known for months. You think they bothered to tell me? Fuck, no! They made sure to cover their asses. And guess who set me up, who narced on me to the police in the first place! Ever think about that, Marguerite?"

A twist of sudden uncertainty begins to niggle at me. He was set up? Even if it was true, Lloyd had still committed a crime.

"No one forced you to deal drugs."

"Yep, no one forced me…but they sure as hell made it sound easy. Easy money, they promised. *Great!*, I was thinking. You think I liked flipping burgers for a living? And then there's Dee, always yapping in my ear about the things she wanted, how I was supposed to step up and be the man and take care of her and the kids. Kids cost money, you know? And I didn't want them growing up the way I did, with nobody around, and always having to fend for ourselves. What was I supposed to do? I would have been crazy to turn down the deal they were offering. For a while, things were good…and then they weren't. But by then, it was too late. I was in too deep to find a way out."

I have such a tight grip on the gun that my knuckles have turned white. Using both hands to keep it steady, I slowly train it away from his chest and down toward his knees.

"You didn't have to get involved selling drugs. If you needed money, why didn't you ask?" I say. "You could have asked."

"I did ask," he mutters, "but she told me *no*."

The truth as he tells it and as I suddenly recall it stings as sharp and fierce as a slap in the face. Lloyd didn't ask Alan and me, but he did go begging a loan from his parents. Margo's vicious recounting of his plea for money had been laced with spite and had thoroughly spoiled our Mother's Day gathering.

And what do I have to say to that? Lloyd tried and he was rebuffed. He was trying to do right by DeAnna and his children, and his back was up against the wall.

"Yeah, I can see what you're thinking," he elaborates. "You think I should have walked away from dealing. You think I should have told them, *thanks but I think I'll pass*. Well, guess what? Say that to some people, and what do you think happens next? Let me clue you in, Marguerite: you start walking, but you don't get far. Hard to walk with a bullet in your brain.

"And now you finally get it, right?" he replies to my horrified stare. "That's the problem with people like you. You think everything's so simple, so black and white. You get off on thinking that you know what's best, and that it's your f-ing duty to share it with the rest of us. You shoot off your mouth, tell everybody what to do, how to live their lives. Right? But just because you got things easy, don't go assuming the rest of the world does. That's not the way it works, Marguerite. You don't get—"

"You think I have it easy?" I cry, suddenly furious. People can't simply pick and choose which laws to obey. Some things are essential, and the rules exist for everyone's benefit. Lloyd doesn't get to choose the ones he doesn't like. That's no different than a rogue driver stuck in traffic who suddenly revs his engine, cuts out of line, and peels down the shoulder of the crowded highway, putting everyone's lives in danger.

"You think I have it easy?" I repeat. "Because if that's what you think, then you're—"

"Hell, yes, you got it easy!" he shouts. "Look what you just did, interrupting me! You don't even bother listening to what I'm saying. You don't care what I think! My opinion isn't good enough. It's not the same as yours, and so it doesn't count. But not you; you've got it all figured out, right? You think you're so much better than me."

"When did I say that?" I demand. "When did you ever hear me say that?"

"I'm not stupid." His face reddens, the thick chords in his neck bulging. "You think I don't see how you look at me? That I don't know what you're saying behind my back? You and that whole damn family of yours, always making fun of me."

"I do not!" I insist. "We do not!"

"You do!" He stabs one finger in my direction, spittle shooting from his mouth. "You never cut me a break! You and your whole goddamned family have always acted like there's something wrong with me. And that goes ditto for the way you treat Dee. Like, she's damaged goods or something, just because she wants to be with me. Like, you think she could have done so much better than to end up with some low life like me.

"And that's never gonna change, right?" He peers at me. "No matter what I say or do, I'll always be wrong. As far as you're concerned, everything will always be my fault."

Who the hell does he think he is? I feel the rage surging through my body, the blood pounding through my heart, knocking down all the pent-up tensions, frustrations, and fears of the past several hours. This is my house, dammit! Lloyd has no right to talk to me like this.

"What about the things you did to my daughter?" I demand. "Explain to me how that's not your fault?"

"What *I* did?" He seems surprised at the suggestion. "I love Dee. I'd never hurt her. Everything I've ever done was for her."

"Including getting her pregnant?" The words rush out of me with abandon, for any filter I might have once had is gone. "Introducing her to drugs and alcohol? She was barely in her teens, Lloyd. She had no idea what she was getting into."

"And you got no clue what you're talking about," he says. "If you think it was me who—"

"Of course it was you. Who else would it be?"

"Seriously? You think Dee was some kind of innocent when she met me? Screw that idea." He levels me with a cold stare. "And let's not forget that precious son of yours in all this…because he doesn't exactly have clean hands."

"Don't you dare bring Barry into this!" My voice shakes with fury. "He's done nothing but try and help his sister. And as for DeAnna…yes, she has problems, but most of them are only because of you! Instead of trying to stop her, or getting her some help, you encouraged her! You provided the booze, the drugs. Thanks to you, her life is a mess."

Lloyd was the one who knotted the rope and built the scaffold. Let him swing in silence, I vow under my breath.

"Now she's in rehab," I rush the words before he can stop me. "*Thank God* she's in rehab, and I hope she stays there until she learns how to live without alcohol. She says she's working on it. She knows she made mistakes. That's a start. At least she's ready to acknowledge that she messed up. I hope they let her stay as long as she needs…until she begins to understand herself and what it is she's been looking for all these years. She needs to gain confidence in herself. She's not a bad person. But she's an addict, an alcoholic. It's just the way she is. Rehab will help her learn how to take care of herself, how to be a better mother to her children— *your children*. Those two little kids are completely innocent, but they're the ones who have suffered the most. And unless things change, they'll continue to suffer.

"I wish you'd been here the day DeAnna left. I wish you could have seen how LJ and Tiffany cried when she told them she was leaving. When the van from rehab pulled up in my driveway and DeAnna climbed inside? It was horrible, watching their faces, seeing their tears. Tiffany cried herself to sleep that night. LJ wouldn't talk to me for two days. I think he blames me for his mother going to rehab."

"You talked her into it?"

I shake my head. "It was DeAnna's decision. Supposedly, she'd been thinking about rehab for some time. Now she's there, I hope she stays as long as she needs. But the kids miss her. I try my best to fill in, but I'm not their mother. They miss her. They have their own issues."

He throws me a hard stare. "Like what?"

"All right, take LJ, for instance," I say. "He's always had a little of the bad boy in him, but after DeAnna left, he got louder and meaner. His teacher at school says he's acting out, bullying other kids. The school counselor and a behavioral therapist are working with him, trying to get him the help he needs. As for Tiffany, she doesn't say much but it's obvious she knows what's going on. When she's here with me, she's always underfoot. She follows me all around, as if she's afraid I might suddenly take off and leave her behind. And at night, when I put her to bed, she always asks if I'll be here in the morning. I tell her I'm not going anywhere, but then she starts to cry, and makes me promise not to leave her. And LJ—"

I break off mid-stream. Maybe it would be better not to share the most recent example of my grandson's acting out. I haven't told anyone, not even DeAnna. Then again, LJ is his son. Maybe Lloyd needs to hear this.

Exactly this.

"LJ has started wetting the bed. Not every night, but often enough. Two or three times a week. I haven't told DeAnna; the last thing she needs right now is me bothering her with stuff like that. Besides, there's nothing she can do about it . Not while she's in rehab. But I can do something. DeAnna left me in charge. I promised to protect the kids, to watch over them and keep them safe. That's all I've been trying to do here, Lloyd: protect DeAnna's kids. *Your* kids."

I've dumped a heavy load on his shoulders, and he hasn't said a word. It couldn't have been easy, hearing what I'd shared. No parent relishes hearing bad things about their children. And as much as I dislike Lloyd, I would have preferred to spare him the truth.

But the truth is what it is. And while it might be hard to hear, there's no easier, softer way.

"LJ wets the bed?"

"Yes," I say quietly.

"It happened to me, too," he finally says. "When I was a kid."

Something deep inside loosens, tugging at my heart.

"I'm sorry, Lloyd." Only as I say the words aloud, do I realize they are true. No child should have to suffer through something like that…including Lloyd.

"How did things get so fucked up?" he asks.

I'm not sure if he's talking to himself or asking my opinion. But what does it matter? This isn't the time for me to start listing all the mistakes he and DeAnna have made, or how they could have been better parents. What's done is done. The only thing left to do is to keep moving forward, preventing further damage.

"Sometimes people take a wrong turn," I say. "Even our own kids. Sometimes it just happens."

It happened to us. Alan and I did the best we could. Barry gave us only a few minor skirmishes, but DeAnna had been a different story. She rebelled against anything and everything since the day she learned to shout *NO!* I still puzzle at how she managed to finish high school without flunking out. Thank God for Alan. He'd seen to that. A swift sudden longing for my husband engulfs me. I've never missed him as much as I do now. If Alan were here, he'd know what to do.

But Alan isn't here. What happens next is up to me. I force myself to concentrate. I can't afford to lose focus.

I tighten my grip on the gun. What did Lloyd hope to accomplish by coming here today? What was his plan?

Did he even have a plan?

Maybe his motivation was simply a desire to see his family.

"I messed up their lives." He rocks to his knees in a slow, lumbering movement, as if genuflecting to something greater than himself. "Those kids are better off without me."

My heart skids to a stop. Is Lloyd suggesting he might leave? That after everything that's happened, he might simply walk out the door and out of our lives?

I discard the notion with my next breath. No geographical cure will solve this problem. Even if he decides to take off for parts unknown, he'll always be their father. And no matter how much wishful thinking on my part, and an overwhelming desire to throw him under the table, what's happened isn't entirely his fault. Bad things have happened, but our family isn't broken. Not yet.

Maybe if we try hard enough, we can pick up the pieces and patch ourselves back together again.

"You're not the only one to blame," I say. "All of us played a part in what happened. You and DeAnna. And me."

Our eyes lock and we stare each other down. And the longer our stalemate continues—the more I contemplate everything he's said, the things I've said, and what the final consequences might be—the more certain I am as to how this conflict between us might be resolved.

It will end with Lloyd, but only if it begins with me.

I must be crazy, thinking that I can pull this off. But my options are limited. They always have been. Still, if I do this, he'll never see it coming. The only thing needed is to put aside my fears and muster up the courage to try. As for Lloyd and how he might react, I can't allow myself to go there. I can't let myself be influenced by *what if I do?*

The bigger question is, *what if I don't?*

Lloyd lumbers to his feet. He sways slightly as he stands before me, staring at me through brooding eyes, as if trying to figure out my next move.

He won't be expecting it.

I take aim, my finger resting lightly on the trigger. My breathing slows as I lock him in as my target.

Center mass. It's the perfect kill shot.

"Steady, Marguerite," he warns, his eyes flashing back and forth between my face and the gun. "Don't do anything stupid."

Too late. What I'm about to do is probably the stupidest thing I'll ever do in my life.

But I'm going to do it anyway. I've made up my mind.

It's the right thing to do.

The only thing to do.

Slowly, deliberately, I lower my hand, lower the weapon, removing Lloyd from the direct line of fire.

Leaning sideways, I place the gun on the table.

CHAPTER TWENTY-FOUR

"WHAT THE FUCK?" LLOYD THROWS me a hard stare as he grabs the gun. "You stupid or something?"

He's right, I think silently, watching as he takes stock of the weapon. I've done plenty of stupid things in my life but surrendering the handgun the way I just did takes the grand prize.

I take a deep breath, think about my grandchildren. By now, the bus driver would be at the school's garage. He'll fire up the engine, head out to line up with all the other buses in front of the school. The final bell will ring. Kids grab their backpacks, crowd through the hallways, sorting themselves into messy lines snaking out the front door into the parking lot where parents in SUVs and minivans jostle for prime position. Other kids dash down the sidewalk, darting around those dillydallying in front of them, intent on getting home. And bringing up the rear are the bus kids, including LJ and Tiffany. Jammed together in little groups, they wait for the big yellow buses to crank open their doors, allowing them to clamber aboard. Then the bus pulls away from the curb and starts the journey home.

Lloyd hefts the gun in his hand, turns it in my direction.

Is this how I die? Right here in my kitchen? In my mind, I watch, cringing as he pulls the trigger. I hear the gun explode, see the blood—my blood!—spattered all over the walls and floor. It won't be long now—maybe ten or twenty minutes—before LJ and Tiffany come slamming through the front door. They'll tear through the house, calling out for me as they tumble into the kitchen…and come screeching to a halt as they come face to face with their father, gun in his hand, all that blood. And me dead on the kitchen floor.

They are just kids. Little kids.

God help them. My eyes fill with tears. How could I have been so stupid to think I could save them? Now it's too late. I can't save them. I couldn't even save myself. What's done is done. I think about Alan, searching for some small sign he might still be with me. If this is the end, I need to feel him near. I can face anything with Alan beside me.

My breaths are rapid, shallow as I steel myself for what comes next.

"What the fuck?"

I open my eyes to find Lloyd standing directly in front of me. He scowls, curses, lowers the gun.

"Why did you do that?" he demands. His face is mottled with an angry red stain and the wild look in his eyes ramps up my panic. I'm still not clear what's happened.

"You had the fucking gun!" He explodes, whipping his arms from side to side with pent-up fury. "The Fucking Gun, Marguerite! Right. In. Your. Hand. You could have killed me."

He's absolutely right. I could have.

"Why didn't you take the shot?" he demands.

"You know why," I reply. "I told you once already. A quiet peace overtakes me and I realize I'm not alone. Alan's here with me…and I can hear him in my head.

Keep it simple, Reet.

The truth is simple.

"I don't like guns." I shrug softly. "So I decided the best thing for me to do was give it back."

"You expect me to believe that?" Lloyd's eyes, big and round, look as if they might pop right out of their sockets.

"Believe what you want. I'm telling you the truth."

But not all of it. The rest, I hold back. He doesn't need to know.

"Nobody gives up a gun without a fight," he says, peering at me. "Not even you, Marguerite."

"Maybe I don't have any fight left in me."

Whatever fight I have left is reserved for LJ and Tiffany.

Lloyd swings his head from side to side, muttering under his breath.

"You're fuckin' crazy, Marguerite. You know that?"

I let go a long sigh. "I won't argue with you."

"And where does that leave us?" he asks. "Right back where we started. Waiting for the kids. *My kids*." He points to the clock. "Won't be long before that bus shows up."

"What happens then?" I ask. How long before all hell breaks loose? "What are you going to do?"

"No need for you to worry about that."

"Do you plan on staying here?"

"Why in fuck would I do that?" he snorts.

"What about the kids?" My voice is barely above a whisper. "Are you going to take them with you?"

He stares at me, and I abruptly realize that's exactly what he plans to do. He'll take LJ and Tiffany with him. The three of them will disappear. God only knows what will happen after that.

"Where will you go? Where are you going to take them?"

"None of your business. They're my kids and they're coming with me."

I nod at his gun. "What about the gun? What are you going to do with that?"

"I'm sure as hell not giving it to you!" he says in a loud burst of laughter.

"If you take the kids, you'll be responsible for whatever happens."

He shoots me a dark look. "What the hell is that supposed to mean?"

"The kids," I remind him. "Someone has to be responsible for LJ and Tiffany. DeAnna did her best after they sent you to prison. And when she left for rehab, she turned that responsibility over to me. Then you show up at my house today, bust your way inside. Now you're here, waiting for them, waiting to take them somewhere, God only knows where."

"Don't try and stop me," he warns. "We both know you can't."

"You're right. You're bigger and stronger than I am. Plus, you're their father. That gives you some rights."

Lloyd has no idea how hard it is for me to admit this truth, even to myself. *It's not fair!* I'm their grandmother. I've loved them from way before they were born, and all I want is to keep them safe. But he's their father, which automatically gives him top standing in the eyes of the law. I need to remember that.

"All I'm asking is that you think things through," I say. "Please don't forget that LJ and Tiffany are just little kids. And kids are curious…especially about things they've been warned not to touch. Things like guns. If something…"

"You think I want to see them get hurt?" he growls. "You think I'd hurt them?"

"No, I don't think you would…not intentionally." Until now, some of my greatest fears have centered around Lloyd doing exactly that. But I no longer believe that's the case. "But sometimes things happen. People get tired. And when they get tired, they can get careless. Accidents happen."

"Nothing's gonna happen. I'm smarter than that."

"Maybe you are, but what about other people? You can't be with those kids 24/7."

I think about the people he's hung with in the past. Drug dealers, crack heads. Are those the kind of people he'll turn to now?

"I'll figure something out. I got friends who'll put me up." He thinks for a minute. "They'll put us up," he corrects himself.

"They're only kids, Lloyd. They count on us to keep them safe."

"Goddammit, Marguerite, quit pressuring me!"

"I'm sorry." I falter, my heart hammering hard against my ribcage. "I'm sorry, I wasn't trying to—"

"Shut up! Shut the fuck up!" His face contorts with rage, and his arms flail around his head, the gun careening wildly in one hand. "You're always talking! Talking, talking, talking!"

I sense him heading closer to the edge. My fault, I've pushed him too far. I begin inching away from him. God help me. God help us all.

"Not so fast!" He lunges forward and grabs my arm. I get a whiff of stale coffee on his breath. Coffee that I made and served him in this very kitchen. He drags me forward to the table, shoves me into a chair.

"You know what your problem is?" he demands, towering above me.

My big mouth. My whole life, this big mouth of mine has gotten me into trouble. Today, the worst kind of trouble. I might not have any more tomorrows left.

"You never give a guy a chance."

I stare wordlessly up at him.

"You never give a guy a chance to fix things," he repeats. "You think I don't know that I fucked up? With Dee, with the kids? You think I don't wish things were different? That I'm happy about the way things turned out?"

"No, I don't imagine that you are," I whisper, surprised at his fury and passion. Abruptly I find myself thinking back to Barry's wedding several years earlier, and a conversation I had that night with DeAnna. A conversation about Lloyd.

"Can I ask you a question?"

He rolls his eyes. "Here we go again…"

"Why aren't you and DeAnna married? She said you've never asked."

"That's bullshit," he quickly challenges. "I've asked her three, four times, but she always comes up with some excuse. A guy can only take so much before he quits asking."

He's absolutely right. "But why would she tell me you'd asked, if you hadn't? That doesn't make sense."

"Welcome to my world." A deep smirk rides his face. "Most of the stuff Dee says doesn't make sense."

Until now, it's always been standard practice for me to give my daughter the benefit of the doubt as to anything Lloyd-related. But now, I'm not so sure as to who or what I should believe anymore.

"Maybe Dee and I could have made a go of it if I hadn't gotten sent to prison. Maybe she wouldn't be so messed up, the way she is now." He stares out the window into the backyard. The swing set and slide are directly in his view. "Maybe my kids wouldn't be messed up, either."

I glimpse the outer edges of a surprising, unexpected truth slowly emerging.

"You love them…don't you?" I ask, though I already know the answer.

He pulls his gaze away from the window, back to me, and nods. "They're my kids."

Certain that we're on the same page, I suddenly don't feel so frightened anymore.

"You know, Lloyd, you do have another choice as to how all this ends. It's a choice that guarantees the kids would be safe."

He throws up his hands in a what-the-hell-are-you-talking-about? gesture.

"You could just go." The words quietly slip from my mouth.

"Go?" He blinks, repeating the word slowly as if tasting the idea on his tongue. "Go?"

"Leave," I suggest, "right now, before the kids get home. No one knows you've been here, and no one needs to know. And they won't…not if I don't tell them."

He rolls his eyes. "Like that's gonna happen."

"I won't. I promise."

"You think I'm stupid?" His eyes blaze with a fierce intensity. "The minute I walk out that door, you're gonna be on the phone dialing 911."

I shake my head.

"How can I call the police? You took my phone, remember? Besides, why would I call them? You told me they let you out on parole." And as I speak the words, I realize I believe him, that what he's said is true. Lloyd didn't break out of prison; the authorities released him. "Being on parole isn't a crime."

"I forced my way into your house," he reminds me. "I've got a gun."

The irony isn't lost on me. I'm offering him a way out and he's reminding me of potential crimes he's committed. Illegal entry. Holding me hostage. Assault with a deadly weapon.

Yet, besides forcing his way into the house and scaring me out of my wits, what else has he done? Nothing much has happened. We drank coffee, we ate lunch. We hung decorations. And we talked. In the hours of this one brief morning/afternoon, Lloyd and I have talked longer and harder than all the other times in our lifetimes combined.

"Think about it, Lloyd," I urge. "It's a peaceful resolution. You and I are the only ones who know what happened here today. You leave quietly. No one gets hurt. You haven't broken any laws…except one."

Both of us stare at the gun in his hand.

"Are you allowed to own that?" I dare to ask.

"Who says I own it?"

"Where did you get it?"

He shrugs. "A guy I know."

"If they catch you with it, what happens then? Do they send you back to prison?"

"I don't know, Marguerite…whatdya think?"

The scorn on his face is enough to convince me to cut my questioning short.

"You could leave it with me," I blurt out.

"If you think I'm giving up this gun, you're nuttier than I thought."

"It was merely a suggestion," I say in a small voice. It would be a major victory if I somehow manage to persuade him to leave the gun behind. At the very least, I'd no longer need to worry about the potential threat of LJ and Tiffany being caught in a salvo of gunfire.

"You got this all figured out, don't you?" he says. "I hand over my gun, and I'm free to take off and do what I want."

I keep my mouth shut.

"What makes you think I'm gonna do it?" he presses.

"Because it's the right thing to do," I finally reply. "I don't think you came here looking for trouble. I think everything happened just the way you said. Someone told you DeAnna was here, and you came looking for her. But when you found out she was gone, after you pushed your way inside my house, things got more complicated than you expected."

More complicated than either of us expected. I think back to this morning. The doorbell ringing. My mad dash down the hallway. I'd yanked open the door expecting to see the UPS man, only to find Lloyd standing there instead. Harsh words exchanged between us, my refusal to allow him in. Him shoving the gun in my face.

The gun changed everything. Once he and his gun were inside my house, I no longer had control over what happened next. Even the most ordinary things had assumed a different perspective. Sunshine splashing across the kitchen floor reminded me that I was a prisoner, no longer free to walk out the door and enjoy the beautiful day. A phone call, the familiar drone of my neighbor's voice, and eventually Millie herself showing up on my porch. I could have reacted; I could have cried out, begged her for help. But instead, I kept my mouth shut. Lloyd never would have spared her and she would have ended up a hostage, just like me.

Except that Millie isn't here. But I am. And how this eventually plays out is entirely up to him. Lloyd came here looking for Dee and his kids, only to end up with me. But I'm not the one he wants, and it's highly possible this won't end well.

He still has the gun.

It's still pointed at me.

I have always been expendable.

I lift my hands, palms extended outward, in a gesture of sincerity and conciliation. My fate is in his hands. There isn't much time left.

"I never thought about it," he says slowly, as if he's confused, and as if we have all the time in the world. "Dee was always bitchin', complaining how she had it so hard, how none of it was her fault."

"We're all at fault," I say.

"You mean *me*," he challenges. "You're talking about me."

"Not just you. And not just DeAnna. We all played a part in this, Lloyd. You, me, Alan, DeAnna." But even as I speak the words, something worms away, niggling at the back of my brain. Something he'd said earlier. Something I'd dismissed.

And then I remember.

"And Barry," I add. "Somehow he's involved in this, too. Am I right?"

He shoots me a hard look and I have my answer.

"What happened?" I say softly.

"You're asking the wrong guy," he advises. "He knows what he did, and so does Dee. She's no angel. You wanna know what happened? Ask them."

My son and daughter? The mere suggestion boggles my mind. Could it be true? Did DeAnna seek out her brother and beg his help? Had Barry decided to get involved at some point? Did one or both of them contact the police? Lloyd earlier had hinted he'd been betrayed by someone who knew his whereabouts, who'd acted as a snitch. I'd assumed it was the people he was working for, the people he thought would protect him.

There is no valor among drug dealers. But does the same apply to families?

Whoever cast Lloyd as the bad guy in our family script came up with the wrong scenario. We've all taken turns at playing the villain, including me. So many years wasted. And I've treated Lloyd unfairly, allowing my emotions to color my perspective, rushing to judgment. So much could have been prevented if I hadn't been hellbent on insisting DeAnna stay away from him. No wonder she's so messed up. I didn't give her much choice. And what arrogance on my part, assuming that merely because I was her mother, that I was the one who ultimately knew best…that *my* ideas, *my* opinions and attitudes, were the only ones with validity.

My way or the highway.

I am just like my mother. The realization comes as a painful truth, and it's something I'll have to live with for the rest of my life.

Lloyd shifts the gun back and forth in his hands, squinting at it as if unclear as to its make and model. Finally, he looks back at me.

"What if I do?" he asks.

"You mean, if you leave the gun with me?" I feel a tiny bit of hope flicker inside, setting off little fires of faith.

"Yeah." He eyes me speculatively. "What would you do with it?"

"Well, that depends," I say, caught off guard that he's actually considering my suggestion. My mind is racing. What about LJ and Tiffany? Is he thinking about leaving them behind, too? "Maybe I could say that I was cleaning out a closet…that I found the gun buried inside a box high up on a shelf. I could give it to Barry, tell him it was Alan's. Barry knows how much I hate guns. He won't ask questions."

Oh, but he would. Guaranteed my son would have plenty of questions. Especially if he were to find out about Lloyd being here today. *Why was he here? Why did you let him in?* And knowing Barry, the questions wouldn't stop there. He'd sniff around, searching for a whiff of something gone bad… something I wasn't telling him. And he wouldn't stop until he pried the information out of me. Once that happened, all hell would break loose. Barry would never agree with my decision to keep things hushed up, of allowing Lloyd to quietly disappear into the night. He'd insist that we contact the authorities, alert them to what Lloyd had done, how he'd violated the terms of his parole. Possession of a gun. Breaking and entering. Holding me hostage. When the police caught up with Lloyd, he'd be sent back to prison, with more time added to his original sentence. Another five years. Maybe ten. LJ and Tiffany would be adults before their father saw the light of day as a free man once again.

Is that the best way for this to end? To witness him handcuffed, sent back to prison? To know that he's locked away, that whatever influence he once had over DeAnna and the kids has been reduced to nearly nothing? I'll admit, the notion is tempting. I'm only human. He's caused our family enormous pain. But what about the rest of us and the part we've played? Knowing Lloyd was locked up again would be tremendously satisfying, but there would be a cost to pay. More anger, more resentment. When does the cycle stop? Would forcing him back into prison solve any of our problems, or simply add to the suffering we've already lived through?

So many questions, begging better answers than I can find in my heart.

Except for one…the question I started with.

How do I want this to end?

Six hours ago, I might have answered differently.

Might have? Surely I've learned something from today.

I take a deep breath, exhale. My mind is made up.

No one needs to know what happened here today, and that includes Barry. He can ask all the questions he wants, but that doesn't mean I have to provide answers.

Meanwhile, I have plenty questions of my own for Barry.

Lloyd's pistol is no longer pointed at me. I'm not aware of when he dropped his aim, or when I ceased being a target. He sinks into a chair, places one hand on the weapon, presses a button low on its side. The gun's magazine drops into his other hand.

I stare at the gun, then back at him. "What are you doing?"

"Making sure I don't leave you with a loaded weapon." Racking the slide, he checks to verify the gun is empty, then opens the magazine, fishes out the bullets, and drops them in his shirt pocket.

"Shades of Barney Fife," I say in a shaky voice as I realize what's happening. He's leaving the gun behind.

"Who?" Lloyd checks the chamber one last time, then peers at me.

"Barney Fife. He was on a tv show a long time ago. There was this little town called Mayberry, with a sheriff and a deputy named Barney. They carried unloaded guns, but Barney kept his bullet in his pocket."

Lloyd snorts. "Lot of good that would do him."

"It was a good show," I say, my thoughts slipping back to a time when things weren't so complicated. No 24/7 news coverage with sensational headlines, no reality tv constantly pushing boundaries. People had time to sit back, mull things over, talk among themselves, reminiscing about people, places, and things. To dream a little dream or two and hope it all came true.

Just like Mayberry.

Lloyd carefully places the gun on the table.

"Thank you, Lloyd," I say.

"For what?"

"Doing the right thing."

"Yeah, whatever." His mouth contorts in a grim smile. "But why in hell am I doing it?"

"Maybe because you're not as bad as you want everyone to believe…and that includes you. You like to paint yourself as a bad guy. But if you look hard enough, I think you'll discover there's a good guy deep inside you waiting to bust out. Why not give him a chance? He might surprise you."

He eyes me across the table. "Sometimes, Marguerite, *you* surprise me."

I give a small laugh. "Sometimes I surprise myself."

"I never meant for any of this to happen," he says abruptly. "I came over here looking for Dee, but then you opened the door. You acted like you were so much better than me, like I had no business being here. You wouldn't tell me where she was. And when you ordered me off the porch, that's when I lost it. I got mad and I pushed my way in. I knew it was wrong, even while I was doing it, but I didn't let that stop me. But pulling the gun on you, threatening you like I did?" Lloyd pauses, swallows, shakes his head slowly. "That was messed up, Marguerite. I never should have done it. And just so you know: I never would have pulled the trigger. I was mad, but I wouldn't have pulled the trigger. Never."

Hearing such contrition stops me cold. Six hours ago, when he forced his way inside, I was ready to do anything, given half a chance. And if I'd had managed to grab his gun, I might have pulled the trigger. But everything has changed. And sitting here in my kitchen with Lloyd, I'm convinced he means every word. He's offered me the closest thing to an apology that he knows how to make.

Isn't it time I made amends, too?

"Can I tell you something?"

He regards me with wary eyes.

"It's nothing bad," I assure him. "And it's not about you. It's about me."

He shrugs, which I take as a signal he's willing to listen to what I have to say. That never would have happened earlier. Clearly, we've gained some ground, Lloyd and me.

"You talked about this morning, how you rang the bell, how you weren't expecting me to be the one who opened the door. Well, that goes ditto for me. When I opened the door, you were the last person I thought would be standing there in front of me. I assumed you were still in prison. And when you told me you were looking for DeAnna and the kids, that's when—in my head, at least—things fell apart. I didn't want you anywhere near them, and…and I let that one idea color everything I said and did. That was my fault, Lloyd. I made things worse.

"I could have been honest with you. I *should* have been honest," I admit. "I should have told you right up front that DeAnna was in rehab, and that the kids were staying with me. But I didn't tell you…partly because I thought you didn't deserve to know. That was me, judging you. And so, while I didn't exactly lie, I deliberately held back on telling you the whole truth. I knew what I was doing, and I'll always regret it. That's on me, Lloyd. And I'm sorry."

Our eyes meet briefly, and then he nods. We've reached an impasse of sorts, mutually agreeing in our silence to let things be. And maybe that's the best conclusion of all. Lloyd and I will never be friends, but the two of us don't need to be sworn enemies, or constantly butting heads.

Lloyd stands, pushes in his chair. "I gotta get going."

I glance at the clock. The little engine has reached the three o'clock hour.

"What about LJ and Tiffany?" I say. He still hasn't mentioned if his plans include them. They'll be home soon. I have to know.

He stares at me a long moment.

"You okay with keeping 'em?" he finally says.

My heart catches in a fierce rush of happiness. He's going to do it! Lloyd's decided to leave them behind with me.

"Yes, that's fine," I reply. "They're good kids, Lloyd. They're always welcome."

He nods.

Surrendering LJ and Tiffany into my care is a huge give-away for him, especially since he's leaving without having seen them. But his kids will always be a big draw. Sooner or later, he'll show up again. There's nothing I can do to stop him.

But there's something I *can* do to make the next time around easier on us all.

"What are you doing tomorrow?" I ask.

He throws me a pointed stare, like *who-are-you-to-be-asking-me-questions*?

"I was thinking maybe you could stop by, see the kids, eat some birthday cake."

My offer seems to catch him by surprise.

"You sure about that, Marguerite?"

"I'm sure." This is something I need to do. For my grandchildren. For myself. For him, too. "You're welcome to come over and see them. After all, they're your kids. Kids do better all-around when they know they're loved and accepted for who they are. That's what they need…what any of us need, right?" I take a deep breath. "We have to start somewhere."

He gives me the go-ahead with a small nod.

"The kids," he adds. "Don't tell them I was here today. They don't need to know."

"I promise. Not a word."

Another promise I'll need to keep.

"And Dee? When you talk to her, when she gets out…" He hesitates, scratches his chin. "Tell her I'm around, okay? She has my number. Ask her to call me."

"I will. But there's no telling when that might happen. We don't know when she'll get out of rehab."

"Yeah, I get it."

"Do you know where you're headed?"

He shrugs. "I got friends. Somebody will put me up."

"What about your brother? Didn't you say that your mother is—"

"Nope," he says in a tight voice. "Last time I saw her was in the courtroom. She showed up for the sentencing, and then she turned her back on me."

But I was in the courtroom that day, too, watching from my seat in the second row. I remember Margo's face, how it twisted as she heard the guilty verdict pronounced. She gripped the bench railing, pulled herself to her feet, steeling her shoulders as she watched her son being led from the courtroom in shackles and handcuffs.

And I remember Margo's tears.

A mother's heart always remembers, I silently muse, even as the irony of my own situation occurs to me. My mother was a hard, bitter woman; but in contemplating her faults, I'm only wasting time. What would it gain me? My mother is dead and buried, and I'm very much alive. By trying to be a better woman, a better mother to my children, than my own mother was to me, then that will be the best lesson my mother taught me.

"Who knows? Maybe someday, you'll feel like giving your mom a second chance."

"There you go again, Marguerite, getting all preachy." Lloyd wags a finger at me.

"Old habits are hard to break," I say with a small smile. "Then again, *don't go burning bridges*."

"You get that from Barney?"

"Barney?" I puzzle, then laugh as I finally get the reference. "No, not Barney Fife. Alan used to say that. He was always reminding me not to burn bridges. I guess I need to work on that."

"Walk with me," Lloyd says, and heads out of the kitchen.

I trail him through the house, down the hallway, into the living room. Everything feels slowed down, and the notion that he intends to simply walk out the door is hard to grasp. His jacket still lays in a crumped heap at the bottom of the staircase, exactly where it had fallen from the banister hours earlier. He bends to retrieve it, shrugs it on.

"I don't suppose I can have my phone back?" The odds of him handing it over are practically nil, but it doesn't hurt to ask.

"Sorry, Marguerite, no can do." He pats his shirt pocket. "I know you promised not to call 911 but—"

"And I won't," I assure him. "A promise is a promise."

"Yeah, well, I'm still going to keep it. That way, you're not tempted, and I've got a head start."

"You won't need it," I reply as I walk him to the front door.

Lloyd reaches for the handle, pulls the door open. Late afternoon sunlight floods the hallway but the air is frosty with a hint of coming weather, and I suspect that soon my front porch will be covered with snow. He stands in the doorway for a moment, his gaze turned outward. Out on the street, his junker car sits exactly where he left it, sloppily parallel parked next to the curb.

"Be careful," I say without thinking. It's something I would automatically tell my own children. Why not him?

He gives me a short nod.

"See ya, Marguerite. It's been real."

Real? It's been that, and much, much more.

"Good-bye, Lloyd. Take care of yourself."

"Yep." He starts out the door, then halts, straddling the threshold; one foot on the porch, one foot still inside. He turns once again to face me.

"Earlier, when we were eating lunch…what I said about the grilled cheese sandwiches?"

"I remember," I say, thinking back to how he'd dissed my cooking, how I'd burned with anger.

"I lied." A sheepish half-smile tugs at his mouth. "The truth is, Marguerite, you make a mean grilled cheese…way better than mine."

And before I can reply, he turns and walks out the door.

Just like that, Lloyd is gone.

CHAPTER TWENTY-FIVE

T HE HOUSE SEEMS STRANGELY EMPTY. Alone in the hallway, I close the door. Lloyd being here triggered so many emotions. Anger, resentment, betrayal, confusion…most of all, fear. But simply because he's gone doesn't mean things have automatically reverted back to normal. Any concept of what qualified as *normal* was busted wide open during the past six hours. And while I'm no longer afraid, the confused state currently occupying my brain feels surreal and disorienting. It's almost as if I'd drifted off to sleep, only to fall into a nightmare…Lloyd busting into my house, holding my dreams hostage.

But it wasn't a dream, that much I'm certain.

Lloyd *was* here.

And now he's gone.

I retrace my steps from earlier, wandering through the empty rooms as if to reassure myself it all really happened. The living room with its staircase and banister. Lloyd stood at the bottom, tossed his jacket and missed, leaving it where it fell on the floor in a crumped heap. The dining room with colorful ribbons and streamers, a myriad of birthday balloons floating from the chandelier. With me too chicken to climb a ladder, those balloons are Lloyd's handiwork. In the kitchen, leftover dirty dishes in the sink; soup bowls soaking, my old cast iron skillet waiting to be handwashed. An empty pickle jar sits on the counter, and beside it, a gaily wrapped box. The birthday gift Millie hand delivered for Tiffany. And next to the coffee pot, my phone's empty charger, its black cord still plugged into the outlet.

No phone to charge. Lloyd took my phone with him.

A gun on the table. Lloyd took the bullets with him.

Holy crap, what do I do with that gun?

I grab a glass, fill it with water from the faucet, and sink into a chair. Not my chair, any chair will do. The water tastes cool and refreshing, but I sip slowly. I still don't trust myself and I don't want to choke. My head is throbbing, and I'm desperate to lay down. But that will have to wait. It's past three o'clock and the school bus is on its way. LJ and Tiffany will be home any minute.

The kids are safe, I remind myself. No more reason to feel anxious or afraid. *The kids are safe and so are you*. But repeating my mantra over and over does nothing to quiet the jittery thoughts or to stop my hands from trembling. I hug myself close, trying to warm myself up. Since Lloyd left, the inside temperature of the house feels as if it's dropped ten degrees. I pull my sweater tighter. As soon as I'm sure that my legs will hold me, I'm heading for the thermostat and turning up the heat. Cost be damned.

And since I'm splurging, why not carry it further? Starting with dinner. No way am I cooking tonight. Lloyd took my phone, but there's still that landline in my bedroom.

I can call for delivery, order pizza.

I can call Millie, apologize for being rude.

I can call 911, report Lloyd and his crimes.

But before I make any calls, there are two things urgently demanding my attention.

I need to use the bathroom, and I need to figure out what to do with the gun.

Convincing myself to pick it up isn't easy, even though I know it's unloaded. I watched Lloyd remove the bullets. But a gun is a gun is a gun, and the mere sight of it there on my kitchen table continues to unnerve me. When I finally do manage to pick it up, again I'm surprised at its hefty weight. Maybe Barney Fife was right. A gun, even one without bullets, is still a lethal weapon. Used as a hammer, it could break a person's kneecaps or ribs. Hit someone just right on the skull, and this gun could easily bash their brains in. I shift back and forth from one foot to the other, gingerly holding it at arm's length, trying to decide what to do. But with each passing minute, my urge to use the bathroom grows more desperate.

It's now or never. I don't have a choice.

I head down the hallway with the gun still in hand. The kids might get home before I'm finished, and I don't want them seeing the gun or being anywhere near it. I reach the little bathroom Lloyd and I used, step inside, lock the door behind me. I carefully place the gun on the vanity, point its muzzle in the opposite direction. I pull down my pants, sink down on the stool and finally let go. I drag in some deep breaths as I begin to relax. Then I catch sight of the narrow window near me, and I'm reminded how, only a few hours earlier, I'd briefly considered it as a possible escape route. Good thing I didn't try, for now it's clear enough to see that I never would have fit. Stuck there, trapped between inside and out, I would have had no choice but to cry out to Lloyd for rescue.

The notion of him busting into the bathroom, his likely astonishment at seeing me stuck in the window is all it takes, and I break out laughing as I sit there on the toilet. *What was I thinking?* I laugh so hard that tears fill my eyes, spilling over and down my cheeks. Never in a million years would I have fit through that window. Not even if I somehow managed to lose thirty pounds!

But the one thing I *didn't* lose today?

My life.

Thank God I am still alive. Thank God neither of us were hurt.

I grab some toilet paper, take care of business. I think about Lloyd, where he might be headed. He mentioned staying with friends. Most likely they live here in town, which means he'll be close by. What if he decides to take me up on my invite, shows up tomorrow for birthday cake? And what if, after spending time with LJ and Tiffany, he decides that he's changed his mind, that he wants his kids, and he whisks them away? What then? What do I do?

Exactly what I should do now. All I have to do is run upstairs, grab the landline, punch in three easy numbers.

911.

But if I make that phone call, I'd be breaking my promise to him.

The threat of violence is gone, but my dilemma remains. Do I contact the authorities and turn Lloyd in, or do I allow him to simply walk away? I think about the hours that the two of us spent together here in my house today. What really happened? What did he do? Yes, he scared me. But he was running scared, too. Yes, he forced his way into my house. But only because I taunted him. I upped the ante with my rudeness.

He held me at gunpoint. But aren't I guilty of doing the same thing? When I managed to grab his gun, I turned it on him.

Eventually, though, I put the gun down.

Eventually, Lloyd did, too.

I pull up my pants, flush. At the vanity, I scrub my hands clean, my eyes still on the gun. Lloyd surrendered it without a struggle and then he walked away. What about me? How long do I continue holding on to the anger and resentment I've nurtured against him all these years? Breaking my promise, turning him over to the authorities. Doing that would be yet one more example of my incessant need to be in control…it would be me trying to prove to myself that I know better than anyone else, and that my decisions are righteous and just.

Far down the hall, the doorbell rings.

The kids? But they never use the doorbell.

Lloyd? It could be Lloyd! What if he's changed his mind and he's come back to take the kids?

And the gun! What do I do with the gun?

My eyes sweep the bathroom, frantically searching for a place to stash it. There's no place under the vanity, not even behind the spare rolls of toilet paper. Too easy to spot.

The doorbell rings again.

With only seconds to spare, I take one last wild look around, and suddenly realize exactly where to hide it. I lift the tank lid and drop the gun in the water. It sinks quickly, settling on the bottom, completely submerged in the tank, safely resting on its side.

No one will find that gun now.

The doorbell rings again. Shrill and insistent. Whoever it is, they're not going away.

I reset the lid, then hurry down the hall toward the front door. There's a strong sense of déjà-vu. Six hours ago, I'd hurried down this same hallway to answer the doorbell. I'd been waiting for the familiar brown delivery truck in the driveway. A truck with a unique yellow logo. The truck I'd been expecting since yesterday, and the only reason I'd flung the door open this morning without using the peephole. If that truck had shown up when it was supposed to, my front door would have been locked today. When Lloyd rang the bell, I would have spied him through the peephole and I never would have opened the door. None of this would have happened.

And yet, it did. Was it random happenstance, or were the stars aligned in some pre-ordained cosmic intervention designed to teach me some uncomfortable truths? I learned a lot about myself today. I'm stronger than I think. Stepping outside my comfort zone was scary, but today taught me that I can manage difficult situations, difficult people, difficult conversations. I think about the conversation I plan on having with DeAnna and Barry sometime in the very near future. A conversation about how, and why, and where, and when, and the possible roles each of them played in Lloyd's arrest and conviction. Insisting the three of us sit down for that particular conversation will be difficult, but I'll be able to handle it. I can handle myself. I can even handle a gun. Well, sort of.

But I didn't fall apart. I did all those things, and I didn't fall apart. For that, I am grateful.

Grateful, too, for the time I spent with Lloyd. Granted, it would have been easier without his gun. But given our conversations, and the things I learned about him, I have a better grasp of where he came from, and what he's all about.

There's a famous quote about how if you want to understand a person, you should try walking a mile in their shoes. While that won't be happening for me and Lloyd (according to DeAnna, he wears a size 17), I think I can empathize how difficult it must be for him finding shoes that fit.

Maybe it's the same with families. There's no such thing as a perfect family. Just like shoes, families can be difficult. Despite all the squabbling, one might prove the perfect fit, while another ends up pinching your toes and heart. But wear them long enough, and usually they'll stretch out to be a comfortable fit. Not perfect, but comfortable. Doable. Wearable.

If Lloyd and DeAnna were married, he'd be my son-in-law. But they're not, and he isn't. And while Lloyd and I might never be *family* in an official capacity, he'll always be the father of my grandchildren. The guiding concept here should be our love for those kids and in doing the right thing.

Which is exactly what Lloyd did today.

Did these past few hours change us? Time will tell. Maybe we'll know as soon as tomorrow. If he shows up at my door under the pretense of birthday cake, swaggering into my house full of his usual bluster, trying to bully his way back into our lives, I'll know he's just the same old Lloyd. But somehow I have a feeling that's not going to happen.

Trust your eyes. Trust your gut. Trust your heart.

Lloyd did that today. And maybe I can, too.
The bell shrills again and this time I don't hesitate.
I open the door.

ABOUT THE AUTHOR

Kathleen Irene Paterka is a bestselling author of Women's Fiction. Her latest novel, ***Saturday Night Sisters***, delves into the shadowy world of women's friendships and longstanding secrets, while her bestselling Women's Fiction novel, ***The Other Wife***, explores the lives of two different women of two different generations, betrayed by the same man. Kathleen is also the author of the acclaimed series *The James Bay Novels*, including ***Fatty Patty***, ***Home Fires***, ***Lotto Lucy***, ***For I Have Sinned***, and ***Deep Fried Reservations***. Kathleen is also co-author of the non-fiction books ***For the Love of a Castle*** and ***For the Love of a Castle ~ The Romance Continues***. She and her husband live in the beautiful north country of Michigan's Lower Peninsula. Kathleen loves hearing from readers. Visit her website at https://www.kathleenirenepa-terka.com/